SORRENTO Beach

DAVID GROTE

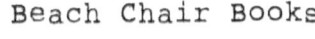

Beach Chair Books

Manhattan Beach, California

Sorrento Beach drawings by Kelsey Grote

Author photograph by Matt Grote

Substantive editing by June Eding

First printing 2012

ISBN: 0615599672
ISBN 13: 9780615599670

Manufactured in the United States of America

Published by Beach Chair Books.

To Sherie, whose courage and optimism inspire me daily.

SORRENTO Beach

PROLOGUE

Muncheberg, Germany
April 17, 1945

Isaiah Rosenberg awoke to the rumbling of military tanks on the gravel road which passed his uncle's farm, about two hundred meters in front of the two houses. Twenty-six year old Isaiah brushed aside his shoulder length, dark brown hair and peered from his bedroom window. He identified small Russian flags attached to the rear of the tanks. Isaiah's pulse quickened and a wide smile began to form. *The Russian Army! Yes! Heading to Berlin to end the war! The fear and hiding … over!*

SEVEN YEARS before, Isaiah, his wife Rachel, and their newborn son Adam, had moved to Ethan and Danye Rosenberg's farm to escape the mandatory registration of all Jews in their hometown of Muncheberg. Isaiah's parents, Abe and Hannah, had sensed something sinister in the new regulation and made the bold decision to defy the law and come to Abe's brother's house about ten miles outside of town.

Rachel Rosenberg, formerly Rachel Langer, was the oldest child in a family of three girls. She had known Isaiah since they began at the same school when they were five years old. Isaiah had secretly admired the beautiful, dark haired girl since he was ten years old, having the kind of childhood crush that can be all consuming for a young boy. When they were older, Isaiah fifteen and Rachel still fourteen, the infatuation became mutual and turned into something more, loving each other with the kind of intensity reserved for teenagers. Both sets of parents disapproved, worried their children were spending too much time together, too serious at such a young age. But this love did not pass like many teenage romances. At eighteen, they were married, and Rachel became pregnant shortly thereafter. Baby Adam was born February 18, 1938, just missing Isaiah's birthday by one day.

THE ENDLESS line of tanks continued west past the farm. As his wife and son slept, Isaiah moved to the front porch for a better look. Three of the soldiers, on foot, caught his attention. Their uniforms were not the clean and neat outfits he remembered the German soldiers wearing from his younger days in Muncheberg. These soldiers were disheveled, shirts untucked and unbuttoned, carrying long rifles at their sides as they walked unsteadily towards Ethan's farmhouse.

Isaiah hurriedly slipped on his shoes and jogged the thirty meters to the main house to tell his parents. The Russians were here, coming to give them news of the war. His balding, heavy-set, sixty year old father answered the door. Abe's eyes widened upon seeing the approaching soldiers.

"No need to worry father, they're Russian."

But in spite of Isaiah's excitement, Abe pulled Isaiah into the house, slammed the door, and rushed to wake up Hannah, Ethan and Danya.

"Father, what's wrong?" Isaiah shouted down the hall.

Abe ignored him as he ordered the women to stay in the bedroom and remain quiet.

Against his father's wishes Isaiah left the house and walked a few steps on the dirt path to meet the soldiers, eager to hear of the war's progress.

Nearly a year earlier they had been heartened to learn of the Americans arrival on the coast of France. By spring of 1945, American troops had driven the German army out of France and were crossing the border. From the other direction, much closer to Muncheberg, the Russian Army had retaken Poland, liberated the camp at Auschwitz, and was advancing toward Berlin. These were hopeful times at the Rosenberg farm. Successfully hiding for nearly seven years, avoiding the fate of most Jews in Europe, help was now on the way and defeat of the Nazi regime seemed certain.

THE SOLDIERS ignored Isaiah's happy greeting, stepped onto the front porch, not bothering to knock, just walked in, speaking Russian, and laughing amongst themselves. The stench of the soldiers was overwhelming, plus they reeked of alcohol, which Isaiah thought strange for so early in the morning.

"What do you want? Why do you come in to our house like this?" Abe demanded angrily.

Ignoring Abe's reproach, they began going through the house, each of them in a different direction, one going upstairs, and one to the kitchen. The other ripped out the drawers of the desk in the living room, emptying the contents on the floor, papers scattering everywhere.

Taller and leaner than his brother, and with a little more hair, Ethan Rosenberg entered the room. "Stop this! Leave my house immediately!" he yelled.

The soldier glanced at the red-faced Ethan, said something in response he did not understand, and continued wreaking havoc. The heavyset one walked down the hallway towards the bedroom. He barged into the room to find Hannah and Danya huddled closely together on the bed, obviously frightened. He yelled out a cheer as if he had found what they had been looking for.

He walked to the bed where they sat as the other soldiers came to the bedroom to have a look at the two women. Danya was the prettier of the two, had long black hair, and was about ten years younger than her sister-in-law. One of the slightly built men started towards Danya, but the heavy one yelled at him, stopping him before he reached her. The slight one then yelled back, some kind of disagreement over the fate of Hannah and Danya. The heavyset soldier grabbed Isaiah's short, gray haired mother by her upper arm, roughly pulled her out the door, closing the door behind him. The soldier he had yelled at stayed in the room with the slender, cowering Danya.

As the other soldier kept his rifle pointed at the men, Hannah was pushed into the kitchen area, the soldier behind her. The Russian made it clear that he was hungry, and motioned for her to get him something to eat. Isaiah noticed his mother trembling as she hurried into the pantry to retrieve a loaf of rye bread that she had baked yesterday. As she set the bread on a cutting board and brought it to the table, they heard for the first time the muffled screams from the bedroom.

Ethan bolted down the hallway upon hearing his wife. A shot exploded from the soldier's rifle, stopping him before he could reach the door. Ethan cried in anguish, crumpled to the hallway floor, holding his left thigh. His khaki colored pants slowly turned crimson as the blood flowed from his upper left leg.

In the kitchen, the foul smelling, heavyset soldier sat at the table. He watched Hannah, who was still dressed in her loose fitting nightgown, as she lifted a roast beef from the icebox.

The Russian who had shot Ethan, keeping his rifle trained on Isaiah and his father, joined his comrade at the table, waiting for Hannah to serve the beef. Isaiah grimaced. Awful cries from the bedroom and the agonized moaning of Ethan filled his head.

"Father, what can we do?" he whispered.

"Nothing. There is nothing we can do except wait for them to leave."

As Hannah sliced the roast, the seated soldiers lit cigarettes and shared a joke. Their laughter was tortuous for Abe to endure, but he stood with his son, every muscle tense, as Hannah placed the food on the table. The soldiers motioned for her to get them something to drink and she retrieved beer from the pantry. The third soldier emerged from the bedroom to cheers and more laughter from the other two, nonchalantly kicking Ethan in the ribs as he walked by. He joined the others at the table. After serving the beer, Hannah rushed to her husband's side and the three of them watched and waited, eager for the Russians to be gone, Isaiah's expectation of them being friendly terribly wrong.

MINUTES LATER, one of the slight soldiers, apparently having had his fill of bread, beef, and beer, got up from the table and walked towards Hannah with his rifle in hand. She shrunk behind her husband, but the soldier violently grabbed Abe by the shirt and shoved him aside, knocking him to the floor. Hannah recoiled a half step as he grabbed the neckline of her gown, and with a quick motion, tore the fabric all the way to the waist, exposing her breasts. Isaiah leaped on the soldier, pulling him from his shrieking mother. The rifle clattered to the ground. Abe struggled to get to his feet, but one of the other soldiers pushed him back to the floor with his muddy boot and held him there. The other struck Isaiah across the shoulder with the butt of his rifle, sending a piercing pain down his right arm and causing him to lose his grip on the soldier.

At this very moment, with Hannah in tears, Isaiah standing guard in front of her, Abe still pinned to the floor, and the three soldiers eyeing Isaiah's mother, Rachel and Adam walked in the front door. After awakening, the noises coming from the other house's kitchen had made them curious. The heavyset soldier looked lustily at Rachel, grunted something unintelligible, and started towards her.

"Rachel! Adam! Run! Run!" Isaiah yelled.

Rachel reacted immediately, assessing the danger of the situation. She scooped up her slight, dark haired son in her arms and ran out the front door the way they had just come in. Rather than head back to her house, she smartly turned the corner, ran along the side of the house and continued away from both houses towards the thicket of forest, half a kilometer away. Although he was small for his age, Rachel quickly had to set Adam down so they could run separately. At seven years old he was nearly as fast as his mother. The large open field which separated their homes from the forest, cleared of trees for planting by Ethan many years ago, was now a mixture of planted wheat and vacant land, filled with weeds and wildflowers. While the soldiers were distracted with Rachel's escape, Isaiah managed to slip out the back door, running to catch up with them.

As he approached, he screamed, "Don't stop! Keep going as fast as you can! We need to get to the forest to hide ourselves!"

His panicked legs churned as he quickly caught up to his wife and son. Isaiah stole a glance behind him to see if any of the soldiers had followed. Two of them stood on the porch, their rifles raised, looking through sights directly at him. Suddenly Rachel fell in his path. It was after she fell that the sound of the rifle reached him, and not until he tried to help her up, did he realize the bullet had found her.

Then, two more cracks of the rifles. Adam cried out in agony. "Help me, Papa. Help me! It hurts Papa!"

Isaiah crawled to his son as bullets whizzed past. The hideous laughter from the porch cruelly teased him.

"No, no! Not my son. Please God, not my son."

They were fully exposed here, the weeds providing no protection and the taller wheat plants ten meters to their left. Adam was bleeding badly and beginning to lose consciousness. Isaiah tore off Adam's shirt and used it in an attempt to stem the flow of blood from the wound, just below the shoulder blades. Adam whimpered softly as his father held the wadded-up shirt to the gaping hole where the bullet had entered. He gently turned him over and was horrified by the even larger hole where the bullet had exited the middle of his chest. Adam was no longer breathing and had no pulse.

Isaiah crawled back to his wife, who laid face down and motionless before him. The gush of blood ... she had been struck in the back of her head.

"Oh, my sweet, sweet Rachel. God help me," he said through his tears. He had also lost his beloved wife.

As bullets continued to whiz past him, Isaiah lay face down in the dirt and cried uncontrollably. A few minutes passed without any shots. Slowly he lifted his head ... no soldiers on the porch. Another half hour passed before Isaiah allowed himself to leave the lifeless bodies of his wife and son and venture back to the house. Still battling through a fog of grief, he arrived at the rear of the home, peeking through the side window into the main bedroom. Not detecting any movement, he cautiously moved to the front, held his trembling hands to the window, shading the light so he could see inside. There, in the kitchen area, the bloodied bodies of his father, mother, aunt, and uncle lay sprawled on the floor. He staggered through the front door. All were dead. He crumpled to his knees, at first fighting the urge to end his own life, and then, his strength returning, resolved to somehow, some way, exact revenge.

I

On July 17, 1977 at ten after ten in the morning, Jack Rosen disappeared.

The day started out normally enough. The morning air was perfectly still and warm, and you knew that when it felt like that at nine o'clock, you were in for a scorcher. By noon, the sand would be too hot to play and everyone would move down to the water's edge, where it was ten degrees cooler. I arrived early, first one on the beach, knowing that I had to be at work by one o'clock and wanting to get in the most games I could. As I was walking toward the courts from the parking lot, I could see that I was actually in second place: there was a man cuddled in a raggedy sleeping bag up against the wall. He lay motionless except for the rhythmic rise and fall of the bag, convincing me he was, in fact, alive. Likely one of the homeless who lived in the friendly confines of Santa Monica, he, like many others, chose the beach over the streets or the shelters. The cops didn't bother them here and I guess I would do the same if I were them, at least in the summer. The protection from the wind offered by the Sorrento wall provided a perfect place to spend the night.

I set down my beach bag and cooler in the shade of the magnolia tree against the wall. Then, to get the juices flowing, I jogged in the deep, soft sand toward the shoreline, fully two hundred and fifty yards from the wall to the water. The construction of breakwater walls in Santa Monica Bay decades ago had enabled sand to build up, creating the long trek.

"What's happenin' Billy?" I said to Bill Hayes, the regular guard at Tower 14, as he propped up the wooden window covers, opening his station for the day.

He hooked the last cover, then looked down at me from his ten foot high platform. "Hey Paul, how are ya? Just firin' up for a crowded, busy day. You're here early."

If Central Casting was searching for a lifeguard, Bill would be their choice. In fact, a beach-going talent agent spotted him at work a while back and landed him several modeling jobs. I nearly got in a wreck last month driving down the 405 freeway, when I looked up to see Lifeguard Bill occupying an entire billboard wearing nothing but Calvin Klein underwear.

I sidestepped further from the tower onto the wet sand. "Tryin' to get a game or two in before it gets too hot," I said. The foamy whitewater rushed over my feet, splashing up to my knees, still colder than I would expect for July. I bent low and quickly dunked my head in the water—better to wake you up than a cup of coffee, I always thought. Beyond the small shore break, waves were almost non-existent, as if they had been tamed by the heat of the past few days. A solitary surfer paddled about, hoping against hope for a swell large enough to propel him.

"Betcha the hot days bring out all the crazies, huh?" I yelled, moving my lanky, six foot four frame out of the surf and closer to the tower.

Bill unfolded his wood and canvas chair, setting it up on the small front porch. He settled into the chair and put his feet up on the railing, binoculars in hand. "Oh yeah, we'll get the full assortment today."

Back near the courts, I recognized Doug Williams walking from the parking lot toward the wall. I wished Bill luck and commenced the jog back. Doug would be up for a game. Now we just needed two more.

"HEY LJ, you get in a fight with your barber?" I greeted Doug, noticing that his locks looked quite a bit shorter than yesterday. With his long, shaggy brown hair, reddened and lightened by the daily dose of sunshine, Doug bore a resemblance to Michael Landon on Bonanza, so we took to calling him Little Joe, or just LJ.

He smiled sheepishly. "Just a little disagreement … it's not that bad, huh?"

"Nah, I'm just givin' you crap. Plus, you're married. Whadda you care? Now if it was me that got that cut, I'd be …"

Screeeeech! The tires squealing on the pavement of Pacific Coast Highway, a mere sixty yards from the wall, interrupted me. Doug and I looked at each other, listening. No crash. We exhaled, relieved. The colliding of cars was audible about once a week at Sorrento Beach, and though a common occurrence, it always put a lump in my throat when I heard the awful crunch of metal.

"Wanna go check it out?" I said.

LJ and I walked around the condo complex to get a view of the highway. There, in the middle of the road sat Jack Rosen's Mercedes.

"Holy shit, it's Jack!" LJ said, as we began jogging to get a closer look.

A dark blue sedan, positioned perpendicular to Jack's car, blocked his way. Cars quickly began to back up northbound and southbound as they slowly passed the two stopped cars. Then, as abruptly as it had stopped, the sedan sped away, leaving Jack standing next to his car, screaming obscenities with nobody to hear them. He got back in and drove the Mercedes the short distance into the beach lot. LJ and I moved toward his parking spot to hear the story.

The door swung open wide and out climbed Jack, all five foot eight and two hundred and twenty pounds of him, already puffing on a cigar at nine in the morning. Although overweight, Jack had the healthy glow of a beach bum, just like the rest of us. His plump, round shaped face had less wrinkle lines than it would have because of his weight, making him look ten years younger than his fifty-eight years. I gave him a quick embrace, our daily ritual upon first greeting each other.

"Did you see that asshole? About gave me a stroke. Races along beside me, slams his brakes, spins, and stops right in front of me. Then I get outta my car to see who the hell this guy is … he just takes off!"

"Maybe some idiot kid racing down the street lost control. You're lucky you didn't slam him," LJ said.

Jack opened the trunk and got out his umbrella, beach chair, and a lunchbox-sized ice chest. "No shit, and I just got this car yesterday. It's a '66 250S, a real beauty … already got a buyer lined up."

Jack made a living out of traveling to Germany from time to time, buying several older Mercedes automobiles, shipping them to Los Angeles, converting them to California standards, and then reselling them at three to four times what he paid for them. In Germany they were just old used cars, and there were lots of them. In the United States, the Mercedes name was magic. The beautifully crafted wood interiors and classic lines of the older models commanded a premium, especially in Southern California where people love their cars and have plenty of money to spend on them. Jack spent minimal time doing all of this. He hired people to do the conversion and restore the cars to immaculate condition. Together with an occasional acting job in television commercials, he was able to make a decent living and spend most of his days at Sorrento.

"Here, make yourself useful, boy." Jack handed me his old wooden umbrella, probably manufactured in the 1940's when all the metal was being used in the war effort. It had a heavy duty white canvas top, designed to last and to block all the rays of sunshine, unlike today's lightweight plastic and nylon umbrellas. Over the years, all the regulars at Sorrento, and a few privileged visitors, had taken the magic marker that Jack always carried with him and signed their name to the canvas, some with a note, like the back of a high school yearbook in the form of a beach umbrella. Every inch of the old and yellowed canvas was covered. Mixed in with our worthless signatures were the autographs of famous actors and sports stars who had frequented Sorrento's sands over the years.

"What happened to you? Hope that barber of yours gave you a discount," Jack said with a grim expression, touching his fingers to LJ's shortened hair.

"Ah, screw you guys," LJ said, as we stepped off the asphalt and onto the sand.

Jack and I looked at each other and laughed. "Hope we get a fourth pretty quick. It's really starting to heat up," I said, feeling the warmth under my feet.

"Marlowe should be here any minute. I saw him walking out of Norm's right after I exited the freeway," LJ said. Norm's was a popular coffee shop on Lincoln Boulevard.

I set the umbrella down and got down on my knees to dig the deep hole needed to keep it upright for the day. Jack plopped down next to me in his beach chair.

"You're here early. You spend the night with your buddy over there?" Jack motioned to the man still asleep in his bag.

I laughed. When I first started coming to Sorrento Beach over three years ago, Jack had taken me under his wing, not so much to teach me volleyball, but to make me feel welcome. The Sorrento regulars were a tight knit group, many having grown up together in Santa Monica and others gaining gradual acceptance based on their volleyball skills. Most had been coming to this beach for years and years. For a novice beach volleyball player fresh out of Kansas it was intimidating, and like most newcomers, I was not openly welcomed in the beginning. Jack however, was friendly from day one. He made certain that I got to know everyone, always asking me to play if he needed a partner, or setting me up with someone else if he knew they needed a partner. We became close during the course of the many hours spent together playing volleyball, talking, and just relaxing on the beach. I relied on him for fatherly advice, whether it be about school decisions, career direction, or financial wisdom. We talked about politics, religion, happiness, and the meaning of life. Our relationship developed such that I began calling him "Pops".

"You get a haircut too?" Jack asked as I packed sand around the wooden pole.

"No, just went down to the water and stuck my head in." The curly, blond hair which normally covered my ears was wet and tight to my scalp.

Our conversation awakened the heavy set, bearded man who had been sleeping a few feet away from us. He crawled out of his dirty bag, gathered up a few of his belongings, and trudged through the sand northward, probably to find new solitude and continue sleeping off whatever he had been drinking last night.

Jim Marlowe walked into view, coming toward us along the wall. Marlowe was one of six or seven guys in the Sorrento crowd able to make money playing beach volleyball. Playing in the twelve professional tournaments held up and down the California coast from Santa Cruz to San Diego every year, Marlowe made enough money to avoid working, at least for the summer. Jim had accumulated more wins on the professional tour than any other player, and this particular summer, with Andrew Lee, had won all six of the tournaments that had been played thus far.

Jack tapped some ashes off his cigar into the sand as he eyed Marlowe walking up. As soon as he was within earshot, he yelled, "You and me, Jimmy boy … Court One. These young-sters are in for a whippin'."

About twenty yards from the wall were a row of three volleyball courts and beyond them another row of three more. The courts (unlike at most other beaches where nets and ropes were put up and taken down on a daily basis) were permanently set up with heavy duty nets and thick yellow ropes to mark the boundaries of the thirty foot by sixty foot playing area. The nets hung from a tightly stretched metal cable connected to two eight by eight wooden posts, sunk deeply into the sand nearly as far below the surface as the ten feet they protruded above the surface. White paint on the posts had mostly chipped away, revealing the previous light yellow color. Posts on each court were stenciled with the numbers one through six, the closest court to the wall being #1 and the furthest away in the second row marked with a #6.

"MOVE! You fat old Jew! *Move* for the ball!" Jack berated himself after another of LJ's dinks landed just out of his reach. Midway through our game, he had a look of disgust on his face as he ducked under the net moving to the south side of the court.

"Relax. Just worry about your corner. I'll take care of the rest," Marlowe said. When Marlowe played with Jack he covered three-fourths of the court, leaving his partner with a fifteen by fifteen foot area that he was in charge of. Jack loved playing with Marlowe mainly because he was able to win without expending too much energy. But today was a different story.

"Alright boys, see this? The cigar is taking a courtside seat." Jack discarded his cigar next to the post, a sure sign he would be giving it his all.

LJ's next serve went to Jack, who passed it well. Marlowe set the ball a few feet back from the eight foot net, necessarily further away because of Jack's short stature and negligible jumping ability. Jack, playing on the right side, moved sideways a step to the outside rope, positioning himself behind the descending set. Holding both hands together and raising them over his head, he lofted a short, angled shot, a "cut shot" we called it.

"Short! Go, go, go!" I yelled in vain trying to encourage my partner, the shot landing well in front of him.

"Take *that,* you little cowboy!" Jack gloated, referring to Little Joe's occupation on Bonanza. Jack puffed out his chest, raised his right arm in the shape of an "L" and flexed, displaying a puny bicep.

A couple sideouts later, it was my turn to serve. I jogged a few yards to retrieve the leather, Spalding Top Flite Eighteen ball, the brand of choice for all the good beach players. Starting back to the court, my attention shifted to someone in a dark gray suit, red tie, and black dress shoes walking from the parking lot through the sand towards our game. I held the ball at my side, resting it on my hip, staring at the strange sight.

"Who the hell is that?" I said, as the large man continued to approach.

Marlowe and Jack, on the south end of the court with their backs to him, now turned around, hands on their hips, eyeing the stranger. He had light brown hair cropped in a crew cut, and a long rectangular face that blended with his thick neck such that it was hard to tell where the face ended and the neck began.

"I am looking for man by name of Mr. Jack Rosen," the man announced in a heavy accent I would describe as Eastern European or Russian.

Jack, as mystified as the rest of us, said, "That's me. What can I do for you?"

Stopping about twenty yards from our court, standing stiffly with his arms at his sides, the man said, "I need speak with you in private, Mr. Rosen."

Annoyed at the man's abrupt manner, Jack turned away from him, facing the net as if to resume our game. He said loudly, "I'll be with you in few minutes. We're right in the middle of a game here."

The suited man's voice turned more serious. "No, I'm sorry, Mr. Rosen. It cannot wait. Please come with me right now."

The increased volume and tone of his voice did not leave room for disagreement.

Who is this guy? Taken aback by this unusual visitor and the ominous way he carried himself, we asked Jack if he needed our help. He said not to worry, that he would be right back. So the game stopped as he followed the man toward the parking lot and out of our sight around the condominium building.

That was the last we saw of Jack that day. He never returned for his beach chair, umbrella or cooler. His car remained in the parking lot as the sun dipped below the horizon. He had simply disappeared.

Blonde haired, blue eyed Nancy Williams walked into our apartment late Monday morning. The shorter, dark haired Susan McCarthy came in right behind her.

"So this is the bachelor pad, eh guys?" Nancy said.

Tommy Ruderman and I shared a small one bedroom apartment across the street from the UCLA campus on the corner of Gayley and Kelton Avenues. Tommy had met the Kappa Kappa Gamma sorority sisters the night before at a party in the next door apartment building. We knew most of the Kappas from having worked at the sorority house a year ago as hashers. We served lunch and dinner to the girls, and cleaned all the dishes, pots and pans—fifty beautiful girls and eight of us. But these girls had just finished their freshman year and so were not in the House when we worked there. At the party, Tommy had invited them to stop by sometime to see the apartment. Eager to get to know my tan, muscular, sandy blond haired roommate better, they took him up on his invitation the very next morning.

Tom replied, "Yep. This is the den of iniquity. Meet my roommate, Paul."

I wasn't used to looking at girls eye to eye, but Nancy must have been about six feet tall. She extended her hand. "Hi, Paul." Then she cocked her face to the side and frowned. "Anyone ever tell you, you look like Clint Eastwood? You got the high cheek bones, steely blue eyes, about the right height. Just need to darken your hair a bit and age you about ten years."

I paused for a second, a big grin on my face, not sure how to respond. Finally I said, "Really think so? Well, thank you. I'll take that as a compliment." I liked this girl already, but in the back of my mind I was thinking that this was the one Tommy was going after.

"Nice to meet you, Paul. What a cute little place," Susan said.

My eyes eventually shifted down to Susan after she finished her sentence, and I extended my hand to her. She got it half right. The apartment was little. I could stand in the center of the kitchen and reach everything from the highest cupboard shelf on one wall, to the lowest shelf in the refrigerator on the opposite wall, without moving my feet. But cute would not be a word I would utter in the same breath as Apartment 239. The dark orange shag carpeting, even with our low standards, should have been replaced two tenants ago. Our questionable housekeeping had not helped. The peach colored, vinyl tile flooring in the tiny bathroom, intended to color coordinate with the carpet, was bubbled up and cracking. The best feature of the place was the living room. Located on an inside corner of the building, one wall of the room had large windows overlooking the central courtyard of the large complex and the west-facing side of the room had a sliding glass door opening up to a balcony.

The girls walked into the living room, with Nancy leading the way. She wore green plaid shorts just above her knees, and a yellow t-shirt with *Santa Clara Swim Club* emblazoned across the chest. An episode of *The Three Stooges* played on our fifteen inch television screen.

Nancy said, "Oh, cool ... Stooges! This is the one where they're all trying to sleep in one bed on the train, and Moe keeps sitting up and conking his head on the ceiling." She planted herself on the floor in front of the TV.

"You're a Stooges fan?" Tom asked, disbelieving.

"I love the Stooges. I used to watch them all the time with my brother and his friends," she replied.

Tom crouched down to her left. "Okay, one very important question ... Shemp or Curly?"

"Most people like the ones with Curly, but I prefer Shemp. Cracks me up when he sleeps." Then she inhaled, making a snoring sound, and exhaled, "be-be-be-be-be-be-be ..." a la Shemp.

Tom settled in next to her on the carpet, an amazed look on his face. "I don't think I've ever met a girl that liked the Stooges."

The show was right at its end however, and a minute later, both got up. Tom turned the TV off and Nancy joined Susan, bravely sitting on our tattered and stained couch which we had rescued from a trash bin down the street. I sat cross legged on the floor opposite the girls and Tommy camped in his favorite spot, on the sill of the open window. He had taken the screen out to give himself more room to sit, with half his behind hanging out the window.

Susan was dressed less casually than Nancy, wearing a button-up, light blue blouse, neatly tucked into a cream colored, mid-thigh length skirt. She brushed aside her straight, silky smooth hair and glanced toward the sliding glass door. "What's with the mattress on the balcony?"

I answered, "Oh, that's for guests. We roll out a sleeping bag. Sometimes we drag it into the living room and sometimes they sleep out there. So if you ever need a place to stay …" I glanced at Nancy, but she was busy talking to Tom.

"Thanks, but I think I'll pass," Susan replied, not seeing the humor.

My pride was bruised, getting the strong sense that Susan would have rather been somewhere else. Since she felt that way, and since I'm a guy, and therefore it is my job to point out every perceived flaw in a girl, I will tell you that her nose and her hips were a little on the big side. So now I could feel better about her rejection, knowing I wouldn't want her anyway.

The truth about the mattress was that *I* used it more than anybody, getting kicked out of the bedroom by Tommy whenever he had a "guest". I couldn't remember the last time I had a "guest", and it wasn't for lack of trying.

"So what brings you our way?" Tom asked.

Nancy, whose deeply tanned face was only interrupted by the tender, pink, peeling skin on her nose, said, "You said stop by sometime, so we're stopping by. What are you guys up to today?"

I unfolded my legs, stretched them in front of me, and leaned back against the wall. "Thinkin' about heading down to the beach. By the way, Tom, what'd the guys have to say about Jack after I left yesterday?"

"Oh, everyone thinks it is something to do with his car business. Probably something got screwed up in one of his deals and he had to go make it right," Tom said.

Nancy moved forward, now on the edge of the couch. "What are you guys talking about?"

I said, "Oh, sorry. Yesterday at the beach we were playing a game and this man in a suit and tie approaches us and says he has to speak with Jack. Jack's a friend of ours, an older guy. So Jack goes off and never comes back. Leaves all his stuff there— umbrella, chair, everything. Even his car is still there at the end of the day."

"He probably just came back late, after you guys left," Susan said, leaning back and crossing her legs.

"I'll bet he's pissed off cause he thinks somebody stole his umbrella and chair," Tom said with a chuckle. "I was one of the last guys to leave so I put his stuff in my car."

"Well, I'm sure we'll hear the whole story from the horse's mouth when we get down there today. You guys wanna come?" I said.

"Thanks, I'd love to, but I've gotta work," Nancy said.

"Where do you work?" Tom asked, as he rocked back and forth on the window sill.

"Ships, down on Wilshire. Waitressing. I started there when Spring Quarter ended."

"How about you?" I said, looking at Susan. "You wanna brave it alone with us?" I was really just trying to be polite and didn't expect her to want to come.

"I've already got plans to go up to Malibu with a couple friends,"

"Now why would you want to go to a place like that when you could be with us?" I said, making one last effort to get her to smile.

Tom added, "Yeah, there's a total of about five girls that go to Sorrento. You guys would … w-w-whoa."

Before finishing his sentence Tom seemed to lose his balance on the window sill. He grabbed at the window frame with his left hand as his right leg kicked up. But he couldn't quite grip the frame because of the odd angle. As the girls sat stunned, Tommy's entire upper body disappeared out the window and his legs quickly began to follow. Terrified, I made a last ditch dive across the carpet in an attempt to grab his left leg. But it had happened too fast.

Susan screamed, *"Aaaahhh … my gawd!"* as Tommy hurtled downward.

Horrified, the girls froze on the couch. Next came the sound of his body crashing into water, like when the fat boy does a cannonball into the public pool. Unbeknownst to our guests, who had never been to our apartment complex before, a large swimming pool was directly below our window. Tommy had perfected this stunt, successfully scaring the daylights out of unsuspecting first time visitors. This time it had scared me too. Seeing how awkwardly he was falling out, I had made a real effort to grab him.

Tommy walked up the stairs and through the front door, soaking wet, blue eyes sparkling, and a big grin on his face. "I'm so sorry," he managed to get out while both of us struggled to keep from bursting out in laughter.

Susan was finally able to speak, her face pale. "That was terrible. I can't believe you did that. You almost gave me a heart attack, I swear."

Nancy, the Stooges fan, stood behind her friend, giggling to herself. They said good-bye to us a few minutes later, Susan managing a smile as they walked out the door, but not with the same enthusiasm she displayed when they first arrived.

They were several yards down the hallway when Tommy poked his head out the door. "Hey Nancy, can I talk to you for a second?"

She walked back toward our apartment, Tom meeting her halfway. Tom said, "What are you doing tonight? You wanna maybe catch a movie?"

Her eyes widened, a look of shock on her face. "Tonight? You expect a girl like me to be free on such short notice? I'm sorry, I highly doubt it. I'll have to check my calendar."

She sounded so serious, Tom's confident smile disappeared. "Actually, I seem to recall that I have an opening tonight. Let me give you my number." Then she laughed, as much at Tommy for his stunned reaction, as at her own joke.

Tom went back in the apartment, found a pencil and tore off a piece of a grocery bag to write on. He walked back out and she recited her phone number as he wrote.

"Wow, I must be special to deserve your finest stationery," Nancy said.

"Yeah, only the best for you. So, how about if I call you around six or seven?"

"That'd be good. See you tonight." Nancy rejoined her friend and proceeded down the open air walkway towards the stairwell.

Before they turned the corner, an off-key voice echoed against the apartment house walls. "Hey hey mama said the way you move, gonna make you sweat, gonna make you groove." The girls stopped in their tracks, looking in every direction, then back at Tom, shrugging their shoulders.

With a dismissive wave of his hand he yelled out, "Just ignore it. It's only Singin' Sammy."

Sam Hobart, one of the few non-students in the complex, lived at the end of the hall in Apartment 221. He was a bit unbalanced and had a habit of breaking out into song at random moments. The girls must have inspired his rendition of *Black Dog* as they sauntered down the hallway. Singin' Sammy, with long, scraggly, orangish red hair haphazardly framing a weather beaten face, could usually be found wandering the apartment building wearing a skimpy Speedo swim suit and nothing else. It didn't matter the weather, his attire remained unchanged. On occasion I saw and heard Sammy on campus, traipsing down Bruin Walk or sunning himself in the Quad between Royce Hall and Powell Library. His lack of clothing usually prompted the University Police to "encourage" him to visit elsewhere. But as far as I could tell, Sammy was harmless, and endlessly entertaining, whether it be because of his lyric-perfect serenades, or his habit of scaling the walls like a chimpanzee from the ground floor up to his second floor balcony. Since he didn't like to carry a key, and regularly locked himself out of his apartment, he would make the climb to enter through the sliding glass doors.

Tommy re-entered the apartment, grinned at me and said, "Could be a good one, Townie—even likes the Stooges. But boy, if looks could kill, I'd be dead by now. The other one didn't like my little leap one bit. Whadda you think, Clint?"

"I think that when you lose interest, which I know you will, Mr. Eastwood here is going to give it a shot."

In the years I had known Tommy, he had never lacked for female companionship. But he also had never had what I would call a girlfriend, always dating a girl for a month or two, then moving on to the next one.

I HAD MET Tommy nearly four years earlier in my third week at UCLA. I had just turned eighteen years old. A recent arrival from my home town of Winfield, Kansas, I was moving into Sproul Hall, one of four seven-story dormitories housing over

800 students each. Tommy, at six foot three a bit shorter than me, was at UCLA on a volleyball scholarship, and lived across the hall from me on the seventh floor. I was a late arrival into the dorms, since I'd been on the waiting list. I walked the length of the hall loaded down with my belongings. A tall, lean boy, dressed in flowered beach trunks, flip flops, and a t-shirt that said *1973 Manhattan Open* across the front moved toward me with a grin on his face.

"So you the new guy moving into 741?" he asked me.

"Yeah, that's me. I'm Paul Townsend." I shook his hand, struggling not to drop any of my stuff.

"I'm Tom Ruderman. Nice to meet you. Here, let me help you with some of that."

Arriving at Room 741, I set down everything in the hall and used my new key to open the door to the surprisingly spacious two person room. All the rooms at Sproul Hall had ten foot ceilings which, especially for a tall guy like me, made them feel larger than they actually were. One side of the room: perfectly organized with books lined up in a row on the desk, the bed neatly made, and somewhat disturbingly, a poster of Barbara Streisand on the wall. The other half: an empty desk and a mattress on the floor.

"What happened to the bed?" I asked, as both of us dumped my belongings on the floor.

I noted a trace of excitement in his voice as Tom said, "C'mere, I gotta show you."

He led me to the end of the hall where a large window gave a beautiful view of the campus. When we arrived at the window Tommy pointed down at my bed frame, firmly lodged in the branches of a big pine tree, about the level of the fourth floor.

He spoke like a ten year old boy telling his parents about the "A" he just got on his math test. "Some of us guys got a little drunk the other night and for some reason we decided it would be a good idea to toss the bed out the window. But I saved your mattress. That was my idea."

"Thanks ... I think," I said.

That was my welcome to Sproul Hall and the beginning of my friendship with Tom Ruderman.

AFTER TOMMY'S pool stunt had scared away Susan, dragging Nancy with her, we fixed ourselves some peanut butter and jelly sandwiches, threw a couple apples into our lunch bags, and headed out the door on our way to Sorrento Beach. Tommy drove today, his 1964 Ford Falcon, always an adventure. The brakes worked intermittently, the tires were bald, the seat belts only the lap kind—no shoulder harness, and the dashboard metal. It was a little after twelve when we hopped on the Santa Monica Freeway toward the coast.

We exited on Lincoln Avenue, traveled north about a mile and parked in the residential area up on the bluffs above Pacific Coast Highway to save the five dollar parking fee that the public lot at the beach charged. As Tom locked the car, I looked up in the clear blue sky and took a deep breath, invigorated by the clean, crisp coastal air, and thankful to have arrived in one piece in the Death Trap, my nickname for the Falcon. We walked across Ocean Avenue and started down the long stairway which meandered down the eroding cliff sides upon which the city of Santa Monica was perched. We had gone down no more than a dozen steps before we both stopped in our tracks at the sight below us. In the Sorrento Beach parking lot, a police car was parked next to Jack Rosen's Mercedes. A crowd of twenty or twenty-five people milled about as the police went through the car. Tommy and I exchanged a glance without saying a word, but we both had a terrible feeling in our gut that this was not good.

Doug Williams called the police when he arrived at the beach that morning, noticing that Jack's car was still in the lot. Normally the police wouldn't have sent a squad car for a missing person. Instead you'd have to go into the station to make a report. Plus, Jack had only been gone for a day. But Marlowe knew one of the captains and LJ knew one of the cops from high school, so they sent somebody. After he met the police in the parking lot and gave them a quick rundown, LJ had driven up Temescal Canyon Road about a half mile to Jack's house.

"So you were up at Jack's, huh?" I asked LJ as Tommy and I joined the crowd milling around Jack's car. "Did it look like he'd been home?"

"Nope. The morning paper was still there. No answer when I knocked. I went around to the backyard and looked in the windows—no sign of life." LJ stood with his hands on his hips, his shortened hair only partially controlled by the blue Dodgers cap he wore. "I talked to his neighbor and she remembered seeing him Sunday morning leaving for the beach, but not since. I don't know guys, I'm kinda worried. Where could he have gone? It's just weird."

"Maybe he went somewhere with that guy, they started drinking, and he couldn't make it back cause he was too drunk," Tom said.

I tapped Tommy's shoulder with the back of my hand. "You know, that's probably it. That's gotta be it," I said, excited that he'd come up with a likely answer. LJ nodded in agreement.

Marlowe drove back to his apartment to retrieve a photo of Jack sitting in his beach chair. The police said they would make copies and distribute them to all the street cops. They put us at ease by telling us that in the large majority of their missing persons cases, especially when it has been for such a short period, the person usually shows up wondering what all the fuss is about. By the time we had finished our discussion with the police, we thought it likely that Jack would be waddling down the palisades stairs at any minute, asking who in the hell took his beach chair and umbrella.

The policeman climbed into his patrol car, readying to leave, when I approached and knocked on the window. When he lowered it, I asked, "Is it okay to leave his car here until he shows up?"

"Yeah, no problem. I'll tell the attendant it's okay," he said, then drove off.

"Hey Tom, you really think he went off drinkin' with that guy?" I wanted to believe it, but my gut was telling me otherwise. He just didn't seem like the kind of guy Jack would voluntarily choose to socialize with.

"Probably didn't even need to call the cops if you ask me," Tom said. "I still think that guy'll be dropping off Jack down here anytime now, hung over as hell."

After half an hour in the parking lot, we finally made our way over to the wall, sack lunches in hand, and took a seat on the sand. Jim Marlowe and Harvey Darnell, our resident multi-millionaire, had just finished winning a game on Court One and with no challengers, Tommy and I jogged out to the court to warm up.

Nobody knew for sure how Harvey became so wealthy, but at forty years old and spending nearly half his days at Sorrento Beach, most of us assumed it was inherited. He was evasive when asked about his money, so we eventually gave up trying to find out. His nickname, Rabbit, had nothing to do with his quickness on the court, believe me. Somebody, may have been Jack, saw an old movie in which Jimmy Stewart befriends an imaginary six foot tall rabbit named Harvey. Well, the next day Jack starts calling Harvey "Rabbit", and pretty soon everybody's calling him Rabbit. And it stuck.

"Okay guys we're ready to go," Tom yelled to Marlowe and Rabbit, both sitting under LJ's umbrella.

"We finished over here," Marlowe said as he and Rabbit arrived at the court, ducked under the net, and made their way to the north side. The winning team started out the game on the same side of the court that they finished the previous game.

"You go ahead and serve," I said to Tom, knowing his serve was tougher than mine. I tossed the ball to Tommy and he walked back to start the game. I said, "Hold on a sec. Who's that? Oh no, don't tell me it's one of those paparazzi guys." I spotted what looked to be a paparazzo, walking in from the north, the opposite direction of the parking lot.

The second house north of the condo complex was owned by Jennifer Ryan, a beautiful, sexy, television and movie actress who became famous starring in a television sitcom about ten years ago. She graduated from that to making romantic comedy movies, which made her a mega star. Now, at thirty-two years old and single, the tabloids kept close track of her. I fell in love with Jennifer Ryan when I was fourteen and still was infatuated with her now, seven years later. Not alone in my desires, all my friends in Winfield were in love with her, too. When I first started attending Sorrento and found out that she lived right there, I wrote letters to a couple of my friends to brag about it. I utilized a little poetic license in my writing, saying I ran into her all the time, but the truth of the matter was that I had only seen her once, exiting the gate that led from her backyard to the sand.

About a year ago, she had been with another woman I didn't recognize, and both had walked down to the water for a dip in the ocean. I remember that day like it was yesterday. She emerged from the gate, her wavy, light brown hair blowing in the breeze. I froze in the middle of a point, letting the ball drop to the sand. She wore a plain white t-shirt, an oversized one, extending down to just above her knees, concealing the perfect, petite figure I had seen on television. My heart pounded against my ribcage. My mouth opened to say something, but no words came out. Walking past our court with her friend, she carried a blue striped beach towel, maybe twenty yards from where I stood. Rabbit was on the north side of the court, much closer to where she walked. He said hello and she smiled at him. I gazed at her moving away from us, my mouth still agape, finally remembering to breathe. About half an hour later, we sat up against the wall, our game finished, and she returned from the water, her t-shirt now damp from the wet bikini underneath. This time several of us said hello, and she waved as she went through the gate and back onto her property. I was star struck for days afterwards. Other than that brief sighting, I was content to have her occupy a favored spot in my fantasy world.

The local paparazzi knew better than to frequent Sorrento Beach. Part of our antagonism toward the photographers was simply because we felt territorial about Sorrento. Though it was obviously a public beach, we were not crazy about outsiders. But probably a bigger factor was our adoration of Jennifer Ryan. Although as I said, she was for the most part a fantasy, she was our fantasy, and being our neighbor so to speak, we instinctively protected her. We had several fights with photographers over the years, some physically violent and some just verbal, some publicized and some not. I assume word had gotten out among the paparazzi crowd that Sorrento Beach could be a dangerous place to ply their trade, and for their own wellbeing they usually stayed away. But here came one now.

"What can we do for you, bud?" Rabbit yelled, though the photographer was still fifty yards away. He didn't answer.

"Can we help you?" This time Marlowe shouted out as he got closer.

He awkwardly walked through the sand wearing white Adidas tennis shoes, tight fitting black jeans, and a white cotton dress shirt, unbuttoned halfway to the waist. The man looked to be about thirty years old, had long greasy black hair combed straight back, and a short black mustache. His lily white skin desperately needed some sunshine. He carried a large bag over his shoulder, presumably his camera gear, and a compact two step ladder.

He said, "Relax, boys. This is a public beach isn't it? I'm just catching some rays."

Emboldened by the like-thinking friends who had my back, I said, "Well catch 'em somewhere else. We don't want you hangin' here."

He stopped walking and glared at me. "It doesn't really matter what *you* want, now does it? Like I said, it's a public beach and I'll go anywhere I damn well please." He sat himself up against the wall and unfolded the step stool. He started to take camera gear out of his shoulder bag as Tommy, Rabbit and I approached him.

"Listen, we don't want any trouble with you. We just want you to get the hell outta here," Rabbit said.

The paparazzo didn't look up, intent on attaching a large lens to his camera. He simply said, "Fuck off."

The dismissiveness and indignity of the curse word set Rabbit off. His neck and jaw muscles tightened and he jumped forward, grabbing the camera out of the photographer's grasp and flinging it about 20 yards towards the parking lot. "Get the *fuck* out of here!"

In spite of the three of us towering over him, the enraged photographer jumped to his feet and pushed Rabbit aside with his forearm, as if he were an intruding vine on a jungle trek. The shove knocked Rabbit off balance, causing him to stumble to the sand. Then the paparazzo moved toward him, hovering over Rabbit with his fist cocked. I rushed at the guy, intending to tackle him before he could throw the punch. I slammed into him, leading with my fist, which landed solidly with surprising force just below his left eye. The blow caught him by surprise. He staggered back a step, then fell backwards. Landing on the sand, his head snapped back and hit hard against the wall. His nose gushed blood from the force of my blow and he lost consciousness from hitting his head against the concrete.

"Holy shit, Townie. I think you killed him!" Tommy said.

LJ sprinted to Tower 14 to tell Lifeguard Bill. I stood there, unmoving, staring at my victim. *Oh my God, what have I done? It all happened so fast.* Marlowe checked the guy's breathing and pulse. He did not need CPR. Within two minutes, the sirens of the paramedic vehicle blared on Pacific Coast Highway. They drove the van through the parking lot, onto the sand, and continued the fifty yards to where we stood, surrounding the bloodied, motionless man. They let him breathe something like smelling salts, which brought him back to life. Then the two paramedics eased him onto a stretcher.

Moving toward the ambulance, the photographer lifted his head, and his eyes locked onto mine ... hateful, furious eyes. He said, "You're going to be sorry you ever met me. You better watch your fuckin' back." Placed into the rear of the van, still pointing his finger at me, the doors closed and he was driven away.

Still out of breath from his quarter mile dash, LJ said, "You know any good lawyers? That guy'll file charges for sure."

It hadn't occurred to me that I could be arrested. I felt numb. My anger of five minutes ago was replaced by the uncertainty of what trouble I might be in.

"No, I don't know anybody."

LJ put his hand on my shoulder, reassuring me. "Don't worry, man. A buddy of mine from my platoon went to law school after Nam and became a criminal defense lawyer. He's really a sharp guy. I'll call him and tell him what happened. You've got witnesses, man. That asshole attacked Rabbit. You were just defending him."

Marlowe added, "Don't sweat it Townie. The Santa Monica cops all know us and they hate the paparazzi. We got ya covered."

The words comforted me but I couldn't shake the haunting look in the photographer's eyes, something about his eyes … soul chilling eyes … *sorry you ever met me … watch your back* ….

4

I arrived at Buck's Sporting Goods still in a fog because of my confrontation with the paparazzo. Work was about the last place I wanted to be. What I really needed was three or four beers in me. I had been working at Buck's since right after my sophomore year, the first summer I had decided to stay in Los Angeles and not go back to Winfield.

"Hey guys," I greeted Ernie Nichols and Ken Slater in a monotone as I made my way through the Ski Department toward the time clock.

"What's wrong with you?" Ernie said, tugging at one end of his light brown mustache.

I glanced back at them and hesitated. "Nothing, why?"

Ernie, thirty-four years old, the manager of the Tennis Department, knew me better than anyone. "You don't look so good. Your eyes are kinda glassy. You okay?"

"No, I'm good. Just a little tired is all."

I continued up the back staircase to clock in and was surprised to see Buck Braddock in his office. Normally by this time he was in his camper in the back parking lot, drinking whiskey, chatting with friends, maybe playing poker.

"Howdy, Paul," Buck said as I reached the top of the stairs. He wore a cowboy hat, embroidered, western style shirt, a shoestring tie, and an oversized belt buckle in the shape of the state of Texas.

"Hey Buck, surprised to see you up here this late."

A little under six feet tall, Buck had curly, bright white hair which usually needed a trim, and the tanned leathery skin of a man who spent a lot of time outdoors. That time out of doors was mostly spent with Emily, his wife of fifty years, at his ranch in Tehachapi, a little community outside of Bakersfield, about a two and a half hour drive north from Santa Monica.

"Believe me, I ain't gonna be here much longer. Had to do a special order for a buddy of mine. Wants a certain kind of backpack for a trip he's takin' to Alaska."

I punched my timecard and it read 2:59. Good to be on time when your boss is sitting right by the clock.

Buck's, which occupied a dilapidated old, frame and stucco building, carried a full line of sporting goods, but the store thrived on two specialties—skiing and tennis. The longer leg of the L-shaped building was mostly filled with ski equipment and skiwear. Beyond the skiwear at the top of the "L" was a relatively small area for hunting, fishing and backpacking. The corner of the "L" was for tennis shoes, skis, and ski boots. The shorter leg was the Tennis Department, where I worked. I had been hired to work in Tennis since I had played quite a bit in Winfield and knew a little about the sport. Plus, I knew nothing about skiing, so I needed to become a tennis expert.

"We got many rackets to do?" I asked Ernie, who was still standing with Ken as I passed them heading toward Tennis.

"Couple more. I saved 'em for you so you wouldn't be bored this afternoon."

"What a guy," I said, loud enough for him to hear, although I didn't look back.

"Just lookin' out for ya," Ernie yelled out as I turned the corner.

I arrived to an empty Tennis Department. There were two rackets—a Head Professional and a Wilson T-2000—hanging from the far left peg, where we put all the rackets due for the day. They were both scheduled for a six o'clock pick up. I took the Head Pro and secured it in the Ektelon stringing machine.

RENEE AYERS, a seventeen year old high schooler, had started working a week ago in the Ski Department. I had just grabbed a set of nylon string from the back shelf, when she turned the corner. Her straight, light brown hair was parted down the middle and extended nearly to the middle of her back. Let me just say this. UCLA has lots of beautiful girls. And the Kappa house, where we worked, allowed me to get to know some of the elite. But Renee Ayers … wow … she took my breath away.

"I'm soooo bored over there. Can I come bug you for a while?"

"I'm available to be bugged by *you* any time you get the urge," I replied, beaming from the attention.

She stretched her arms high above her head, fingers interwoven, and yawned. Her powder blue skirt moved up as she reached, revealing long, slender legs.

"That's so cool, you get to have music over here," she said, bringing her arms down and stepping over to take a closer look at Ernie's stereo system. He had brought in his receiver, tape deck, and speakers and set them up on the shelves directly behind the stringing machines. A Led Zeppelin tape was playing, probably a little louder than it should have been.

"You like doing that?" she said, staring at my fingers deftly threading the strings through the racket frame, tightening and clamping the vertical strings one at a time.

"I do, yeah. Every racket is like a piece of art. Keeping the string in good condition and getting the tension consistent across the whole racket ... it's a real skill, and the top players appreciate a good job. The racket plays better."

She continued to look blankly at the racket. "Doesn't look too thrilling to me."

Ernie stuck his head into the room. "Paul!" he said in a loud whisper. He had an excited look in his eye and spoke quickly. "Kenny and I have been watching this guy for the past ten minutes and he's been lifting a few things. He stuffed a couple knit caps down his pants and a T-shirt under his sweatshirt. Come on over. We might need your help."

The three of us stood in different areas of the Ski Department and not so subtly kept watch on the young man, probably sixteen or seventeen years old, wearing a big, baggy hooded sweatshirt and loose fitting blue jeans. He may have gotten spooked when Ernie and I joined Ken, because he headed for the front door within a minute of us coming from Tennis. As he moved to leave, we edged closer to the door, several feet behind him. Taking one quick glance back at us, he broke into a dead run as soon as the door closed behind him. Ken was first to the door with Ernie close behind. I decided to go out the back door so that if he made a right turn when he got to the sidewalk I would be able to cut him off. The chase was on. He had about a ten yard lead on Ernie and Ken, and was sprinting like a mad man.

We had all been trained to watch for shoplifters and it happened pretty often, seemed like at least once a month. Confronting the person inside the store meant you could get the merchandise back, but you wouldn't be able to charge him with a crime, since technically it didn't become a crime until he walked out of the store. This was true even if you had videotape proof of him hiding the stuff, which we did, since Buck had every inch of the sales floor being videotaped at all times. We would keep a watchful eye on the perpetrator while he was in the store and if we were absolutely sure he had taken something, we would grab him as soon as he walked out the front door. But unlike the majority of people we confronted, this guy meant to get away.

Ken and Ernie lost some ground on the sprinting thief when he made a right turn around the building at the end of the parking lot. He was running on the sidewalk along Wilshire when I leapt out from the back parking lot and stood directly in his path, my heart racing and adrenaline pumping.

"Alright asshole, game's up!" I yelled, as Ken and Ernie quickly closed in from the other direction.

The thief reached into his pocket and quickly withdrew his hand, like a gunfighter from the Wild West. He flipped open a shiny steel blade about four inches long. "Back off fuckers … *back off*!" he said, crouching in a sideways stance so he could see all three of us. Waving his knife back and forth menacingly, he reminded me of a cornered animal.

"Whoa, man. Take it easy," Ken said.

I took a few steps backward, raised my hands in a sign of surrender and said, "You're free to go, man. We're not stopping you."

At that, he ran directly across Wilshire, dodging the oncoming traffic like a tailback, then continued to run north on 10th Street after he crossed. We breathed a sigh of relief.

"I'm not getting paid enough for this kinda shit," Ken said, as we nodded in agreement.

BUCK HAD called the Santa Monica Police shortly after we began our chase, but the guy was long gone in the five minutes it took for them to arrive. The cop put out a call to all the units in the area but I never heard if they caught him.

When I returned, Renee stood by the swimsuit rack, mindlessly rehanging and organizing the suits. *Communication Breakdown* blared from the speakers.

"Did you catch him?" she asked.

I raised my eyebrows and paused before answering. "Uh … no. He had a knife."

Renee gasped and pressed her hand to her mouth. "Oh, my God."

I leaned over the swimsuits, both hands firmly gripping the stainless steel, circular bar that the suits hung from. "Yeah, first we asked him if he would like some more clothing, a tennis racket or two, our wallets maybe? Then we told him to have a nice life and bid him farewell."

Hanging a final swimsuit, Renee stepped away from the rack. "Did he get close to you guys with it?"

"No, not really. We backed off and he took off running." I shook my head and moved over to the stringing machine to pick up where I had left off. "One fight a day is my limit."

"Whadda ya mean? Who else did you fight?" she asked, taking a step toward me.

"Nobody … just a little misunderstanding at the beach. It was nothing."

Renee eyed me warily, not really believing me, but letting it go.

"Well, why don't you take me to a movie after work? Get your mind off all your battles." She stood in front of me, swinging her arms restlessly and casually clapping her hands. "*A Star is Born* just came out last week. Let's go see that."

I stopped weaving the nylon string and looked up at her. "You're kidding, right?"

"No, it's supposed to be really good."

"Tell you what ... I'd love to take you to *A Star is Born*."

"Really? You'll take me?"

"Yep. I'll take you ... then come back a couple hours later and pick you up." Now the truth of the matter was that I could sit through any movie, even a Barbra Streisand one, if I was next to a girl as beautiful as Renee. But I wanted to try to get her going a little bit, see what kind of spunk she had.

She put her hands on her hips and looked defiant. "Ha ha, very funny. And what would you like to go see, Mr. Opinionated?"

Knowing in advance her probable reaction, I said it anyway. "How about *Kentucky Fried Movie*? I've already seen it, but I'd go again."

She rolled her eyes, and said, "Oh, please. Now *you've* got to be kidding ... sooo infantile. You just went down a notch in my book, Mr. Townsend."

I turned around and decreased the volume of the Zeppelin tape. "Ah, c'mon. Do you even have a sense of humor? Name a funny movie you've seen lately."

"*Annie Hall* ... saw it last week."

"Yeah, okay, sorta funny. Nowhere near as good as his earlier funny movies, though. *Take the Money and Run*, now there's a classic."

"Oh, my God. I can't believe you would say that." She put her palm to her forehead, a look of disbelief on her face.

"Maybe we should just go to dinner," I said.

She did her best to hold back a smile. "I don't know. After hearing your taste in movies, I'm starting to wonder if you'll be able to hold an intelligent conversation."

"See, I was wrong. You do have a sense of humor," I said, patting her on the shoulder.

"Okay, dinner it is. But you look pretty tired. Maybe next time we work together. How about sushi?" She reached out to shake my hand, closing the deal.

Leaving her hand waiting, I said, "Sushi? You're kidding right?"

It was called The Big Press. Two weeks ago at Christmas my big present from Santa Claus was a toy printing press that operated just like the real ones. When you hand cranked it, the red plastic printing plate lowered, pressed against the ink pad, and as you kept cranking, the stack of paper slid under the plate as it lowered for a second time to print the letters and pictures on the print plate. At age eight, being the budding entrepreneur that I was, I utilized The Big Press to its fullest commercial utility and printed a weekly newspaper. Every shred of news and gossip I could dig up in my neighborhood I meticulously spelled out with tiny rubber letters fitted onto the printing plate. I proudly printed up several copies of the Neighborhood News and sold them door to door for five cents each.

Our neighbors were used to me coming to their door selling something. It started about a year earlier when we had more pomegranates on our tree than our family could eat, and Mom had already made a ton of pomegranate jelly. So I loaded up my wagon with pomegranates and went a few blocks in each direction until they all sold. Looking back on it now, I'm sure most people bought them because they couldn't turn down the cute little seven year old boy, but hey, whatever works. Next, there were the flower and vegetable seed packets I ordered from some company that offered prizes if you sold enough. Then, last summer, I took a bucket, dish soap, and some rags door to door, offering to wash cars for a dollar. I didn't get too many takers on that one, probably because that same kid that was too cute to turn away with his wagon full of pomegranates, was just a little young to turn loose on the family car.

This particular day I was home with my older brother Mark, a sixth grader. My sister Cathy, thirteen years old, was over at a friend's house working on some school project. I had written a story about the Carlsons, our next door neighbors, and how their English Terrier had threatened to take a chunk out of the mailman's leg. Granted it would have been a bigger story had the dog actually bitten the mailman, but I took what I could get, and this was the biggest news in our neighborhood that week. I was positioning some of the larger size letters into the plastic printing plate to spell out the title of the story, *Dog Almost Bites Mailman*, when my brother walked in.

"I can't believe you're spending so much time with that thing," Mark said.

I fit a capital B into the rubber slots, then looked up. "It's a weekly newspaper and tomorrow is Saturday, delivery day."

Mark scratched his head, disturbing his perfectly combed, dark brown hair. "People actually buy them?"

I gave my head one definitive nod. "Last Saturday was my first edition and I sold seven copies–made thirty-five cents."

Mark hovered over me, examining my typesetting. "Seems like a lot of work for thirty-five cents."

"Heck, I can get seven packs of baseball cards for thirty-five cents. Plus, I like doing it. It's fun." I shrugged my shoulders.

"Well, it *is* a pretty cool printing press," Mark admitted.

I stood up, deciding to save the rest of the job until later. "When are Mom and Dad getting home?" I asked.

"Mom left in a hurry and said she was going to Dad's office. I'm not sure why she went there, but they should be home pretty soon. I'm getting hungry," Mark said with a frown, patting his tummy.

WE ATE DINNER at home, as a family, pretty much six nights a week, the seventh night being Friday night, our night to go out somewhere, usually Me n' Ed's Pizza Parlor, or DiCicco's, an Italian restaurant, or Perry's Smorgasbord. Friday night was a kind of celebration of the end of the school week and work week for Dad. But the other six nights, Mom would always cook, going into the kitchen around four-thirty or five so it would be ready when Dad got home at six o'clock.

My dad, Robert Townsend, worked as a tax accountant in a small office building in downtown Winfield. Dad worked hard. He worked all day at the office, then came home and worked some more. If not accounting, then he was doing yard work or some house repair. He didn't spend much time doing stuff with me or Mark, but he was always there, never too busy to answer a question or help us with homework or whatever. He never left any doubt in my mind that we were what was really important to him. And I always felt like I was his favorite. Don't know if that was the case, but I think it was. One

of my earliest memories was him reading me a bedtime story
when I was four years old, squeezed in next to me on my bed.
He finished the book, said good night, and told me never to
forget that I was his special boy, more important to him than
anything in the world. That's why I think he liked me better
than Mark or Cathy.

Marsha Townsend, my Mom, worked until two o'clock
every day at Betty's Bake Shop, the most popular bakery in
Winfield. My sister, brother and I definitely reaped the benefits of Mom's job as she would daily bring home leftover cookies, cinnamon rolls, cakes and pies. It was a wonder we hadn't
turned into tub-o's, eating all those desserts, but our whole
family was skinny as rails.

NOW IT WAS CLOSE to eight-thirty, and not a word from
Mom or Dad. Mark and I had eased our hunger by melting
cheddar cheese on toast, cutting some salami slices, and having
chocolate chip cookies and ice cream for dessert. Moments after
we polished off our second helping of Rocky Road, the sound
of a key in the front door brought us to our feet. At our ages,
we didn't run to greet Mom and Dad when they arrived like we
had when we were younger. But tonight we did.

"Mom! Dad!" we cried in unison.

I hadn't said much to Mark, not wanting to be a baby
about it, but I was worried about Mom being gone so long
and Dad not coming home at his regular time. Judging by
how fast Mark ran to the door, I got the feeling he was pretty
worried too.

Mom opened the door. Black streaked down her face from
tears that had ruined her makeup. Her eyes red and puffy, she
broke down and began sobbing. She hadn't said a word, and I
had no idea what was wrong, but tears came to my eyes too. She

reached out with both arms and embraced Mark and me, burying her face on Mark's shoulder.

"What's wrong, Mom? What is it?" I asked.

Mark backed away from the hug and looked out the front
door. "Where's Dad?"

Between sobs, Mom answered, "Your father ... had a ...
heart attack ... at the office. He didn't make it."

I can still remember playing in the sandbox in kindergarten. It was my number one favorite thing to do at recess. Maybe that is part of the allure of the beach—something very basic, taking us back to our childhood. Add to this the competitiveness of beach volleyball, and you've got an intoxicating formula for a young man. You dig your opponent's hard hit ball, then go up and smack it down to the sand right in front of him. You puff out your chest a bit, and for a moment, you are the conqueror. The combination of the sun, sand, ocean, good friends, and great sport, is ... why so many of us went to Sorrento Beach day after day.

THE SAND was damp from the fog that rolled in late yesterday afternoon and hung over the coastline all night long. The gentle offshore breeze brought a musty, briny odor with it. A little before noon, the sun started to break through the gray armor of clouds. I had just made the walk down the palisades stairs, and laid my cooler and bag up against the wall. Marlowe and Andrew Lee were playing on Court One against Matt Jackson and Fred Shaw, from Manhattan Beach, probably the second best team on the tour this year, having gotten second place in three of the six tournaments.

"Whoa! Man! Unbelievable," LJ said to no one in particular. Jackson had just crushed a ball straight down but Andrew stuck out his left arm and the ball popped straight up. After a nice set from Marlowe, he softly put the ball away with a precise cut shot out of reach of a diving Fred Shaw.

"I can't believe you boys drove all the way up here just to get beat up on," Andrew said, readjusting the blue bandana he always wore to keep the shoulder length dark brown hair out of his eyes.

"Shut the fuck up and serve the ball," Shaw said, still brushing the sand from his arms.

Andrew stood behind the back rope, raising the ball to serve. "Okay, which one of you pretty boys wants it?"

"Just serve the fuckin' ball," Jackson said.

Andrew had honed his trash talking skills in the NBA, having played four seasons with the Milwaukee Bucks before being cut and returning to volleyball, a sport he had grown up playing on the beaches of San Diego.

The next serve went to Jackson again, who passed the ball well, got a nice set from his partner, then took out his building anger on the ball, swinging at it mightily. Unfortunately for Jackson, he mistimed the hit slightly and the ball sailed a good ten feet beyond the end line.

"*Fuuuuuck!*" Jackson screamed.

Andrew approached the net with a big grin. "Hey Matt, c'mon man, this is a family beach. Watch your language there."

Jackson stormed to the net and jabbed his finger in the middle of Andrew's chest. "Fuck you, man, *fuck* you! You're a fuckin' asshole, you know that?"

Andrew backed up a couple steps, still grinning, his hands up in a show of surrender. "Calm down, Matt. The sun's out. We're at the beach. It can't be all that bad."

Shaw came up to restrain his partner and after a few seconds they were ready to continue playing. Andrew could have that effect on people. He backed up his brashness by always winning, and that made him even tougher to stomach.

There were about thirty people on the beach but nobody was playing on the other courts, everyone wanting to watch the action on Court One. I sat down next to LJ, who told me he had come down earlier and already played a couple games. I picked up a handful of sand and let the grains slip through my fingers.

"So what's the count?" I asked.

"I think it's 6-4 Marlowe," he said.

I enjoyed watching the top players in the sport, and in fact emulating them was one of the best ways to improve your volleyball, but at the moment I was itching to play a game myself. "You up for a game?" I asked LJ.

"In a bit, yeah. I wanna watch these guys another fifteen or twenty minutes. Is that cool?" he answered.

"Yeah, that's fine. I'll grab somebody and go warm up," I said. You're already warm right?"

"Yep, just finished playing," LJ said.

SEEMINGLY the only people at the beach not watching Court One were Michelle Santos, Scott Rodgers, Beverly Smith, and June Richards, all engrossed in a game of Uno, the card game of choice at Sorrento. I walked over to ask Scott if he wanted to play.

He looked up from his hand and said, "Count me in. Give me five minutes here. I'm almost done whipping these girls."

"Hah! Yeah, right. You mighta dreamed last night about whippin' us, but it had nothing to do with a card game," Beverly said as the other girls roared.

Scott just smiled and ran his fingers through his short, curly brown hair.

Beverly and June were older, maybe in their mid-fifties, and had been playing volleyball regularly at Sorrento for a long time. Michelle was only twenty-six and learned the game a couple years ago, after her divorce. But she had grown up playing tournament tennis and her athleticism made her a quick learner.

"Or maybe it was the three of *us* whipping you? Is that what you're in to?" Michelle continued the harassment. Michelle was a little over five feet tall, very busty, with slender hips and muscular legs. She wore her straight, dark red hair with bangs, just long enough to be feminine looking.

Poor Scott was outnumbered and the laughter persisted at his expense as I walked away. I carried with me a mental image of Michelle in skimpy lingerie wielding a leather whip.

It took about fifteen minutes instead of five, but Scott eventually finished the card game and walked over to where I was sitting with LJ.

"So, did you put them in their place?" I said.

"No, I'm afraid they squished me like a bug. I think they got pleasure out of seeing me eat my words," he said with a look of resignation.

"So how long you here for?" I asked, as he took a seat next to LJ.

It seemed to me that Scott Rodgers had the perfect job. On the surface, being a U.S. Postal Service worker may not fit your idea of a great job, but consider that he got to work outdoors, got a good amount of exercise, usually accomplished his eight hours of work in about five or six hours, and had the flexibility to do the work when he wanted to, as long as he was finished by day's end.

"Oh, I got time. Long as I'm outta here by two or so. Everything's sorted and in my truck. I just gotta deliver it. Usually takes about four hours," the six foot two inch postman replied with a yawn, patting his large belly.

In spite of the daily exercise from his work and the volleyball, Scott was overweight. Not Jack Rosen overweight, but overweight nonetheless, especially for a young man of twenty-eight. Were it not for his weight, he would have been one of the best players at Sorrento, not counting Marlowe, Lee and the other tournament guys. He had been a tremendous athlete at Samohi, playing football, basketball, and baseball. We went out to Court Two to hit the ball around.

"HEY, WHAT ARE the cops doing here again?" Scott asked as he spotted a squad car driving across the lot and stopping at the sand.

I stopped bumping the ball, held it in my hands, and turned toward the parking lot. "I dunno. What do you think? More questions about Jack?"

Two uniformed officers exited the car and began making their way toward the group watching the action on the main court. The game stopped, and everyone stood frozen in place as the officers approached. They chatted briefly with LJ who had walked over a few steps to see what they wanted.

"Hey, Paul, come on over here," LJ yelled at me.

Still thinking it must be related to Pops, I jogged over to where they were standing. The officers were all business, no pleasantries. The officer in charge directed his hard gaze at me. "Are you Mr. Paul Townsend?" he asked.

A wave of apprehension enveloped me. "Yes, sir."

The same officer continued, "Mr. Townsend, we need to ask you a few questions related to injuries suffered by a Mr. Carl Sedgewick."

My shoulders sagged as if a load of bricks had been dumped on them. Carl Sedgewick had to be the paparazzi guy and this meant he was pressing charges. But I asked anyway, "Who is Carl Sedgewick?"

"He's a photographer who has filed a report saying that you assaulted him yesterday afternoon. We're going to need you to come with us to the station, Mr. Townsend," the officer said.

I swallowed hard and went to the wall to grab my stuff. I put on my t-shirt and followed the officers off the beach. I got in the back of the squad car and we headed onto Pacific Coast Highway and up to the police station. There was little conversation during the ten minute drive to the station. I was nervous about saying something I shouldn't, not wanting to incriminate myself. My rapidly beating heart wanted to explode from my chest. *Could I go to jail? Could I get kicked out of school?* I regretted not getting the name of LJ's lawyer yesterday when he brought it up.

LIKE A FISH out of water, I entered the sterile, formal, Santa Monica Police Headquarters in my beach trunks, T-shirt, and flip flops. The vinyl tile floors, steel desks, and heavy fluorescent light fixtures protruding from the "cottage cheese" ceiling weren't designed to give you a warm, fuzzy feeling. The room they led me to contained four, heavy wooden chairs, one large metal table, and nothing else within the barren, faded yellow walls. One of the walls had a large mirrored window which I assumed was a one way window, allowing them to observe the interrogations without being seen.

After a nervous wait of several minutes, a man in a white shirt and tie entered the room. "Hello, Mr. Townsend, I'm Captain Wentworth. I need to ask you a few questions about the incident at the beach yesterday afternoon." No handshake was offered.

Fearing the worst and a little jumpy, I asked, "Do I need to call a lawyer? Am I under arrest?"

I detected a thin smile as Captain Wentworth replied, "No, you are not under arrest at this point."

At this point? What is that supposed to mean? That there'll be plenty of time to arrest me after they're done with the questioning?! My mind raced. *Should I stop talking?* My instincts, rightly or wrongly, were telling me not to make Wentworth angry, but to cooperate and get on with it.

"OK, what would you like to know?" I asked, folding my arms tightly across my chest.

He tapped his finger steadily on the cold, metal table. "Just tell me what happened when the photographer came to the beach yesterday ... from the beginning."

Growing up in the Midwest, I had been taught to respect the police, that they were your friends, and that you could trust them. I decided to tell Wentworth exactly what had happened. Anxious and speaking quickly, I said, "The guy walked onto the beach carrying his little step stool and started to unload all his camera gear. We asked him to please leave, cause we don't think it's right for him to start taking photos and invading people's privacy. Well, he started cursing at us, so Rabbit lost his temper and threw his camera across the beach. That's when he knocked over Rabbit and went to go slug him. Then I jumped in to help Rabbit. I hit him in the face and he lost his balance and fell backward and hit his head on the wall. We told Lifeguard Bill and he called the paramedics. And that's the whole story."

Captain Wentworth eyed me intently as I spoke, probably trying to determine if I was being truthful. Not saying anything for a few seconds after I finished, he picked up a nearby pen and twirled it in his hand. Finally he spoke, "Mr. Townsend, let me make sure I understand clearly. Why did you ask him to leave? Was Mr. Sedgewick harassing anyone?"

"Not till he knocked over Rabbit," I said.

"Let me put it another way. Was he bothering anybody with his picture taking?"

I unfolded my arms and rested my elbows on the table. "No, he hadn't started taking any pictures."

"I see." The Captain shifted in his chair, paused again and then continued. "How did you even know he was a paparazzo?"

His questions twisted it to make it sound like it was all *our* fault. My nervousness diminished, and I began to get irritated by Wentworth's attitude. "I could tell. We all could tell. It was pretty obvious."

"You know, Mr. Townsend, there is nothing illegal about taking photos of someone's backyard. He was on public property."

The helplessness of the situation was becoming apparent. Nothing could be gained by disagreeing with him. I simply responded, "Yes sir."

At this point the policeman leaned forward, looked me directly in the eye, and lowered his voice. "Paul ... what you did could very well be felony assault. If he had hit his head a little harder on that wall, it might have killed him, and then you'd be looking at manslaughter."

I felt the blood draining from my face, suddenly feeling dizzy.

Wentworth continued, "Last night I got a call from Jim Marlowe. Jim and my son have known each other since grade school and were good friends in high school. He told me the same story that you did. He said you guys at Sorrento all hate the paparazzi and do your best to keep them outta there. Well, let me tell you something. I'm not crazy about 'em either. I wish to God they would make it illegal, some of the stuff they do." He lowered his voice a bit more and said, "I'm going to recommend that we do not charge you with anything. As far as I'm concerned, you were just doing what you had to do to defend your friend. And according to Jim it sounds like you've got about twenty witnesses to attest to that."

At that point I could have given Captain Wentworth a big hug and a kiss, but instead said, "Thank you sir, that is a big relief."

"Okay, you're free to leave," he said, rising up from the table.

My first instinct was to get out of there as fast as my two little legs would carry me, before they changed their mind and locked me up. But as I walked out the door I turned around and asked, "Have you come up with anything on Jack Rosen?"

"I'm sorry, who is Jack Rosen?"

"Oh, I thought you would know. He disappeared a couple days ago from the beach and we reported him missing," I said.

"Stay here a minute. I'll get somebody from Missing Persons," he said as he left the room and closed the door.

Not eager to stay in that room any longer than I had to, I nevertheless waited with eager anticipation for news about

Jack. After another ten minutes, a slender black man in gray slacks and a light blue dress shirt with the sleeves rolled up, entered the room.

"Hello, I'm Detective Streeter. Can I help you?

I pushed back my chair with a squeak of wood on linoleum and walked around the table to where the slightly graying, middle-aged detective stood. "Yes, I was wondering if you had any news on Jack Rosen. We reported him missing a couple days ago."

"I remember the name. He's in our system, I know that. All the street officers have been informed and are on the lookout for him. But we don't have anything yet," Streeter replied.

"Do you assign a detective to the case or anything? To look for clues?" I asked.

"I'm sorry, I didn't get your name," the detective said.

"Paul ... Paul Townsend," I answered.

"Paul, to be quite frank, we have hundreds of missing persons, and hundreds of crimes we are investigating. The missing people take a backseat to the unsolved crimes, and we've got way more of those than we have detectives." Streeter took a seat on top of the table. "So the best I can do is tell you that every cop on the street is aware that Mr. Rosen is missing. They have his photograph and carry it with them in their squad car as they go about their business. Chances are he will show up sooner or later on his own accord ... most of 'em do. But in the meantime, that's about all we can do."

THIS EXPLANATION did not instill confidence. If Jack was in any kind of real trouble, it was going to be up to his friends, and not the police, to get him out of it. Captain Wentworth spotted me as I left the room and I took him up on his offer to give me a ride back to Sorrento. We climbed into a squad car and I was allowed to sit in the front seat this time.

"What's your son up to these days ... the one that's friends with Marlowe?" I asked, trying to make conversation on the ride back.

"Moved to Hawaii with his girlfriend about a year ago. Lots of surfin' and just enough work to get by I suppose." Wentworth sighed.

"Doesn't sound half bad to me," I said.

"Me neither ... maybe I'm just jealous," he said, glancing over at me with a smile.

He pulled into the parking lot and the attendant waved him through. I thanked him again as I hopped out of the squad car, and he told me to say hello to Jim and to try to keep my fists to myself. As I walked through the sand from the parking lot to the courts, a wave of gratitude washed over me. Were it not for the phone call from Marlowe, I might have been in serious trouble.

I walked straight up to Jim and interrupted their game as he was about to serve. "Thank you, thank you, thank you. You saved my ass for sure. I really appreciate it, man."

"So Wentworth was cool?" he said, as he set the ball to himself.

"Yeah, he scared me at first, then told me he had talked to you and that you were friends with his kid. Then he told me I could leave. I was so happy to get the hell outta there."

"You owe me one, Townie. Owe me one big time."

I moved off the court and toward the wall. Everyone crowded around, wanting more details and peppering me with questions. After a few minutes, people returned to their games and their beach chairs. I settled down next to Tommy against the wall. I grabbed the bottom of my t-shirt with both hands and used it as a towel for my sweaty face. "Tom, I think we're going to have to try to find Jack ourselves." I explained to him the bleak manpower situation at the Santa Monica Police Department.

Tommy said, "What are we supposed to do? I have no idea what happened."

"I don't either, but I've got the feeling that Jack needs us. I've gotta do something. I can't just sit around and wait," I said, as much to myself as to Tommy.

Half an hour later Tommy and I climbed the steps together, heading toward our parked cars. We had decided to go to Jack's house and see what we could find. It may have been the blind leading the blind, but we had to start somewhere.

1

We found the key to the front door of Jack Rosen's house where it always was, underneath a large stone near the mailbox. We grabbed the Tuesday newspaper laying on the front porch, emptied the mailbox and walked into the house, locking the door behind us. We were hoping to find a clue, any clue, as to what might have happened to Jack.

Tommy scanned the house crammed full of Jack's belongings. "Oh jeez, look at all this crap. Where do we start?"

"Good question. I'll take the bedroom. Why don't you take a look around the house for any names and numbers he has written down. Could be on a note pad or a scrap of paper, anything you can find."

Jack's small, two bedroom house was an old one, built in 1918. Typical of the bungalows built near the beach early in the century, many of them served as part time summer or weekend homes for the wealthy living further inland. The practice of living full time at the beach didn't become common until years later. It looked like a house occupied by a single man, a man not overly concerned with tidiness or cleanliness. He was too cheap to hire a cleaning lady, and it showed. The hardwood floors which extended throughout the house felt gritty underneath our bare feet, a sprinkling of Sorrento sand inadvertently deposited here by Jack, no doubt being the cause. The two dark brown leather couches were a step above our apartment couch, but that wasn't saying much. Hundreds of books of all shapes and sizes were arranged haphazardly on the many bookshelves in the living room, den and bedroom. The Sunday paper was scattered on a table in the kitchen. Above the table was a bulletin board covered with layers upon layers of papers, notes, photographs, receipts, and postcards. All in all, it gave the impression of a very comfortable existence, but one certainly devoid of any female influence.

My first thought was to go to his desk and try to find something among his business papers that would give us some direction. I walked into the bedroom and gazed at the old oak rolltop with at least forty stuffed-to-bursting pigeonholes. I sat on the battered swivel office chair and slid open the long, shallow drawer underneath the writing surface. This was the catch-all drawer, with paper clips, pencils, pens, pads of paper, a take-out menu from Chong's Chinese Food, a tattered old address book. *An address book!* I set the leather covered, pocket sized book aside, knowing this was the type of thing we were looking for. Done with the first drawer, I started perusing the three drawers that extended down the right side of the large desk. In the top one, I found a year's worth of bank statements bound by a large rubber band, and put them next to the address book. I also spotted a check register booklet with "Jan–Jun

1975" written in blue ink on the outside cover. I lifted the rubber band and stuck the booklet in with the bundle of statements.

"Hey Tom, having any luck?" I shouted out, not knowing where exactly in the house he was.

"Yeah, there's quite a bit in the kitchen. I'm just taking anything that looks interesting and stuffing it in my pockets. I got a few notes that were taped on the fridge and some scraps of paper with names and numbers that were laying on the counter by the phone. How about you?"

"Got his address book, some bank stuff. Now I'm pulling out some files for his cars, it looks like." I removed several files from the bottom drawer that appeared to contain documents and notes from Jack's many car purchases and sales. I stacked these in a pile next to the bundle of bank statements and the address book. I planned to take all of these back to the apartment where we could take some time to look through everything.

I moved away from the desk, still sitting in the swivel chair and rolling it over to the bookshelf to begin looking at some of the additional files he had stacked there. Tom was several feet away in the kitchen.

Glass shattered. I froze in place.

Tommy whispered loudly, "Holy shit! What was that!"

"Quick, get in here!" I whispered back.

The old wooden window frame screeched. *Somebody is breaking in!* The only two escape routes, the front door and patio door, were in plain view of where the burglars were entering. *We're trapped!*

"Under the bed!" I said. I had the forethought to grab the pile of stuff I had set aside, and then scooted head first through the dust and trash populating the floor underneath the queen sized bed in Jack's bedroom. Jointly maneuvering ourselves diagonally so that our feet were not sticking out the other end, our faces were but a few inches from the bed's edge. We flattened ourselves on our stomachs as best we could, but our backsides still scraped the support boards of the box spring above. Two men spoke in a foreign language outside of the room. In the dim light under the bed, I saw Tom's frightened eyes, and I imagine he saw the same thing looking at me.

Cupboards were opened, drawers dumped, and papers scattered. We stayed silent and motionless as one of the men entered the bedroom, his black leather shoes moving about. I said a prayer to myself. Clothes from the dresser landed everywhere on the floor. Two times he left the room and then returned. Now the second man joined the first in the bedroom and began rustling through Jack's papers. *What language is that?* Nothing I had heard before. The voices became agitated. Books and folders were thrown about. It occurred to me that I had already found what they were looking for. The two sets of shoes surrounded us, inches from our faces one minute, then to our sides and behind us. In spite of the chilly air, beads of perspiration rolled down the sides of my face. *Can they see my feet?* I imagined that we would be dragged out and unceremoniously killed. I struggled to retain my composure and fought the urge to crawl out from under the bed and run for my life. My neck ached from the awkward upward position I held my head. *What are they doing now?* To relieve the tense muscles I turned my head to the side and rested my cheek on the floor. I resigned myself to waiting, helpless to do anything but that.

Tommy fidgeted beside me. *The burglars will surely hear the movement.* One of the men left the bedroom, the talking between them ceased and only one pair of feet now moved about. More anxious minutes passed. The remaining man walked out the door, leaving Tommy and I alone in the bedroom. I breathed a sigh of relief, hoping they were finished in the bedroom. We dared not utter a word, still hearing them in the house. A door opened and closed. I assumed it to be the door leading to the patio and backyard. But dishes, pots, and pans crashed in the kitchen, the other guy still inside. When the second guy returned, the conversation increased in volume, an argument about something. The heated discourse continued, but in the midst of it, the front door opened, and the voices became more distant. We stayed where we were, listening intently, and after another minute or so, a car started and was driven away.

Tommy whispered softly, "I think they're gone."

"I think so too. Let's get the hell out from under here."

Our legs were useless because of the tight squeeze under the bed, so with our hands flat on the hardwood floor in front of us, we used our arms to pull ourselves out. We cautiously poked our heads outside the bedroom door. No sign of them. I turned around and embraced Tommy. "You alright?"

"Yeah, I'm good. How 'bout you?" Tom replied, breathing a sigh of relief.

"That could be the closest I've ever come to crappin' my pants," I said. "I thought for sure they were going to check under the bed. Hell, they tore apart every other square inch of the house."

The house had been thoroughly ransacked. Kitchen cupboards and drawers were open, desk drawers removed and papers strewn about.

"Man, oh man, these guys mean business." I finally spoke again after a moment of stunned silence.

Tom sat down on one of the leather couches. "We should call the police, Townie."

I flashed back to my visit to the police station earlier that day and replied, "Tom, I'm tellin' you, the cops are so overloaded with stuff, this will just be another case on a long list for some overworked detective. We'll call 'em, but first let's search a little more ourselves."

WE CAREFULLY waded through the mess, trying not to disturb the crime scene as best we could. Walking into Jack's bedroom, it was more of the same—drawers removed from the dresser, clothes thrown everywhere, papers and books scattered about. I got down on my belly and reached under the bed to retrieve the address book, bank statements, and files.

I set down the papers and brushed the dust off my shirt. "Let's not waste time looking through this stuff right now. Anything that looks interesting, we'll take with us and examine it in detail back at our place."

"Yeah. It's giving me the creeps being here. I'd rather get out of here sooner than later," Tom said.

There wasn't much else to find, but we did take a couple more files from car deals and some pay stubs from commercial acting work. About an hour passed until we satisfied ourselves that we had found everything of importance. Only after all of the paperwork was secured in the trunk of my car, did we call the Santa Monica Police to report the break-in. We told them that the burglars had left a couple minutes ago, not wanting to explain why we had waited an hour to call. Carefully avoiding the broken glass, we sat down on the front porch to wait for the police to arrive.

THE SUN WAS LOW on the horizon, obscured by a low fog rolling in once again. There would be no beautiful sunset this evening. The neighborhood was quiet—no people out in their yards and no cars passing by. It had already been a long day and I hoped the police would get there quickly. Tommy sat with his knees pulled to his chest, arms wrapped tightly around them, trying to keep warm. The temperature had dropped at least ten degrees since we arrived and we were both cold, wearing only our beach trunks and t-shirts.

"Maybe I'll be wrong about the cops," I said. "It was foreign guys that broke in and it was a foreign guy that left with Jack from the beach. Maybe they'll put two and two together and realize this is something serious. How long has it been since we called?"

Tom looked at his watch. "About half an hour. I sure hope they get here soon. I'm starving."

But they didn't get there soon. We moved back into the house to wait where it was warmer. Tom helped himself to some peanut butter and jelly, about the only choice in Jack's refrigerator. *Where the hell are they?* Another hour passed before the squad car pulled into the driveway. I reminded myself to be respectful, but I was tired and cranky by the time the cops got out of their car and approached us.

"Which one of you is Paul Townsend?" one of the cops asked.

"That's me. I'm the one who called. What took you so long?" I asked, unable to hide my impatience.

The officer, not pleased at the question or the tone of my voice, answered curtly, "We got here as quickly as we could. It's been a busy day. Now please give me your full name and address, Mr. Townsend."

Tommy and I gave him our names, Kelton address and phone number, then told the officers everything that had happened.

As one of the officers continued to write notes on a clipboard, the other asked in an accusatory tone, "Explain to me again what you were doing in the house?"

Even though we had told him the entire story of Jack's disappearance, the cop seemed to be suspicious of us being in Jack's house. I turned my head away from him and rolled my eyes.

Exasperated, I said, "I told you sir, we were trying to find information which might help us locate Jack."

The policeman glared at me. "Mr. Townsend, I think you should let us do our job. I would hope for your sake that you do not get into the habit of entering people's homes without their permission."

"Yes sir," I said blankly. "May we leave now?"

"Yes, you both may leave. We'll call you if we need further information," the officer said.

Tommy and I got into our separate cars and headed home to the apartment, the "further information" secure in my trunk.

"What an asshole that guy was," I said, as we entered the apartment. I looked at the living room clock ... 9:55. My hands were full, carrying all the papers we had taken from Jack's. Tommy's were full carrying the bag full of Fatburgers and fries we had picked up in Westwood on the way home. I walked to the table in the living room and laid everything out. Tom was right behind me with the burgers. The living room table would do double duty as desk and dinner table. A little ketchup, mustard, or grease on the paperwork wouldn't keep me from doing what I needed to do.

Tom handed me my burger as I squeezed ketchup from the small plastic bag onto a napkin.

"Yeah, you guys didn't really hit it off," he said.

"Hit it off? Hell, he was more worried about you and me breaking into Jack's than trying to catch the other guys." I dipped three fries at once in ketchup and stuffed them in my mouth. "I'm sorry, but those cops are worthless. Jack will be dead and gone before they figure it out. It's up to me, Tom ... you and me."

Tommy set down his burger and looked me in the eye, an unusually serious expression on his face. "Can I ask you a question?" he asked.

"Sure, what?" I said.

"Why are you taking this so personally? I mean, it seems like you think it's *your* responsibility to save Jack. Why you? Like that cop said, why not let them do their job?"

The question surprised me and I didn't have an immediate answer. He was right. Logically I knew he was right. I took a big bite from my burger and chewed it slowly, thinking. I picked up another fry, waved it towards Tom, and said, "I don't know why. I really don't know why. But it's something I have to do. Something inside of me is driving me to do this. I can't explain it. I don't understand it. But it's something I have to do."

Tom smiled thinly, shaking his head as I struggled with my explanation. "Well, if it's that important to you, I'm with you every step of the way, you know that. We'll be like those detective brothers, what's their name? The Hardy Boys. Yeah, that's it, we'll be like the Hardy Boys."

Holding my cheeseburger inches from my mouth, I paused and chuckled. "Probably be more like Laurel and Hardy."

EVEN THOUGH it was late and it had been a long day, I felt energized to start going through the files that we had brought home with us. I felt sure these men had something to do with the car importing Jack had been doing for several years. But what could they have been so desperate to find in his house? And had they kidnapped him? What purpose could that possibly be serving? I had no clue what language they were speaking—could've been German I suppose. *Is Jack into drug smuggling?* I had heard about people filling up tires with cocaine or sealing drugs into door panels of shipped cars. But from Germany? I couldn't imagine that Jack would be involved in something like that. In any case, I began with one of several files that Jack had created, one for each car he brought over. As I carefully leafed through the paperwork, I jotted down names and phone numbers with the thought of calling people to see if I could dig up clues. I completely finished two files and set them aside. An hour passed. Tommy was camped in front of the television watching Johnny Carson's monologue at low volume so as not to disturb me. The tediousness of going through the paperwork made me sleepy and ready to crawl into bed. But I was curious about the stack of bank statements rubber banded together and decided to take a look at a statement or two before calling it quits.

"Hey Tom, look at this." I had opened Jack's bank statement from July of 1975 and noticed a deposit of $50,000. "Where in the hell would he get that kind of money?"

Tom got up from the floor and looked over my shoulder at the statement. "I dunno. How much does he sell those cars for?"

"Not that much. He always said that he bought the cars for four or five grand and sold them for ten to fifteen."

"Well, maybe he sold three or four of 'em at once."

"Maybe …"

Feeling a new energy, I opened several more statements and saw that every three or four months there was a deposit ranging from $40,000 to $70,000. I made a timeline and wrote down all of the large deposits for the two year period for which we had statements. Next, I went through all of the files we had for his car purchases and subsequent sales. As best I could determine from the information in the files, I blocked in the time periods when Jack had traveled to Germany in search of cars. The pattern revealed on the timeline was startling. *Every one of the large deposits is made after his return from a trip to Germany! If the money had been from selling the cars it would have been deposited after he had been home for a while, but these deposits were made within a day or two of his return. What does this mean? The man at the beach, the men that broke into his house, these deposits ... are they related? What is Jack involved in?* At 2:15am I finally made my way to bed, exhausted. Tommy had already been asleep for an hour.

THE DIGITAL CLOCK read 4:03am when Tom woke me up. "Townie! Wake up! Townie! You're having a bad dream," he said as he stood over me and gently shook my shoulder.

My pillow was wet with tears when I woke. The noise of my crying had woken Tommy. "Oh jeez, what a dream. Sorry, man," I said.

"Wow, you were crying up a storm. What were you dreaming?" Tom asked, returning to his bed to sit down.

I sat on the edge of the bed and buried my face in my hands. Then I looked up and began to explain. "I dreamed I was in my house in Winfield with my Dad, sitting in our living room. I was the same age I am now. It was great to see him—it was so real. I haven't dreamed about my Dad since right after he died. Then this big guy barges into the living room. I don't know where he came from. He grabs my Dad, holds a gun to his head, and starts dragging him away. I tried to go help him but I couldn't move my feet. Our living room was full of sand ... deep, thick sand. And I just couldn't move my legs or my feet. It was like I was stuck in cement. My Dad kept calling my name, but I couldn't move. That's when I started crying. And the kicker ... the guy that was dragging my Dad away ... was the guy in the suit that went off with Jack."

"The Alpha Theta Girls Club of Rosedale High School is proud to announce that we have chosen our basketball coach for the annual game against the Tri Delts. By unanimous vote we have chosen ... Paul Townsend!" Cynthia Fernandez, president of Alpha Theta, made the announcement at the monthly school assembly. I stood up and acknowledged the applause, not surprised by the news since Cynthia had told me before the assembly that I had won the vote of club members. She told me ahead of time just in case I decided to turn down the opportunity.

There were two girls' clubs at my high school, the Alpha Thetas and Delta Delta Delta. The high school equivalent of sororities, they did community service projects and held monthly meetings that were mostly social gatherings. Pretty much every cute girl in my high school was in one club or the other. Once a year they played against each other in a fund raising basketball game in the school gymnasium. Two thousand people usually packed the gym for the big event. Traditionally, each club chose one of the seniors on the boys' varsity basketball team to be their coach, which was of course an honor, but also not a small amount of work since there were three practices a week for a month before the big game.

I was terrified at the prospect of being alone with fifteen high school girls, but at the same time, excited by it. Kind of like that first school dance that your mom made you go to in the seventh grade. You really didn't want to go, were a little scared to go, but you knew it would be good for you, so you went. Or that speech you had to give in front of your fifth grade class on photosynthesis. You were frightened by the very thought of getting up there in front of everybody, but you knew you had no choice, so you did it.

I needed practice, but not basketball practice. I needed girl practice. I had never had a girlfriend, and in fact had only ever gone out with a girl once in my life, a year and a half earlier on the first weekend after getting my driver's license. It had been a disaster. The experience so traumatized me that I hadn't asked a girl out since.

Being the Alpha Theta basketball coach was a chance for me to interact with the opposite sex on my own turf, so to speak—be in my element—since if I knew anything, I knew basketball. I had been playing organized basketball since the fourth grade and by the sixth grade it supplanted baseball as my prime reason for living. The hours and hours of practice and the fact that I continued to grow and grow—all the way to six foot four as a senior—made me a pretty decent high school hoopster.

Lori Lewis ran up to me as the assembly ended. "Congratulations Paul! It's going to be so much fun having you as coach."

Lori Lewis! Lori Lewis had never even spoken to me. I didn't think she knew my name. Maybe she had just learned it when the club was voting on a coach. But I knew who she was. I had always put Lori in my Top Five. That would be the top five hottest girls at Rosedale High. I kept a running list, which changed from time to time, but Lori had been solidly on it since she started at Rosedale a year after I did. Not that I ever attempted to speak to anyone in my Top Five, let's get real, but I was expert at admiring them from afar.

She put her hand on my forearm, stood close to me as the students rushed around us to get out of the auditorium. I inhaled the richness of her perfume. My body tensed and my throat went dry as I replied, "Thanks for choosing me. I'm really looking forward to it."

"I'm looking forward to it too. You're such a good player. I'm sure you'll teach us lots of good stuff," she said, striking me dumb with her captivating, deep dark brown eyes.

Lori Lewis is standing here talking to me! After a long pause, I finally said awkwardly, "So ... guess I'll see you around." I moved away, still facing her, but taking a few steps backward and giving a little wave before turning to walk to my next class.

Lori yelled after me, "Don't forget. First practice is next Thursday night!"

"Oh, I won't forget." And then to myself I said, "Damn right I won't forget."

I HAD BEEN anxiously awaiting it all week and now the time was here ... the first Alpha Theta basketball practice. We had been allotted two hours of gym time from 6:30pm until 8:30pm in the school gymnasium, after the volleyball team finished their practice. I made the decision a couple days ago to take this seriously. The temptation was to make it all fun and just have a good time. But they wanted to win, and in order to be successful, they needed a lot of conditioning and training in some of the basic skills. The Tri Delts were assumed to be the favorite since they had a couple of seniors who starred in last year's game. I arrived at six-fifteen just as the last of the volleyball girls were heading into the locker room. I helped Coach Taylor take down the net and remove the metal poles from the slots in the hardwood floor. He showed me how to lower the backboards from the rafters with the hand crank so that we could finish the conversion from volleyball to basketball facility. Coach Taylor also brought out a rolling stainless steel rack full of basketballs for the girls to warm up with.

It is six-thirty. Thirteen girls dressed in gym shorts and tank tops. I can hardly stand it! I'm spellbound by the long legs, the short shorts, the tight fitting shirts, the flowing hair. I must be sex crazed, probably doomed to be a sex offender. I'm not sure any of these girls would be safe with me for more than a few minutes.

Cynthia Fernandez broke my trance, stopping her warm up and walking up to me. "So whadda ya got in store for us, Coach Paul? Should I get everyone over here?"

Time had flown as I sat gazing at the frolicking, nubile bodies. It was six forty-five and Cynthia was right—time to get started. "Oh, thanks Cynthia. No, I got it."

"Everybody come on over here and sit down," I shouted out to the group. They gathered around and quieted, all eyes upon me as I started in with my opening words of wisdom, carefully prepared and memorized in the last two days. "First of all let me say that I really appreciate this opportunity and am so happy you chose me. I hope I can live up to your expectations." My voice cracked when I said "expectations". I detected a murmur of giggles.

Embarrassed and nervous, I continued. "We've got exactly ten practices before the big game. That's not a whole lot of time but if we all work hard and stay focused, it should be enough. My goal will be to condition you so that you can run hard for an entire game. I know some of you already know the basics, but we're going to spend a lot of time working on fundamentals—dribbling, passing, shooting—so that they become second nature to you. Lastly, and maybe most importantly, I want you to learn how to play excellent defense, because that alone may be enough to enable you to win the game."

Relieved to have made it through my opening speech with only the one glitch, albeit a mortifying one, I looked at the sea of faces and exhaled. "Are there any questions so far?"

Several hands shot up, but before I could call on anyone, the questions came hard and fast. "Yeah, how tall are you?"

"Are you dating anyone?"

"Do you have a secret girlfriend or something?"

"The girls at Rosedale aren't good enough for you?"

I stood petrified in front of thirteen giggling girls, blushing a deep shade. My mother would have said, "They're not laughing *at* you, they're laughing *with* you." *Yeah, right.* If they were laughing *with* me, that means I should be laughing too. *Hey, wait a minute. I'm the coach. I'm in charge. We'll see how funny they think I am.*

"Okay, everybody up! Let's start by taking five laps around the gym. Let's go! Let's go!"

After they finished running, I started them off with some passing drills, then some full court dribbling. We spent the entire two hours doing conditioning and drills with no actual shooting of the basketball. By eight-thirty no giggling could be heard. I had successfully worn them out and the girls probably thought they had made a big mistake in choosing me to be their coach. I said good night to all the girls and headed home, kind of worn out myself.

No sooner had I stepped out of my car in the Buck's parking lot to clock in for the morning shift, than I heard the chorus from the guys in Ski Repair.

"Macho, macho man, I've got to be, a macho man. Macho, macho man …" They all sang in unison.

"Can I hire you to be my bodyguard?" Ken Slater, the twenty-four year old manager of the Repair Shop, yelled out.

Totally bewildered, I locked my car and started toward the Repair Shop entrance.

"Oh God, here he comes! Don't hurt me! I didn't mean it when I said you were a shitty racket stringer," Larry Ashworth, another Repair Shop worker, said as he cowered behind Ken.

All three of the Repair guys stood by the door with big grins on their faces as I walked up.

"Have you gone completely off your rockers? What the hell is going on?" I said.

Ken stood in the middle of the other two, carefully parting, and then combing, his greased, brown hair off to one side. "Don't tell me you haven't seen it yet," he said.

"Seen what?" I asked.

"The Daily Outlook." He was referring to the Santa Monica Daily Outlook, a local paper which Tommy and I did not receive at our apartment.

He stuck his comb in the back pocket of his tight fitting blue jeans as I followed him to the rear of the workshop. The smell of the solvent used for removing old wax from skis filled my nostrils. He found the paper on the workbench. "Check it out."

There, on the front page of the second section, was my photo. An article detailing the incident with the paparazzo occupied about a quarter of the entire page. The reporter singled me out as "a local volleyball player who got into a fistfight with a photographer because he was trying to take photographs of Jennifer Ryan." The article dramatically explained that the paramedics had to come to take the photographer away. They made it sound like I had almost beaten him to death with my fists. Somebody at the beach must have called the paper. LJ and Rabbit, who were quoted in the article, were the likely culprits. Wanting to publicize that the Sorrento crew had vanquished another member of the paparazzi, they had "enhanced" the facts.

"Nice photo, Paul," Ken said. I'm not sure who at the beach had provided it, but The Outlook had used a photo of me taken about a year ago at Sorrento, sitting up against the wall. My hair was long at the time, kind of ratty and going every which way, after a windy day at the beach. Although I couldn't exactly remember, I had probably had more than a couple beers, had a crazed expression, and was giving my best wild man pose for the camera. The picture portrayed a mass murderer, easily capable of mutilating a photographer.

I leaned over the bench, bending down to get a close look at the photo. "Jeez, I look like a thug."

"Camera doesn't lie," Ken said.

Leaving the paper behind, I went back to the front of the shop. "And it didn't happen the way they said at all," I protested.

"C'mon, it makes you sound like a stud. Just go with it— you're a hero. Nobody likes the paparazzi," Larry said, as he secured a ski in a vise, readying it to begin sharpening the edges.

"You're right about that," I replied, as I proceeded out to the parking lot, and then into the front entrance to go clock in.

My timecard read 9:03am after I punched the time clock. Scheduled to work until six, I looked on the list for Renee, and saw that she would be in at noon. The anticipation of seeing her put me in a good mood for the rest of the morning. When I walked down to get started, Ernie was already working on the first racket. He had finished the vertical strings and was just starting to weave the horizontals.

Approaching him from behind, I said, "Wow, what time did you get here? You're already half done with that."

Ernie glanced over his shoulder, looked at me with sleepy, hazel colored eyes, and gave me a nod. "I was giving a lesson early up in Rustic Canyon and decided to come straight here when I finished. So how are *you* doin'? I half expected to see you all busted up and black and blue after I read that article."

I walked over to the rackets to be done that day and chose a Slazenger wood racket due at 11am. "It wasn't like what they described at all. He was going after a friend of mine so I jumped in to stop him. When I slugged him, he fell over and hit his head on the wall. And that was it."

"Well, good job, tough guy. Didn't think you had it in you," Ernie said, as he clamped the bottom horizontal string.

THE MORNING crept by, with not a lot of customers except for a couple people picking up their rackets. Luckily, quite a few rackets were due, and that kept Ernie and me busy for the morning. Right before I was set to leave for my lunch break, laughter drifted in from the Repair Shop. Being only a few yards from the Tennis Department, I left my half-completed racket and walked over. Ken and his two cohorts crouched down below the window line, peeking out the window and trying their best to stifle their laughter. It was July, and not a lot of people were getting their skis tuned-up in the middle of summer. With too much time on their hands, the Repair Shop guys were getting creative.

"Get down, Paul! Get down!" they whispered to me. They had attached a dollar bill to some nearly invisible small gauge fishing line, set the dollar on the sidewalk out near Wilshire Boulevard, and then run the line about thirty yards all the way back to the repair shop.

An older woman, probably in her sixties, walked eastward on the sidewalk, fast approaching the dollar bill. At first she didn't notice it, but after passing it by, she retreated a couple steps and bent over to pick it up. Her hand was no more than a foot away from the money when Larry gave a little tug on the line, "blowing" the bill just out of her reach. Staying in her bent over posture, the woman took a couple steps towards the wayward bill and made another attempt to corral it. The four of us giggled like schoolgirls as Larry once again pulled the dollar out of her reach. Now the woman got out of her crouching position and stood straight.

"She's going to step on it!" Ken said.

Larry kept the bill just beyond her step as she chased in high heeled shoes through the parking lot towards the Repair Shop entrance. We were beside ourselves, and apparently, not so quietly. Hearing our guffaws, the woman stopped in her tracks, her head turning upward to find our faces peering out the window. Her embarrassed look told us that she knew we were enjoying her futile efforts to capture the bill, but I don't think she figured out that we were the ones powering the runaway money. Having four people watching and laughing was enough to make her give up the pursuit. She straightened her skirt, gave us a wave and a shrug of the shoulders, and went on her way. I thanked the guys for the humorous interlude and returned to Tennis, while Larry went out to the parking lot to retrieve the dollar bill and carry it back to the sidewalk so they could do it all over again.

"HEY ROCKY," Renee teased as she walked into the Tennis Department. "So that's the other fight you weren't telling me about. Are you crazy? What happened?"

Ernie and I were busy working on rackets. I looked up and smiled at Renee, dressed in a powder blue skirt and matching striped top. "Yeah, just call me Clark Kent. But seriously, it wasn't like that at all." And I proceeded to tell her the real course of events, so unlike how the paper had made it appear.

Giving my forearm a squeeze, she said, "Wow, I think I can feel those Popeye-like muscles in there. Bet you couldn't take me though." Then she made a fist and hit me playfully on my arm.

An attractive middle-aged woman entered Tennis and directed her question at Renee. "Young lady, can you help me pick out some ski pants?"

"Sure, be happy to," Renee answered and then walked with the customer into the Ski Department, leaving Ernie and me to ourselves.

"Well, she's not being *too* obvious," Ernie said as we continued stringing the Jack Kramer wood rackets.

"Whadda ya mean?" I replied, playing dumb.

Ernie crouched down to get a better view as he stuck an awl through one of the holes in the wood frame, clearing out a little room for the next string. "C'mon, she's all over you like a two dollar banlon. You're lucky. She's cute, smart, and I hear her parents are loaded. What more could you want?"

I stopped stringing for a minute and looked at Ernie, dressed in his tennis whites, same as I was. "Think about it, Ernie. She's *half* as old as you. She's seventeen years old for crying out loud!"

Ernie put the clamp on the last vertical string. "Hey, don't give me crap about how old I am. And it's not *me* she likes, unfortunately. Heck, when I was on the circuit, I was twenty, twenty-one, and there were seventeen, eighteen year old girls everywhere."

Ernie was formerly a professional tennis player. The number one player for USC in 1963, he left school early to go pro the following year. But then a shoulder injury, a rotator cuff, ruined his ability to compete at a high level, and he retired at the ripe old age of twenty-three.

"Yeah, and what'd you do about it?" I said, still looking at him.

He ran the fingers of his right hand through his styled, tan colored hair. "What any red blooded American male would do—messed around with 'em. But no sex—not worth going to jail."

I began stringing again. "Glad to hear you've got *some* morals."

Hearing him mention the tennis circuit reminded me how tough it had been for Ernie. One day he's a successful tennis pro and then the next day he's giving lessons to some arrogant fourteen year old kid and stringing tennis rackets at Buck's Sporting Goods.

"Look, you're only twenty-one. In four years you'll be twenty-five and she'll be twenty-one. What's wrong with that?"

"Nothing wrong with that … in four years. But now is now and she's still only seventeen."

Ernie hung his head and said, "I'm telling you, man. Girls like her don't come along too often."

I WOVE IN the final string at the top of the racket and cranked it to seventy pounds tension. Then I clamped it close to the edge of the racket, thread the gut string through the next hole and neatly tied a knot onto one of the vertical strings to finish off the job. I released all of the clamps, removed the racket from the stringing machine, and placed it on the peg with the other finished rackets waiting to be picked up.

"I'm gonna go grab something at Pinnochio's, you want something?" I asked Ernie as I headed upstairs to clock out for lunch.

Ernie's eyes got big and he replied, "Oooh! Can you get me some lasagna? Pinocchio's sounds *so* good right now."

"Meat or veggie?" I asked.

"Meat, baby. Here's five bucks."

I took the money, clocked out, then headed out the back door to walk to Pinnochio's, a little Italian restaurant about half a mile from Buck's. I went there all the time, and usually took my car, but today I decided to take the walk, it being such a beautiful sunny day, and knowing I wasn't going to make it to the beach for any exercise. Twenty minutes later I returned and went to Tennis. Ernie and I enjoyed an uninterrupted lunch, our only challenge being not to drip any tomato sauce on our tennis whites.

BY THREE-THIRTY we had finished all the rackets and there was no need for both of us to stay. I could not get my mind off Jack. I walked out to the trailer to ask Buck if I could leave early, anxious to go home and continue going through the papers we had gotten from Jack's house. I climbed up the two steps on the fold-out stairway that protruded from the trailer door. I poked my head in to see Buck sitting by himself, sipping on what I assumed to be a whiskey and water, his favorite drink.

Buck looked up as if I had interrupted a deep thought. "Howdy Paul, what's up boy?" he greeted me.

"Hey Buck, sorry to bother you. I'm supposed to work until six but we're done with all the rackets and Ernie's gonna be here, so I was wondering if I could leave early."

Buck's bright white, tousled hair looked as if it needed a brush run through it. "Okay by me—not a problem. You got something important to do?"

Burdened by all the information I was keeping to myself, without any forethought, I decided to confide in Buck.

"Well, actually something very important," I answered after a pause.

I think Buck could sense from the tone of my voice that I wanted to talk. He said, "Well, come on in and have a seat. Let's hear it."

So I ducked my head, entered the cramped confines of the trailer and had a seat across from him at the table.

"Can I get you a drink? You're twenty-one aren't you?" Buck offered.

"Thanks, but no. I've gotta drive home," I said.

He closed the copy of *Field and Stream* he had been reading and slid it to the end of the table. "What's so all fired-up important that you want to hightail it outta here early?" Buck asked.

I proceeded to tell him the whole story, from the initial disappearance, to the break-in at the house, to the discovery of the large deposits in Jack's checking account. Buck listened quietly to my story, sipping on his drink. It felt good to tell someone. And I trusted Buck, in a grandfatherly kind of way.

"That's pretty much it. I'm just not sure what to do now."

Buck remained silent for a few seconds, his drink still at his lips. Then he set down the glass and looked at me. "The cops wouldn't like it one little bit that you were takin' stuff outta Jack's house before you called 'em. That's known as disturbin' the scene of the crime. But you've told the cops everything you know about the case, right?"

"Except for those big deposits. They don't know about that."

Buck retrieved the last cigarette from his pack of Camels and put it between his lips. "Well, you should probably tell 'em."

I rhythmically tapped all ten fingers on the yellow formica. "I know I should. This case just doesn't seem to be very high on their list."

He cocked his head to the side and scrunched up his face, looking out the small window in the back of the trailer. He removed the still unlit cigarette from his mouth, and said, "Well, I hear ya, Paul. It seems to me like you have to start hollerin' at everybody in his address book, every vendor on every invoice, every name and number on every slip of paper you found. And when you call people, just tell 'em the truth—that Jack disappeared from the beach and you're tryin' to figure out what happened to him."

Buck was right. This was the only way to gather more information. I had intended to start calling people but I had hesitated, maybe subconsciously not wanting to get more deeply involved. Once you did that, things could get more complicated. But it was the only way.

I said, "You're right. I had been thinking about doing that."

Buck added, "If you had any sense in you, you'd turn everything over to the cops, let *them* worry about finding your friend, and stay out of it. But I've lived long enough to know that some good sense you listen to and some good sense you can't live with."

I nodded in reply, a smile forming on my lips. Buck understood.

"I can tell you're bent on doing this. Just know you could be playing with fire." He struck a match to light the cigarette, then chuckled at the timing, holding up the small flame.

"I know, I know. One look at what they did to that house tells me that," I said.

Dismissing me with a wave of his hand, he said, "Well then, go on. Get outta here and start making those calls."

I arrived at our apartment, fired up to begin making phone calls after the pep talk from Buck. The door was unlocked, meaning Tom was back from the beach.

"Hey man, what's the good word?" I said, seeing Tommy seated at the table facing the balcony, his back to me. Tommy said nothing in reply, barely acknowledging my entry with a slight lift of his chin. I walked to the table and sat heavily in the chair opposite him. He had a sullen expression, his eyes cast downward, looking at a dirty fingernail he was trying to clean using another fingernail.

"You know, sometimes I'm envious of you, losing your Dad at a young age," he said, not looking up.

I stared at him without speaking, trying to digest his words. I quickly realized this was not about me.

"I hate him. I just hate him so much. I can't tell you how many times I've wished he were dead." He lifted his head and looked at me for the first time with angry, bloodshot eyes. "I think he thrives on making the people around him feel like shit. I can't remember one thing I've accomplished that he didn't think was a waste of time."

"What happened man? What did he do this time?" I wondered what could have launched Tommy into this mood.

"Nothing happened. I just got off the phone with the asshole. He doesn't understand why I'm wasting so much time playing volleyball, since I'm not good enough for it ever to make a difference in my life." He raised his hand to wipe away the wetness in his left eye. "He doesn't think I'm smart enough to get anything out of UCLA. Says I should just face up to it, get a job and make some money. He's just chock full of encouragement."

I reached over and put my hand on his shoulder. "Shit, man. Just stop talkin' to him."

Nodding in agreement, Tommy continued, "I know. You're right. But he's my Dad, you know? Why does he hate me so much?"

I couldn't remember seeing Tommy this upset. I did my best to console him, saying in a lowered voice, "He doesn't hate you. He's the one with the problem, not you. C'mon, let's get out of here. Walk down to Westwood with me and we'll get a burger."

Tommy met my eyes and said, "Thanks, man. But I need some time alone. I'm going to walk around campus for a while."

A few minutes later, Tom took off by himself, trying to lay to rest some of the demons wrought by his father.

ALONE IN the apartment, I sat down on the couch and exhaled, looking up at the ceiling. I thought about Tommy and his relationship with his father—thought about my short-lived relationship with my father. My mind drifted back to a time nearly three years earlier when I lived in the dorms: About a month after the school year began, Sproul Hall had a tradition of having Mother-Daughter and Father-Son dinners. They would set up the recreation room with long, rectangular, linen clothed tables. The Mother-Daughter dinner was first, then a week later they would have the fathers. The first year I lived in the dorms, the dinner was pretty much right after I had moved in, since I had been on the waiting list and gotten in late. My new friend, Tommy Ruderman, was my date, since I had no father and Tommy's just didn't want to come.

The second year, Tommy was out of town with the volleyball team, so I was on my own. I considered just not going, but they were serving a steak dinner, far superior to whatever was being dished up in the cafeteria. Plus, it was a free event, or I should say, it was already included in the cost of our meal plan. Thirdly, John Wooden was to be the featured speaker, and I didn't want to miss that.

I had been at the event no more than ten minutes when, observing a roomful of fathers and sons, and already having explained to two different fathers that my own had passed away, I began to feel very sad. My feelings totally caught me off guard. I hadn't really thought too much about my dad in a long time. But boy, it started to hit me like a ton of bricks, and my eyes began to well up. Out of the fear of embarrassment of having all my dorm mates see me bawling, I turned to leave and go back to my room. Just as I reached the door, who walks in but Jack Rosen.

"Heard you might be in need of a pop," he said, a broad smile on his face.

I opened my mouth to reply, but no words came out. The tears that had been gathering came out in a rush as I stepped forward to embrace him.

IT TURNS OUT that Tommy had been discussing the event at the beach and Jack had the idea to surprise me. Smiling at the memory, I got up from the couch and went to the table. I picked up the phone and dialed my own home phone number in Winfield.

"Hello?"

"Hi Mom, it's me. How ya doin'?"

"Goodness gracious, if it isn't my baby boy. Is everything okay? Why are you calling?"

I chuckled to myself. I guess I deserved that kind of greeting since I called so rarely. "Everything's fine Mom, everything's fine. I just wanted to hear your voice."

12

The following morning Tom was back to his old self. I reached up to the highest shelf to get two boxes of cereal, Raisin Bran for me and Cheerios for Tom. Tom got the bowls down and we proceeded to "prepare" our breakfast.

"When did your parents get divorced?" I asked.

"I was four years old when he moved out. I've only got a vague memory of him ever living with us."

I opened the fridge. "Damn, not much milk. I'll split it with you," I said, then poured it in a glass so we could divide what little there was, equally. "Did you see him much?"

"Not much, but more than I wanted to. Seems like every time he came over he'd get in a fight with Mom and tell me I was good for nothing. Mom and me would both be cryin' by the time he left."

We carried our bowls and spoons into the living room. "Man, I can't believe that. I only met him the one time when he came over right when we got this place, but he seemed like a nice guy to me."

Tom sat in the chair nearest the balcony door, still wearing the navy blue, white polka-dotted boxers he slept in. "Oh yeah, he can be charming. Nice to have a beer with, but not nice to have as a father." He put another spoonful of dry Cheerios in his mouth.

I didn't understand the dynamics that went into Rudy Ruderman's problems with his son, but I could guess that his antagonism towards Tom was a result of, and wrapped up in, his poor relationship with his ex-wife. For some reason he was not able to separate the two. And Tommy paid the price, big time.

Using his fingers to comb through unruly, pre-shower hair, Tom finally looked up at me. "Speaking of long lost fathers, did you get through all that stuff from Jack's house last night?"

"As a matter of fact, yeah, I've gone through it all. Now we just gotta make the phone calls." Then I lifted the bowl to my lips, drinking down the last bit of milk, along with a couple of sunken raisins.

I had spent the last two nights sifting through everything we had taken from Jack's house. Tuesday night I found the pattern of payments coinciding with the trips to Germany, but I needed more pieces of the puzzle to determine the significance. Yesterday I had gone through several old check register booklets, searching for payment amounts or names which looked suspicious. I perused the details of every car purchase, every name and every address in his address book. Taking Buck's advice I plunged in and began calling people. We counted over two hundred names and numbers between the address book and slips of paper we had found. There would be additional people to call from the depths of the car deal files. So far I hadn't had much luck, although I had barely gotten started, making a dozen or so calls, leaving messages on answering machines for all but one. The one that I spoke with was an out-of-town friend Jack hadn't seen in years, so he wasn't much help. Tommy wasn't as convinced of the necessity of doing all this as I was, but he knew how important it was to me and so had promised to help. Even with his help, making all the calls would take a few days.

WE LOCKED our front door and began walking toward the stairwell that led to the parking garage. Directly across the open hallway from our apartment's front door was the balcony for Apartment 202. Two very overweight young women lived there. They had the propensity to almost exclusively wear blue clothing and so my roommate had affectionately nicknamed them Blue Whale One and Blue Whale Two. They were sunning themselves on lounge chairs, sharing bags of Ruffles and Oreos.

"Hello, girls. Beautiful day, huh?" Tom said.

"You studs headed to the beach?" Blue Whale One asked.

"That is indeed the plan," Tom replied, as he slapped the palm of his hand on their balcony railing.

"Well, don't wear yourselves out. We're having a big blow-out here tonight. You guys are required to attend."

"Good to know. Thanks so much for the invite," Tom said.

"Yeah, thanks," I added.

"Okay, you better come," Blue Whale Two shouted out as we moved away.

Singin' Sammy approached from the opposite direction, maybe heading down to the pool.

"Hey Sammy, what's goin' on?" Tommy greeted him.

After passing Tom he stepped into my path, blocking my way. He cocked his head, looking at me askew, his tightly closed lips turning upward at the edges into a smile.

"Hey Sam, what's up?" I said.

Again, nothing in reply, but he waggled a finger at me as if to admonish me and started in. "Dreamer, you know you are a dreamer ..."

He sang a couple more lines of the *Supertramp* song, gave me a wink, did a little dance step to go around me, and continued down the hallway without any interruption in his melody.

Tommy looked back at me. We both smiled, shook our heads, then continued to the building's exit.

WE ARRIVED together at the beach, although in separate cars, since I had to be to Buck's by three for the evening shift. We meandered down the Montana Avenue stairs at a little after eleven. It was another hot one. I stopped briefly on one of the landings about halfway down and lifted my head. The sky was still as a painting. Not a single bird dared to fly through the oven-like air.

"Did you remember socks?" I asked as we arrived at the bridge.

"Yeah, I always keep a pair in my bag. We're gonna need 'em today."

It was a rare day that we needed the socks, since our feet had developed a tough, thick layer of skin on the bottom that was impervious to all but the hottest conditions. Making our way across the sand from the parking lot to the wall, we had to make one stop to cool our feet, shuffling them a few inches below the surface where the temperature of the sand was more tolerable.

"No games. Everybody's at the water," I said, looking out at the poles, nets, and ropes, all laying quiet in the heat.

Most of the crew had already made their way to the waterfront, setting up their chairs and umbrellas where they could feel the cool breeze coming off the water. The few people who had not gone to the water were not eager to play a game, so Tommy and I settled in the shade underneath the magnolia tree up against the wall. After five minutes, our bodies glistened with perspiration. Even in the shade, the hot muggy air was oppressive.

"Whadda ya think? You wanna go jump in the ocean?" Tommy asked me.

It sounded good, cooling off in the water, bodysurfing a few waves, but usually I liked to play my games first so I didn't have to play later in wet trunks. I replied, "Boy, I'd love to get a game in first just for the workout. But it's not looking …"

Andrew Lee interrupted me, standing about 10 yards away, peeking over the wall, calling in a loud whisper, "Tommy, Townie, c'mere and check this out!"

Andrew, who even at six foot four, needed to be on his tiptoes to see over the wall, was looking into Jennifer Ryan's backyard. Tommy and I, hastened by his urgent tone, jogged to where he was standing and peeked over the wall ourselves. The centerpiece of the yard was a large irregular shaped swimming pool. There was a man-made cliff side of large boulders on the left, standing about ten feet tall and extending the full length of the pool. A waterfall cascaded directly into the black bottomed pool right about in the center of the length of cliff side. Beyond the waterfall, closer to the house, a jacuzzi was embedded into the rocks. The rest of the large yard was immaculately landscaped with lawn, flowers, and small trees.

"You see her? That's her, isn't it?" Andrew whispered to the two of us.

Also on my tiptoes, peering into the yard, I answered, "Where? I don't see anybody."

"All the way up toward the house, at the far end of the pool on the right," Andrew said.

A small hedge jutted out, partially obscuring the view, but somebody was lying down on a lounge chair a few yards to the right of the pool edge. "Oh yeah, I see somebody. I can't tell if that's her or not," I said.

Tommy said, "Let's move over to the left so we get a better angle."

We moved about fifteen yards to the other side of the tree and again peeked up over the wall. From this spot the view was clear, the hedge no longer in the way.

"Oh jeez, that's her!" Andrew said, a little loudly I thought.

"Townie, I don't think she's wearing anything," Tommy added, excitedly.

This prospect had not occurred to me. I squinted my eyes trying hard to get a better look. "Cmon, you sure? How can you tell from here?" I said.

Then Jennifer Ryan, lying on her back, propped herself up on her elbows, tilted her head back and gave it a shake, so that her hair fell back. *She's topless!* She turned her head in our direction and we instinctively ducked our heads beneath the top of the six foot wall.

"Where's a periscope when you need one?" Tommy said.

But Andrew couldn't help himself and again poked his head above the top of the wall. "She's lying down again!"

Tommy and I followed suit, and with our fingers gripping the top of the wall, pulled ourselves up on our tiptoes once again to take a peek. After a minute or so of muted gazing, we lowered ourselves to the sand and sat with our backs against the wall, taking a deep breath.

"I say we go through the Redmonds' yard and get a closer look," Andrew said. William Redmond was a real estate developer who lived with his wife in the adjacent neighboring house to the south of Jennifer Ryan's. On the other side of the Redmonds' house was a multi-unit condominium development, the one that had been built a couple years ago after they tore down the Grill. On the other side of the condos was the public parking lot.

"We can't do that. What if somebody's home?" I said.

"There's hardly ever anybody there. I'll betcha nobody's home," Tommy said.

Like naughty adolescents, we walked along the concrete pathway that ran alongside the condo development connecting PCH to the beach. We peered through the ivy covered chain link fence that separated the Redmonds' property from the condos, trying to determine if there was any sign of life. There was no movement anywhere that we could tell. As one last test we agreed to go to the front gate on PCH. We rang the buzzer for the intercom. No answer. We rang it again and waited. Still no answer.

"Okay, satisfied boys?" Andrew said.

"I say let's do it," Tommy said, then added, "Damn, this pavement's hot," as he scampered back to the shade of the condo building.

Satisfied that the Redmonds were not there, but still unsure about trespassing, I relented, Jennifer Ryan being a powerful elixir. "I'm in."

Rather than climbing over the chain link fence, which was about ten feet tall and tough on our toes, we went back to the beach, to the rear of the property, and hopped over the wall. All of us easily made it over, but when Tommy landed, he stepped on a dead branch which was laying on the ground. *Holy shit! What was that, a firecracker? Jennifer Ryan's going to be looking over that wall any second now, her eyes will sweep toward us like prison searchlights ... and we'll be dead meat.* We stood motionless for a minute, staring at the wall, expecting her head to pop up any second. But it didn't. Slowly and carefully, across the large lawn over to the solid red brick dividing wall which separated the properties, Andrew led us, making our way closer to the spot we judged would be the best vantage point. The wall was a lot higher than the one at the rear of the property, at least two feet over our heads. Completely silent since Jennifer was just on the other side of the wall, we looked around for a solution. Tommy noticed a stack of firewood up against the house only a few yards away, motioned to me where he was going, and then quietly made his way over to the pile, bringing back a large log. The chunk of wood was about two feet long and six inches wide. When stood on end, Tom would be able to stand on it and see over the barrier. Andrew and I hurried to the woodpile, chose our own logs, and brought them back to the viewing spot.

What we experienced next I cannot easily put into words, but I *will* say that if I had turned to stone because of what I beheld, I would have died a happy man. The three of us stood on our perches, silently gazing upon the most beautiful creature I had ever seen. When God created woman, this is what He had in mind. She was no more than fifteen feet from us, basking in the warm sun wearing not a stitch of clothing. Her long lean legs, perfectly shaped, medium sized breasts, silky smooth skin, and flowing light brown hair draped over her shoulders, kept us entranced for what seemed like an eternity. I examined every inch of her, even noticing the crimson red toenail polish on her neatly pedicured feet. My hypnotic trance was broken when she propped herself up on her elbows like she had done earlier. But this time she rotated her legs to the side of the lounge chair and stood up. A voice inside me said to duck for fear of being discovered, but I ignored the voice, frozen in admiration of her beauty. She slipped on a pair of sandals, walking slowly into the house through the sliding glass door. We got off the logs and slumped to the ground, sitting side by side, still in silence.

"Unbelievable," Andrew was finally able to utter.

"I'm glad you guys are here, cause nobody would ever believe me if I told them about this," Tommy added.

I shook my head slowly from side to side and exhaled. "Whew."

Sandals clicked rhythmically on the other side of the wall, announcing her return. We eased ourselves back up on our logs. Jennifer sat down again, adjusting the angle of the back rest so that she could sip the iced tea she carried in her right hand. Suddenly I felt movement next to me. Tommy grabbed at my elbow.

"Holy shhh ..."

Not balanced quite right on his log, he grasped the top of the wall to keep from falling. But the log tumbled, making a loud noise, and as Tom dropped to the ground, Andrew and I anxiously stared down at the fallen chunk of wood.

Jennifer wheeled around, saw the backs of two heads poking above her wall, and screamed, *"Oh my God! Get ... out! Get out! Oh God!"*

We leaped off our logs, raced for the back wall, and with adrenaline coursing through our veins, easily cleared it with a single hop. Safely on Sorrento sand, we continued our sprint over the baking beach and jumped into the ocean to cool off. We needed it.

The hostess seated us at a table in the middle of a large, crowded room, one of six such rooms within La Barbera's Pizzeria. We settled into the worn, red vinyl covered chairs. Renee leaned forward, her blue-green eyes never so mesmerizing, now that I was sitting directly across from her. Her elbows rested on the red and white checkered tablecloth, hands clasped together with her chin sitting on top.

She said, "So I wanna hear the story about your big fight."

I pulled a breadstick out of the glass container on the table and pretended it was a cigar, something my brother and I used to always do when we were kids. "It wasn't really a fight. I just kinda lost my temper."

The waitress interrupted us and we ordered our drinks, a beer for me and a Pepsi for her.

"This paparazzi guy comes down to the beach and just starts settin' up shop. He was gonna start taking photos over the wall into Jennifer Ryan's house. We went over and told him to get lost, he pushes this friend of mine, so I slugged him a good one." I took my first bite out of the breadstick, shortening the cigar.

"That's all? And the paramedics had to come? You must pack a punch." She punched her fist at the air and tried her best to make a menacing face.

I laughed. "Actually he lost his balance after I hit him, fell down and hit his head on the wall. That's what knocked him out."

"Oh ... " She paused, as if visualizing the scene. "So why did you care so much that he was taking pictures of Jennifer Ryan?"

"I don't know. I've kinda had a thing for Jennifer Ryan for a while." The volume in my voice dropped about halfway through the sentence as I realized how silly I sounded.

"A thing? What kind of thing?"

"You know, just kinda liked her. Ever since I was in Junior High."

"Huh. How old is she?"

"Thirty-two."

She slapped her hands down on the table and leaned forward with her mouth open. "Thirty-two?! Oh my God, she's practically old enough to be my mother."

"Yeah, but that doesn't matter. It's just a fantasy anyway."

"A *fantasy?* Really. A fantasy. So how long have you been fantasizing about Jennifer Ryan?" She had a big grin on her face.

I shifted uncomfortably in my chair. "Oh jeez. Can we change the subject?"

She couldn't stop laughing. "I'm sorry. I didn't mean to give you such a hard time. I just couldn't help myself. You were such an easy target."

The waitress returned with our drinks and we ordered a large Super Deluxe Pizza, a combination with about ten different toppings.

Renee reached across the table and gripped my arm. "Oh, my God! You won't believe what happened to me yesterday!"

"What?"

"Well, I'm taking a summer school class at Marymount and once in a while I walk across the street to UCLA, cause we're allowed to use the library. So I'm walking on the lawn heading toward Powell Library and this old guy starts kind of circling me as I'm walking. And the only thing he was wearing were these white Speedos—first I thought it was his underwear." She closed her eyes and involuntarily shuddered.

"Oh, no. Singin' Sammy," I said.

"What? You know this guy?"

"Yeah, he lives in our apartment building. So, did he sing you a song?"

"Yes! How did you know? He was sorta talking and sorta singing—that song that goes: Wild Thing ... you make my heart sing..."

I lowered my head and laughed.

"It's not funny. He scared me. I didn't tell you the worst part."

"What?" I said, still smiling at the image of Sammy dancing around her singing *Wild Thing*.

"Later that day when I got out of class and was walking to my car, he's there again! At Marymount! He's doing somersaults on the lawn, following me like a big, rolling ... ball. It really freaked me out. I was going to go to the office and have them call the police, but then he just scampered away."

My smile disappeared. I could tell she had really been frightened. "Wow, sounds like Sammy went a little overboard. You know what? I'll go talk to him. I'll make sure he never bugs you again. I'm pretty sure he's harmless, but boy, that is kinda scary. I'll talk to him tomorrow. He's right down the hall from us."

"Thanks. That would make me feel a lot better. Nice apartment building you live in. Any other freaks live there?" she asked, as the waitress set our drinks down.

"You mean, besides me and Sammy? No, it's just the two of us."

USING MY FINGER I drew a tic-tac-toe game in the frost on my beer mug. We interrupted our conversation to play a quick game.

After the game ended in a draw, I erased the x's and o's, and she asked, "So, tell me about Kansas. Do you have any brothers and sisters?"

"An older brother and an older sister," I replied, then picked up the beer and took a long drink.

"The baby of the family ..." She again perched her chin on interlocked fingers and trained her eyes on mine.

"Yeah, that's me, spoiled rotten."

"Where do your brother and sister live?"

"Still back there. I'm the only one who left." A pepperoni and sausage pizza arrived at the table to our left. The wonderful smell made my mouth water. I couldn't help myself and glanced over to take a look in the middle of my sentence.

"My questions boring you?" she said.

"No, sorry, just really hungry," I said, embarrassed that I'd been caught.

"Sounds like you were the black sheep, hightailing it out of town like that."

"Mom was not thrilled, but she understood. I think she always figured I would return there to live my life. When I decided to stay out here a couple summers ago, that probably upset her more than when I first left. I think she realized that I might never move back."

"How about your dad? What did he think?" Renee asked.

"My dad passed away when I was eight years old ... heart attack."

"Oh my gosh. I'm so sorry."

"That's okay, don't be sorry. That was a long time ago," I said. "Tell me about your family."

Renee sighed. "I've got one younger sister, in seventh grade now and a real brat. You know what she said to me the other day? She said, 'If brains were dynamite, you couldn't blow your nose.' She was trying to insult me, but it just made me laugh."

I swallowed a laugh with my beer and choked, coughing and pounding myself on the chest as I continued to laugh. I was finally able to get out, "Now *that's* funny."

She giggled at my reaction. "You okay, there?"

I cleared my throat and nodded.

"So, anyway, my dad is an orthopedic surgeon, and I see him about once a week." She took a breath, lifted her shoulders and let them fall as she exhaled. "Mom is an attorney at a big law firm in downtown LA and I see her a little bit more than Dad. We've got a live-in housekeeper, maid, whatever you want to call her, who's supposed to keep an eye on us."

A beautiful, dark haired girl in a very short skirt walked right past our table with her date to be seated. Although I couldn't help but notice, I learned my lesson with the pizza and willed my eyes to stay fixed on Renee. "Sounds like you've got plenty of freedom," I said.

She slid her forefinger on the edge of her glass, wiping off a drop of spilled Pepsi. "You know, sometimes I think my parents only stay married because they're too busy to get a divorce," she said, then paused, an embarrassed look crossing her face. "Oh my gosh, it feels so petty complaining about my parents knowing that you lost your father."

"Just because I lost my dad doesn't make your family issues any less real. It's not easy is it? But you should give your dad a break. He's probably doing the best he can."

"Well, now that my family has completely depressed you, tell me about UCLA. You're about to graduate right?" she asked.

"I was supposed to have graduated last month but I decided to take last quarter off. I'll graduate after fall quarter in December."

"Why, o' why would you want to do that? Heck I'm taking extra units so I can graduate high school a semester *early*."

"Really? That's impressive," I said. "I don't have a good excuse for myself I'm afraid. I just wasn't ready to leave UCLA, go off and get a real job somewhere. This way I have another summer vacation as a college student and more time to figure out what I want to do."

"You're not going to be like Benjamin are you?" she asked.

"Benjamin?" I furrowed my brow and grabbed another breadstick.

"You know, Dustin Hoffman in The Graduate. He moves back home after graduation, floats around the pool all day long, and then at night ... sleeps with Mrs. Robinson."

"Yeah, but in the end he gets Mrs. Robinson's hot daughter, so he must have been doing something right," I replied with a chuckle.

"So now you're fantasizing about Elaine Robinson?"

"Hmmm, hadn't thought about her, but now that you mention it ... "

She rolled her eyes. "Oh, gawd."

"So what's up with you graduating early? Can't wait to grow up?" I asked.

She smoothed back her long, silky hair, which had a tendency to drop into her drink. "I like Marymount. I'm just ready to move on. The idea of moving away to college is really appealing."

"What do you want to do when you grow up?" I said, only half joking, remembering that she was only seventeen.

"This is going to sound funny after what I said about my dad, but I think I'd like to be a doctor. I've gotten straight A's for as long as I can remember and I loved all the science classes."

I raised my brows in response, truly impressed. "Man, straight A's, huh?"

"Yeah, this isn't just a hat rack." She smiled as she tapped the side of her head with her finger.

The pizza arrived at our table and we both plopped a heavy slice onto our plates. The waitress asked if I wanted another mug of Coors and I readily agreed.

"It's been nice talking to ya," Renee cracked as we both dug into the delicious, cheesy creation La Barbera's was famous for. The conversation did in fact die down as we eagerly went through our first and then second slices. She picked up my beer and took a sip, then made a face as if she'd bitten into a lemon. "I haven't developed a taste for that quite yet."

As I started on my third slice I was secretly impressed that she was keeping pace. Skinny as a rail, but this girl was not picking at her food.

"So I guess it's time for the big question. At your ripe old age, have you ever had a boyfriend?"

"Yeah, if you could call it that. We went out for about three months. He was this super rich, spoiled, baby of the family—oops sorry, didn't mean to cast any dispersions on babies of the family—but you know, he was born on third base and thought he hit a triple. You know the type?"

"So other than that, you really liked him." I couldn't help but laugh at her description.

"And you?" She set down her pizza to give me her full attention.

"Oh there's been a few, but nobody too serious."

"Yeah, I'll bet."

"No, really. My first girlfriend was back home. That didn't last too long—just the summer after I graduated high school. At UCLA there have been a couple that I dated for three or four months each."

She blushed a little as she looked down at her plate and said softly, almost too softly for me to hear, "Well, I guess you're going to be a challenge."

Two pieces of Super Deluxe remained untouched, but she was stuffed and I didn't want to eat like a pig on our first date, so we asked for a doggy bag. Renee understood the value of leftover pizza to a poor, starving college student fending for himself in an apartment, and so offered to let me take both slices. She insisted on paying the bill since she said she had been the one to ask me out. After an uninspired objection, the poor starving college student agreed to let her pay.

We walked out the front entrance, went the short distance around the block to the parking lot behind the restaurant.

"That was fun. We should do it again. And if you pay again, we should do it real soon," I said.

She didn't respond to my attempt at humor, just found my hand and gave it a gentle squeeze. I reached for her other hand

and our eyes met as I leaned back against her car. Her eyes captivated me. Her skin looked smooth and delicate, too beautiful to touch, but it was those blue-green eyes that had me in their embrace. She moved closer, the subtle contours of her body pressed against me. She ran her fingers through my hair, leaned in, her breath warm on my ear. "Okay, now just close your eyes and pretend I'm Jennifer Ryan."

"Oh, shut up," I said softly, as our foreheads touched.

Now her full moist lips were on mine, her body pulsing with eagerness, the passion intense. I held her tight as we kissed.

The suddenness of it, the intensity of it, something about it ... scared me. I moved my head to the side and gave her a hug.

"So when do you work next?" I said, somewhat lamely, trying to lighten the mood.

"When do *you*?" she said, poking her finger in my chest. "I'll change my schedule and make sure I'm there. Or you could call me at my house. We could see each other tomorrow."

Weak with desire, I kissed her again on the lips, then on her neck, cheek, and ear. Like being swept away down a flood ravaged river, I was hopelessly enthralled, holding her, caressing her, wanting to explore every inch of her. I had an inkling the first time we met at Buck's, but this caught me off guard, the powerful, magical forces that had emerged tonight.

I opened her car door, gave her one more quick kiss after she was seated and said, "You know, I just might do that."

After she drove from the parking lot, I walked slowly to my car, sat down in the driver's seat and stared straight ahead. Like a wet blanket tossed over a roaring fire, the reality of her age enveloped me again.

I whispered to myself, "She is unbelievable. Oh, my God. What am I getting myself into?"

14

I was awake, but still in bed, hoping to rest up a little more before starting my day. The clock stared at me, mocking me for trying to fall back to sleep. It was seven thirty-five, Friday morning. I hadn't slept well, excited yet somehow troubled about my dinner and parking lot rendezvous with Renee last night. I could not stop thinking about her.

Finally I surrendered, climbed out of bed and made my way to the sink to brush my teeth. The door to the bathroom was ajar and I saw that Tommy was in there, towel wrapped around his waist. I reached to close the door, but stopped. He was carefully laying a length of toilet paper flat on the water in the toilet bowl.

I squinted my sleepy eyes, and said, "What in the world are you doing?"

He looked up at me through the two inch crack in the door, holding another strip of three squares. "Preventing nuclear splash back," he said.

I leaned over and put my eye to the door opening, checking out the surface of the toilet bowl water, now nearly covered with tissue. "What!?"

"Nuclear splash back. You know, you drop one and the water splashes up and gets your butt wet with toilet water," Tommy said, then completed his preparation by laying down the final strip.

"Oh … yeah, right." I closed the door and shook my head, too groggy with sleep to fully comprehend.

AFTER A GOURMET breakfast of cold La Barbera's pizza, we decided to make some phone calls out of Jack's address book, thinking we might be able to catch some people before they left for work. We divided the calling, each of us doing an hour or two a day. We tried to vary the times we called, hoping to catch people at home or work as the case might be. Tom took the first shift and spent an hour calling people, talking with a few, leaving messages for most. After making each call Tom wrote down who, if anybody, he spoke to, how they knew Jack and what they had to say. One reason for the notes was to keep track of who we had called and assure that we didn't accidentally call people more than once. But more importantly, the notes would help us remember what everyone had said, and hopefully we could look back at the list and see a pattern or clue which would lead us in the right direction.

Before I started making my calls, I decided to pay a visit to our eccentric neighbor. I walked down to the end of the hallway, mentally preparing myself to read Sammy the Riot Act. I knocked on the door and waited. No answer. I knocked again. Still no answer. Moving a few steps to the kitchen window, I cupped my hands so I could see better through the screen of the open window. There, in the middle of the living room floor, was Sammy, doing sit-ups.

"Sam. *Sam*!" I said loudly.

He stopped doing the sit-ups, looked my way, but didn't respond.

"Sam, what's up, man. I need to talk to you about something."

He ignored me, rolled over on his stomach and began doing push-ups.

"C'mon, Sam. I gotta talk to you. There's this girl, Sam, a friend of mine. She says you followed her yesterday. Over near Powell, and then at Marymount. You scared her, Sam. You can't do that. Anyway, I just wanted to ask you to stay away from her. Would you do that for me, Sam?"

Finally he got up and walked to the kitchen. Still not saying a word, he crouched down on the kitchen floor, his arms wrapped around his knees, pulling them tightly to his chest.

"Sam, what are you doing? Did you hear what I said? Stay away from that girl you followed yesterday, okay?"

Suddenly he leaped up and pressed his face against the screen. It happened so fast I wasn't able to pull my face back in time. I could feel his breath, his wild eyes were less than an inch from mine, and he growled like a rabid dog. My heart skipped a beat before I reacted and backed away to the railing.

"*Holy shit*!" I said.

"*Piss off*!" Sam said, then disappeared as quickly as he had arrived.

"HELLO, THIS is Paul Townsend and I got your name and number from Jack Rosen's address book. Please call me at 555-1734. I need to ask you a question about Jack."

I left the message on the answering machine. I had started making my calls as soon as I returned from my near heart attack at Sammy's window. It was tedious, repetitive work and didn't really feel like it was accomplishing much, but it was the best hope we had. If nothing else, a lot of Jack's friends and acquaintances were on the alert, now aware that he might be in trouble.

"Hello?" the voice on the other end said.

After so many answering machines, the live voice excited me. "Hello, is this Jerry Moberg?" I asked.

"Who's this?" the voice responded.

I stood up and took a couple steps, stretching the phone cord to look out at the pool area. "This is Paul Townsend ..."

He cut me off. "What are you selling?"

"Not selling anything, you see, I'm a friend of Jack Rosen and I got your name ..."

I heard a click and the line went dead. "Hello? Hello?" I looked at the receiver quizzically as if it was the phone's fault. I started to write down Jerry Moberg's name in our notebook, then stopped. It occurred to me that he had hung up the phone *after* I mentioned Jack's name. Everyone else, although hesitant in the beginning, not knowing me and thinking I was a solicitor, would settle in and speak with me after hearing Jack's name. I didn't even know for sure it was Jerry Moberg on the line, although if it had been somebody else, they probably would have told me I had a wrong number instead of just hanging up. I called back. The phone rang three times.

"Hello?" the same voice answered.

"Hello, is this Jerry?" Again, the line went dead. This guy did not want to talk.

Climbing from the shower, Tommy had not heard the exchange, so I filled him in. Jerry Moberg's address was written down in faded pencil at the top of the second "M" page. The phone number was written down over an erasure, as if the number had been changed at one point. The lines which followed indicated his home was in Manhattan Beach, about twenty minutes down the 405 freeway. We needed to pay Jerry Moberg a visit.

Tom joined me in the living room, still wearing a white towel around his waist. "Well, there's no time like the present. We know he's home," Tom said.

I sat on the couch, staring at the Moberg entry in the address book. "You're right. We gotta go. Asshole ... hangin' up on me." The more I thought about it, the angrier I got. I couldn't imagine anyone who knew Jack not wanting to help us or even talk to me.

We grabbed our beach stuff so we could hit Sorrento on the way home and took the elevator to the basement parking garage. We jumped into my VW, drove around the corner onto Veteran Avenue, and headed to the freeway on-ramp. The map book was laid out on Tommy's lap. He was my navigator, trying to track down Jerry Moberg in Manhattan Beach. He estimated our destination to be a couple blocks from the beach just off Rosecrans Avenue at the north end of town. Manhattan Beach was a quiet little beach community about ten miles south of Santa Monica.

After exiting the freeway, we made our way westward to the water, then turned left on Highland, which ran north and south, parallel to the coastline. A few short blocks on Highland brought us to 29th Street, but we were not able to turn onto it since Moberg lived on a "walk street" where no cars were allowed. The car access to the walk streets was from the alleys behind the homes, and in the alleys, the only parking allowed was inside people's garages. It made it difficult to have visitors.

We parked two blocks away on Highland and then returned to walk up the steep hill to find his address.

The fourth house on the right matched the address written in Jack's book. We opened the three foot high iron gate and let ourselves in. I said, "I say we play it straight. Tell him our story like we tried to do on the phone."

Tom stood behind me on the lower step. "I'll let you do the talking."

The three story Mediterranean style structure was three short blocks up from the water. Sloping up steeply from the sand's edge, 29th Street provided white water ocean views to everybody within the first three blocks. I rang the doorbell, and in less than a minute, a short, balding man with wire rimmed glasses, looking to be in his mid-fifties, answered the door. "Can I help you?"

"Yes, my name is Paul Townsend and this is Tom Ruderman. We're friends of Jack Rosen and are hoping you can help us find him."

"Find him? What do you mean?" the man asked, holding the door open only about a foot.

"He disappeared a few days ago. He went off with a man who came down to the beach to talk to him and we haven't seen him since.

"What makes you think he didn't just go out of town or something?" he asked.

Tom took a step up and joined me on the tiled porch.

I said, "He left his car in the beach parking lot and hasn't been back to his house. Plus, his house got broken into. We think the guys that broke into the house work with the man that took him from the beach."

At this news, the man who we assumed was Jerry Moberg abruptly ended the conversation. "I'm very sorry to hear that, but I can't help you. I'm really very busy. I'm sorry."

And just like that he closed the door. We rang the bell again ... no answer. Tommy and I stood there, looking at each other, still shocked at how suddenly the conversation had ended. One thing was clear, though. Jerry Moberg knew something and we needed to find out what that something was.

15

"HELLOOO ... BEACH!" Scott Rodgers announced his arrival to no one in particular, as he always did when he first set foot on the sand. Four o'clock approached. A hint of moist, foggy air began to drift in from the shoreline. Several of us grouped together up against the wall, chatting about this and that, the games having ended over an hour ago.

"You're a little late, man. We're pretty much done playing," Tom said to Scott as he trudged toward us.

"I figured as much," Scott replied as he set his bag down, sighed heavily, and collapsed his big body onto the sand. "Can't believe I had to work the whole fuckin' day. Damn."

"Actually you're just in time. We were thinking about moving this party up to TT's," Andrew said.

Tampico Tilly's, or TT's as we called it, was a fancy Mexican restaurant at 12th and Wilshire just three blocks from Buck's.

"I'm in," Rabbit said.

"Me too," Marlowe added.

"See ya there in a few," I said, then gathered up my stuff and walked up the stairs with Tommy to his car to drive the short distance to TT's.

I WALKED into TT's, grungy from a day of volleyball, in my beach trunks, dirty T-shirt and sandals, a little self-conscious, but meeting up with our like-dressed group made me feel better.

"Hey, Townie, Tomboy. Have a seat," Andrew welcomed us.

Around the table were Michelle, Rabbit, Scott, Marlowe, and Andrew, all with a margarita in front of them. They had beaten us there by a few minutes, since we had to make the hike up the stairs, and they had left from the beach lot, all in Rabbit's car.

Andrew got the waitress' attention as she finished an order at another table. "These guys need a margarita soon as you get a chance."

Tommy and I took a seat in the wicker chairs. "Thanks, man. How'd you know?"

"Lucky guess. These things are too good," Andrew said, taking another sip. "And even better cause this guy is paying." Andrew pointed a thumb at Rabbit, seated next to him.

Rabbit looked better than the rest of us, having put on a clean, turquoise golf shirt. He turned our way, nodded at us, and said, "I figure you derelicts rarely get a good meal. I'm doing it out of pity."

Tampico Tilly's was a new restaurant made to look old. It opened a couple years ago in a newly constructed building with beautiful Spanish tile throughout and red brick walls that had been partially plastered to give the look of a 100 year old, elegant hacienda. Our waitress delivered two more baskets of tortilla chips and two bowls of salsa, our compadres having already polished off the first two. I dove into the chips, ravenous from a day in the sun and having had no lunch to speak of. The margaritas were going down easily. Rabbit ordered a second round for everyone before the first ones were empty.

"Little Joe Cartwright! What's happenin', brother? Come join the party." Andrew spotted LJ walking in the front door and yelled across the room. TT's was empty except for one couple sitting in the corner. So what if we were a little loud?

LJ joined us, sitting at the opposite end of the table from me, next to Andrew and Michelle. Rabbit immediately caught the waitress' attention and ordered a double margarita for LJ.

"Gotta catch him up," he said to us after he ordered.

Jim Marlowe, sitting across from me, said, "So Townie, I hear you've been doing some detective work trying to find Jack. What's the news?"

I paused for a second as I swallowed a big gulp of margarita. "Whole lotta nothing. It's frustrating. Tom and I have been making a bunch of calls to people in his address book just to see if anybody knows anything. So far the only interesting one is this guy in Manhattan Beach who won't talk to us."

Marlowe leaned forward in his chair, elbows resting on the table. "Won't talk to you? Whadda ya mean?"

"I mean he hung up on me when I told him we were friends of Jack. Then Tom and I paid him a visit this morning and he basically shut the door in our face."

"And you say he knows Jack?"

I waved a chip around, finally pointing it at Marlowe. "Yeah! We got his name out of Jack's address book."

"Should we go kick his ass?" Marlowe asked, the look in his eye letting me know he was serious.

"Maybe. I'll let you know. I'm still thinking about the best way to approach the guy. It could be that he doesn't want to be bothered. Maybe he doesn't even know Jack very well. But we'll figure out some way to get him to talk."

I overheard Andrew at the other end of the table recounting yesterday's foray into the Redmonds' yard to spy on Jennifer Ryan.

"She was right there. *Right there*!" Andrew said, pointing at the table next to us about ten feet away. "And not wearing a thing! Man, I tell you, that image is etched into my brain for life. Then she gets up and walks into the house. Cutest little ass I've ever seen. Man, I'm telling' ya." Andrew sighed, shook his head, and looked down the table at me and Tommy. "Boys? Am I right?"

The image was fresh in my mind. "No argument here."

"It may have ruined me for other women," Tom said.

"I wonder if she *wanted* someone to see her," Michelle piped in casually, as she munched on a chip.

"Hah! I doubt that, if you could've seen her reaction when she spotted us. Hoo boy, she was pissed," Tom said.

Andrew turned in his chair to face Michelle, a baffled expression on his face. "Whadda ya mean, *wanted* someone to see her."

Michelle continued, "Well, I'm just thinking, there's a little bit of the exhibitionist in all of us, you know. It's kind of exciting to think about someone watching you." Her dark red hair stood in contrast to her eyes, which were an unusual light golden brown, amber, like the eyes of a big cat. Being the only girl at a table of seven guys, she certainly had our attention.

"I'm just saying … maybe she sunbathes nude in her yard out in the open like that, cause it gives her a little thrill."

Andrew turned back to face the table, raised one eyebrow as he nodded his head.

"Michelle, if you're ever looking for a little thrill like that, just let me know, be glad to accommodate you," LJ added, his hand on Michelle's shoulder as he polished off the last of his drink.

Rabbit frowned at Michelle. "Now you got me all worked up. I'm gonna get some food."

"Now there's an idea," Tommy said as we all scooted our chairs out and headed to the special Happy Hour buffet table. I filled my plate with taquitos, mini-enchiladas, and a chili relleno, knowing this would be my dinner. By the time we had returned to the table with our food, Rabbit had ordered up tequila shots for everybody plus a third round of margaritas.

"I would like to propose a toast ... to Rabbit ... for getting us all good and drunk," Andrew said, as we all downed our tequila and sucked on a wedge of lime.

After the shots, holding up his margarita glass, Scott said, "And I would also like to propose a toast ... to Jennifer Ryan ... and Michelle ... for some wonderful mental imagery I can take home with me tonight."

Michelle blushed and giggled, stood up and bowed, accepting the accolades.

"By the way, I almost forgot. Who's the wise guy who called the Outlook and gave them that flattering picture of me?" I said, looking down the table.

"Ahem ..." LJ cleared his throat. "That would be me."

"Well, thanks bud. I look like a serial killer," I said, smiling. "And nice imagination on the story."

LJ just nodded and said, "Thank you. I was pretty proud of it."

"You know," Rabbit said, suddenly serious, shaking his finger at all of us. "It was a great opportunity for us to get the word out to the fuckin' paparazzi to stay the hell away from Sorrento Beach." Then he looked straight at me. "And we knew Marlowe had cleared you with the cops, so why not embellish the story a bit?"

I raised my hands, open palms facing Rabbit. "You know I'm kidding guys. I'm cool with it. Heck, I've gotten congratulations from everyone I've seen."

I finished the last taquito on my plate and got up to reload. Alcohol made me eat like a madman, twice as much as I would normally eat. When I returned from the buffet table, another shot of tequila sat in front of me, everyone waiting for my return to drink theirs.

Marlowe raised his glass and said, "To Jack … may he be well, wherever he is." We all said in unison, "To Jack," before clinking our shot glasses with each other and downing the liquor.

We continued chatting, eating, and drinking for another hour. Happy Hour had long since ended and the dinner crowd was beginning to arrive. I excused myself to go to the restroom and found Scott at the only urinal. "Hey, hurry it up there. You're not at the post office."

"Still shakin' it boss," Scott replied, as I laughed out loud.

We walked out together, a little wobbly, and returned to the table. It was six forty-five when LJ announced that he had to get going.

"Oh, boo. Party pooper. Last one to get here, first to leave." Andrew gave him a hard time.

"I really gotta go too, guys," Michelle said. "Doug, do you think you can give me a lift?"

"Sure, c'mon," he said. Michelle lived in an apartment building on 7th Street, less than a mile from TT's.

LJ and Michelle walked out, LJ still in his beach trunks and Michelle with the T-shirt and jean shorts she had put on over her bikini. I nudged Tommy with my elbow and asked if he was ready to go.

"That's about it for me too. Friday night, not even seven o'clock, and I think I'm done for the night," I said, getting up from my chair. Tommy got up also and we walked out together, first thanking Rabbit for picking up the tab.

Tommy drove us straight back to the apartment. Blue Whale One and Blue Whale Two gave us crap for missing the "party of the year" last night. I apologized half-heartedly then stumbled through the front door, half drunk and fully exhausted. I showered and collapsed in front of the television. Tommy, on the other hand, had a second date planned with Nancy Williams. They had gone out Monday night, hit it off pretty well and planned to go out to dinner tonight. I was thinking he wouldn't need to order much after all those appetizers.

AFTER TOMMY LEFT, I turned off the television and went out on the balcony. The moon was just a sliver, and no more than six or seven stars were visible in the dark blue, early evening sky. I sat on the mattress with my back against the stucco wall, looking out at the rear of the adjacent apartment building. The curtains were open in a couple different apartments. I could see people, probably students, scurrying around, preparing themselves to go out for the evening. My mind drifted to earlier that day, to our encounter with Jerry Moberg. I tried to visualize his facial expression when we told him Jack's house had been broken into. That really seemed to frighten him. That was when he closed the door in our face.

I thought about Jim Marlowe's offer to "kick his ass". I didn't think that would work on Jerry Moberg. We needed to strike fear in him alright, but I had another idea.

Prior to stringing a wooden tennis racket, a good racket stringer must smooth out all the holes that the string will go through. If there is a rough edge that the string passes over, the taut string will grate on the rough spot and, over time, eventually will snap. At Buck's, we utilized a dremel tool, with a drill bit about the diameter of the tennis string, and glided the bit over every hole in the frame to assure a nice smooth path at every point where the string passes through the frame. The craftsman-like job we did when we "drilled out" the rackets was one of the reasons people came from far away to have us string their rackets.

It was Saturday morning and my stomach was asking me why, why did you do it? The tequila from last night was still making its presence known. I was in the middle of preparing a Dunlop Maxply for stringing when Renee walked in. The whining squeal of the drill and the sweet smell of burning maple wood filled the air.

"Oh God, it makes my teeth hurt just to listen to that drill," she said, her face twisted into a grimace.

I turned off the drill momentarily. "Have a seat. I'll do a little work on you. What do you need? A filling? Root canal? I'm very cheap," I said. "Good morning, beautiful."

She blushed perceptibly and answered, "Good morning. I missed you yesterday. You said you would call."

"I said I *might* call."

"Let me give you a little tip, Mr. Townsend. Don't ever say to a girl that you might call unless you're actually going to call. So let's hear the excuse. What were you so busy with yesterday?"

I looked down at my feet, took a deep breath, then looked up, my eyebrows raised. "Well, if you must know, I had a very tight schedule between the beach, Tampico Tilly's, and returning dead drunk to my apartment."

Ernie Nichols made a timely entrance into Tennis, getting me off the hook.

"Good morning," I greeted Ernie.

"Morning Paul, morning Renee. Good to see your bright and smiling faces—more so yours than his." He gave Renee a toothy grin, then turned to me. "We busy today?"

I had already assessed the day's work and told him, "Not really. There's two more to string besides this one I'm doing, a couple string repairs and one new grip."

"Well, I'm going to let you boys play with your rackets while I go back to the Ski Department to do some real work." Renee sauntered away, looking back at me and wagging her finger, scolding me for yesterday's lack of communication.

"She is really a cutie isn't she? Man!" Ernie said, shaking his head.

"I cannot disagree with your assessment, señor," I replied, as I pulled one of the vertical strings to full tension in the Dunlap.

"I'm telling you, forget about her age. She's mature for sixteen."

"Seventeen. Don't make it any worse than it already is," I said, my voice trailing off.

ERNIE AND I finished all the rackets by eleven-thirty and with not a lot to do in Tennis, I wandered over to the Repair Shop to see what trouble the idle hands were getting into today. Ken Slater walked out, a skateboard tucked under his left arm. I got along with Ken, but could never have been friends with him. He was one of those guys who always talked about women. Maybe it was my Midwestern upbringing, but I never fit in well with guys who discussed the explicit details of their latest conquest. Part of it was the arrogance, boasting about who they had and what they did, but more so than that, it just made me uncomfortable talking about girls like that. My good friends felt the same way. I mean, you wouldn't find a guy anywhere more successful with women than Tommy, but he didn't feel the need to brag about the details of his exploits. Ken, on the other hand, was always looking for an audience.

"Hey Paul, you wanna go with us?" Ken said, as his Repair Shop co-workers rode their boards in the parking lot waiting for him.

"Whadda you mean? Where are you going?" I said.

"We're going up to this residential area in the Santa Monica Mountains. They've got a couple streets that go downhill for over a mile. It's awesome. Two of us ride down and the other one drives the car so we have a ride back up."

"Sounds pretty cool, but I think I'll pass. I'd probably kill myself," I said, only partially kidding. Skateboarding, like skiing, was not really my thing.

A LITTLE after noon, I walked to Pinocchio's to pick up an order of eggplant parmigiana. I returned with my lunch and went into the back room to eat. We kept just about everything in this storage area—all the tennis shoes, backup stocks of clothing, cleaning supplies, and the water cooler. It doubled as a lunchroom. I was thoroughly enjoying my meal when Renee walked in without me seeing her and silently approached me from behind. As I readied another bite of eggplant, I suddenly felt the warmth of her body up against me. From behind, she wrapped her arms around my midsection and squeezed her body up against mine. I breathed in the familiar fragrance of two nights ago.

"Hey baby, what's for dessert?" she said.

A smile formed on my face as I slowly turned to face her, her arms still surrounding me. "What did you have in mind?" I asked.

With her chin resting on my chest, she tilted her face upward and puckered her lips. "Maybe a little of this?"

Resisting Renee Ayers was not an easy thing. The rose-petal softness of her skin invited my touch. Nearly giving in to the temptation, but utilizing every ounce of willpower I had, something told me this was not the time or place. "No thank you, miss. I'll just stick with my usual, a big slice of coconut cream pie, please."

Playing along, she answered in her best southern accent, "Coming right up, but next time you visit our fine establishment, you really should try me."

"Are you as good as the coconut cream?" I said, my hands moving down her back.

She turned her head, resting the side of her face on my chest and closing her eyes. "Oh, much, much better," she said quietly.

"Ahem." Stacy Johansen, manager of Skiwear and Renee's immediate boss, cleared her throat. "Sorry to interrupt, but Renee, can you come out here a minute and help this young lady with a ski sweater?"

Renee gave me a furtive glance and obediently left to go onto the sales floor. Stacy looked back at me before leaving, a knowing smile on her face.

I FINISHED my lunch and returned to Tennis. I hadn't been back but five minutes before Buck wandered in, just as I was turning the volume up on a Doors tape. I quickly adjusted it lower.

"Sorry about that, Buck. I don't usually play it that loud," I said, my hand still on the knob.

Buck scratched the two-day-old growth of grayish white stubble on his cheek. "Don't worry about it. I may be an old codger, but I like the Rolling Stones."

Smiling inside, I couldn't bring myself to correct him, and so just let it go.

"Hey Paul, are you busy? I was wondering if you could take me for a little drive," he asked.

Buck had been an actor before he got into the sporting goods business, and he still had connections in the industry. From time to time, a director would hire him to scout out locations for filming, Buck knowing the Southern California area about as well as anybody, after sixty years of living and working here. Buck would have somebody, oftentimes me, drive him around so he could focus on the scenery.

I rested my hand on the empty stringing machine. "Sure, Buck. We finished all the rackets this morning and Ernie will be back from lunch in a bit. You wanna go now?"

Buck took a step toward the back entrance and clapped his hands once. "Yep, let's go."

SO HE CLIMBED into the luxury of my Squareback and we headed out, Buck directing me to go east on Wilshire. I liked Buck. He was an interesting guy. And although I had heard some of it before, I loved to get him talking about his old acting days.

"So tell me again, how did you get into acting?" I threw out the bait, knowing he would take it and run with it.

"Cause Tom Mix took a likin' to me. Came out here from Gainesville, Texas when I was a punk kid of fifteen years old. Got a job at the very first movie studio in Southern California ... Fox Studios, right near where Dodger Stadium is today."

"Fifteen? Wow, why so young?" I asked.

"Wasn't getting along with Mom and Pop and was itchin' to go join the Army. This was 1917 and we had just joined the fight in Europe. Told 'em I was eighteen but they checked up on me and says I'm too young, so I come out to California to get in the movies. Not knowing any better I figured I'd go to the biggest studio in town and tell 'em I wanted to be an actor. Well, they kinda laughed at me. Here I was this young kid dressed funny. I always wore my hat and boots, even back then."

Buck stuck his hand out straight in front of him, thumb extended to the right. This was his way of giving me advance notice that we would shortly need to make a right turn. He usually did this at least half a block before we needed to turn. I had to stifle a chuckle every time he did it—it's hard to explain, but it was just funny to me.

"But I reckon they felt sorry for me cause they gave me a job, not acting of course, but doing whatever needed doing around the sets. This was around the time that Tom Mix hired on to do a bunch of Westerns, all silent at that time, mind you. Well, he was just about as big a star as there was ..." Buck interrupted himself to tell me to turn right on 20th Street, reinforcing the earlier hand signal.

"Well, ol' Tom Mix started asking me to do stuff for him—bring him lunch, get him a glass of gin, clean his boots, you name it."

I stopped at a red light and turned toward him, my elbow up on the seat back.

"In fact he's the one that gave me my name. I was always William Braddock—not Bill, not Billy, just William—till Tom Mix started calling me Buck. Don't know why he called me Buck, and when I asked him, he just said I looked like Buck to him. Well, since it was Tom Mix calling me Buck, pretty soon everyone else started calling me Buck. And from then on I was just Buck. About a year later he let me be in one of his movies. You ever think about gettin' into actin'?"

I turned my body straight again as the light changed to green. "Guess I've thought about it like most people, but no, not really."

"Well, you got the look. I could see you playin' the strong, silent type, kinda like a Gary Cooper. I could set you up with somebody if you want."

Being in LA, the allure of becoming a star was ever present, but if I was honest with myself, I couldn't see myself doing it. I'm just not sure I had the right personality for it. And the only attraction of it for me would be the money.

Buck had me turn left on Olympic Boulevard and drive through the industrial areas near the Santa Monica Freeway. He was trying to find an old metal building with the right kind of look. He said they were going to do a "shoot 'em up" scene in a warehouse building. I drove up and down the streets and Buck snapped photos, even while the car was moving. And he didn't miss a beat with his story.

"Anyway, it was 1927 I think when "talkies" started up. Ol' Tom Mix never really made the transition. And probably because of that, Fox Studios began havin' money problems. So I went over to Paramount and got a job at their big, new studio in Hollywood. They put me to work alright. I did everything from Bing Crosby musicals to Mae West comedies to the big Cecil B. DeMille extravaganzas."

Buck's hand was out again, thumb pointing to the left.

"This was during the Depression?" I asked, then made the left turn.

"Yes, sir. Emily and I were under contract at Paramount— not much money, but we were happy as pigs in the poke just to have jobs."

"How did you get into sporting goods?"

"Oh, that was after the war," he said.

"What did you do during the war?"

He paused for a minute, told me to slow down, then took several shots of an old metal building on the right side of the street. He continued, "I was no youngster—thirty-nine years old when the Japs attacked. But the very next day, December 8th, I went and signed myself up. Emily was madder than a bull lookin' at a red blanket, but she knew my mind was made up."

At that point Buck put his camera back in its case, signaling he was done, and said, "Alright, you can head back now. I've seen all I need to see."

SHORTLY AFTER we returned, two women walked into Tennis and began perusing the rackets. I walked over to ask if I could assist them—my jaw dropped to my chest. I couldn't get any words out. *Jennifer Ryan! Right here in Buck's Sporting Goods and right here in my Tennis Department!* After what seemed like five minutes and was really probably five seconds, I stuttered, "M-m-may I help you?"

"I hope so," Jennifer replied, her blue eyes looking up at me seriously. "I would say I'm between a beginner and an intermediate. I'm going to start playing a lot more and need a new racket. What do you recommend?"

Her friend went to browse through the tennis clothing and left me alone with Jennifer to discuss rackets. *Jennifer Ryan!* Luckily, she asked me a question I had been asked hundreds of times.

"More and more I've been suggesting these oversized rackets," I said, pointing shakily to the grouping of larger headed rackets. I felt like I was having an out-of-body experience. I could see myself talking. I could hear myself talking. I was starring in a movie opposite my heartthrob.

"My friend told me to get a Jack Kramer. Is that one of the big ones?" she said, looking first at the rackets, then at me. She wore a pleated white tennis skirt with a white V-necked top, both with navy blue trim. Her light brown hair was pulled back neatly into a ponytail, serving to accentuate her facial features, the doll-like nose, delicate ears, and small mouth with thin lips. I didn't notice much make-up, and it seemed to me that she looked different somehow than in her movies. Better, definitely better. More beautiful, if that was possible.

"No, here's the Kramer. See the difference?" I said, as I held it up next to the Wilson Ultra, one of the larger frames. My voice sounded high pitched to me. Here I was talking to Jennifer Ryan and my voice was deserting me. "The Kramer is a great racket, don't get me wrong. But you're going to find that a larger racket is easier and more fun to play with." I was suddenly conscious of my height. I felt freakishly tall.

I was probably a foot taller than Jennifer Ryan and it felt like three feet. I tried to compensate by slouching. "You'll have fewer missed shots because of the larger sweet spot."

I survived the conversation because I knew the subject so well. She ended up choosing the Wilson Ultra, then we walked over to look at the selection of gut and nylon strings.

She furrowed her brow and said, "You look very familiar to me for some reason."

A lump formed in my throat, my mind racing to the scene of two days ago in her neighbor's backyard when the voyeurs had been discovered. *She couldn't possibly recognize me from that, could she?*

Her face flashed with recognition and she pointed her finger at me. "Now I know where I saw you. Aren't you the guy who beat up the paparazzo who was on the beach? I saw your picture in the paper."

"That's me," I said, relieved that I hadn't been found out.

She put her hand on my arm and said, "I really, really want to thank you for doing that. I hate those guys with a passion. They make it so difficult for me to have any privacy. You are definitely my hero."

How ironic that she was calling me her hero for protecting her privacy when just two days before I was surreptitiously gazing at her naked body. I calmed myself once again, took a deep breath, and said, "Thank you. It's nice of you to say that. We do our best to keep those guys from snooping around the beach."

"What is your name?" she asked.

"Paul ... Paul Townsend," I said as we shook hands.

"Now that I've met you, I want to thank you properly. Would you be my guest tomorrow afternoon around four o'clock at my place for dinner?"

"Oh my gosh, Miss Ryan, I don't know." I was so stunned by the invite that I didn't know what to say.

She dismissively waved her hand. "Oh nonsense, I'll expect you around four. And please call me Jennifer."

"Thank you. Thank you so much. I'll be there. I'll definitely be there," I gushed, nervously dropping her new racket frame on the floor and quickly picking it up.

Several employees from the Ski Department and Ski Repair had drifted into Tennis to check out Jennifer Ryan. They overheard our conversation and whispered amongst themselves. I finished her racket order, telling her what type of string I would be installing and that I could personally deliver the racket when I came to her house tomorrow.

She extended her hand and said, "Thank you so much, Paul. It was nice meeting you and I look forward to seeing you tomorrow. You know which house, right?"

"Oh yes, I know which house," I said as she waved goodbye and exited the front door with her friend.

The Buck's employees gathered around congratulating me as if I'd just won Wimbledon or something. In a daze, with a silly grin on my face, I took the racket she had just bought and began securing it in the stringing machine.

"I can't believe what I just heard," Ernie said. "You lucky bastard. You fucking lucky bastard." He couldn't say any more, just kept shaking his head.

Conspicuously missing from the revelry was Renee. I walked into the Ski Department and found her folding some T-shirts.

"Well, aren't you special," she said without a trace of a smile.

"Oh, c'mon. You're not upset, are you?"

"What makes you think I'm upset?" she said flatly. "Have a great *hero's* dinner with your best friend, Jennifer." Then she walked away.

"So I see our best and only fan is here again. Who is this guy?"

I had gathered the girls around at the end of our fifth practice, the halfway point of our preparation time before the game, to give them a summary of how we were doing, what we still needed to work on, and so forth. Starting with the second practice and at each and every practice thereafter, a man in blue jeans, white t-shirt and an old Yankees baseball cap, probably in his early twenties, was in the stands for the entire practice. His smooth complexion was pasty white and stood in contrast to a neatly trimmed, short, black beard. He was all by himself and didn't talk to anybody, just watched us practice, then walked out when it was over.

The team was seated on the glossy hardwood floor in front of me. The girls all looked toward Lori Lewis.

Lori said, "I'm really sorry. He's a guy I went out with for a while and now he just kind of shows up different places."

"I thought he was a spy from the Tri Delts," I said, only half kidding.

Lori continued, "Believe me, I wish that's who he was. He's just being a creep following me around. I've told him to stop it but he keeps showing up."

I lowered myself to sit on the floor, facing the girls. "Do you want me to talk to him, tell him he's not welcome? Or I can always close off the gym to visitors."

Lori shook her head as she spoke. "No, he's harmless. He never even says anything to me. He's just a weirdo. I think he'll lose interest eventually."

"Okay, if you say so. Anyway, just to wrap things up," I said, clapping my hands together. "I'm really proud of you guys. That was a great practice. Over the weekend each of you should make the effort to practice on your own. Shoot some baskets in your driveway, play some one on one with your brother or sister. Make that basketball your best friend— hold it, dribble it, shoot it." Lori's ex-boyfriend stood up and stepped down out of the bleachers, continuing out the front entrance. The girls all turned their heads to look at him as he walked out. "I'll see you all next Tuesday, same bat time, same bat channel."

I stood up and gathered a couple of errant basketballs, then put them on the rack, before rolling it to the supply closet. The girls started to head out of the gym and to their cars, or in some cases to their parents' cars, who had come to pick them up.

The gym had emptied except for Lori, who walked up to me and, with a smile that melted me, said, "Paul would you mind walking me to my car? Max has been acting a little weirder lately and I'd feel better if I had some company."

"Sure, Lori, be happy to. Just let me turn off the lights and we'll get out of here."

I was excited and nervous, knowing that I was alone with Lori Lewis. I jogged to the electric panel and switched off the lights as Lori held open the gym door. After locking up the gym, the other girls and their parents gone, Lori and I walked on the sidewalk that diagonally traversed the large grassy area in front of the Rosedale High Gymnasium. There was no sign of her stalker friend Max as we moved toward her car in the semi-darkness, the only light being the dim parking lot lamps a few yards away.

"So how am I doing? I've never really played basketball before," she said, her big, brown eyes looking up at me inquiringly.

I seemed to remember that she had spent a lot of time in dance classes and competitions when she was a kid. Not having done a lot of hand-eye coordination sports would explain why basketball was such a challenge.

"Lori, I think you're doing awesome. You're getting better every practice. You're gonna be great in the game," I lied, as we arrived at her car.

"Thank you, Mr. Townsend, and I think you are an awesome coach!" Lori got on her tiptoes, put her hand on my shoulder and gave me a quick kiss on the cheek. "See ya tomorrow at school. Thanks for walking me to my car."

My heart skipped a beat. It wasn't even the kiss so much as the closeness, the smell of her perfume. *Is it possible that she likes me? It's possible. Not likely, but possible.* "No problem. You're welcome. See you tomorrow."

I never thought I had a prayer with a girl like Lori, so had never even considered it until that very moment. This basketball coaching is a pretty good gig, I thought to myself as I did a little dance on the way to my car.

"Do you like her?"

The voice came out of nowhere and startled me. Max stood about ten yards away in the shadows of the gymnasium building, the shadows created by the parking lot lights.

"Yeah, s-sure ... she's a nice girl," I managed to reply after recovering from the surprise.

"She's my girlfriend, you know," Max said, keeping his distance.

"No, I didn't know that. I thought you had broken up," I replied, my voice weak.

Max laughed in a strange way, almost awkwardly, and said, "No, no, we're still together."

Then, without another word, he vanished into the darkness.

"Tom, I think tomorrow we should pay an early morning visit to our friend Mr. Moberg. Maybe park in the alley down from his house. Hopefully he goes to work like most people in the morning, and when he leaves, we follow him and find out where he works."

It was Sunday morning and Tom and I had just spent an hour apiece making phone calls while the other one did a little apartment cleaning. We had worked our way through about three-fourths of the names in Jack's address book and called all of the extraneous numbers written on slips of paper that we collected at his house. We had left lots of messages and gotten return calls from most, faithfully keeping our log of when and who we spoke to, and what they had to say. So far the only person even remotely suspicious or who seemed to know anything was Jerry Moberg.

"You just keep thinkin' Townie. That's what you're good at."

"Tom, I've got vision and the rest of the world wears bifocals," I said, responding as I always did to the Butch Cassidy line.

Tom was stretched out full length on the couch, his head resting on the pillow, watching me do some pushups. He said, "We've got no other leads so we might as well try to make Moberg talk. But why are you worried about where he works?"

I collapsed on my stomach, catching my breath, my nose buried in the shag carpet. "Not worried, just figured it can't hurt to have more information. He seems a little nervous about us already since we showed up on his doorstep. Once he figures we also know where he works, maybe he'll be convinced we aren't going away. Maybe it'll scare him enough to talk. Boy, did you see his face when we mentioned that Jack's house was vandalized. That really seemed to spook him. He knows something."

I rolled over on my back and pulled my knees to my chest, stretching out my lower back.

Tom swung his legs around and sat on the edge of the couch, leaning forward. "Just thinking out loud here, but what if we just decided we were going to *make* this guy talk. I don't know what it would take ... threaten him or something. Get tough with him, you know, maybe get hold of a gun and scare him."

"I don't know, Tom." I released my knees and laid my legs flat on the carpet. "Maybe if we have to, but not yet ... not yet."

"I guess let's just see how it goes tomorrow and then we'll take it from there," Tom said, leaning back and interlocking his fingers behind his head. "You wanna come down to the beach with me? Or are you gonna rest up in the apartment all day to mentally prepare for your rendezvous with Miss Ryan?"

"Very funny. I'm coming down, but I gotta drive my own car cause I'm gonna take a change of clothes and go straight from the beach to her place. And do me a favor ... don't tell any of the guys. I don't want everyone giving me a bunch of crap. I'll give everybody all the gory details tomorrow."

"Alright superstar. Mum's the word," Tom said.

WE PARKED within a block of each other on Palisades Avenue, and walked together down the stairs, across the bridge, and onto the sand. All the big boys were gone today, it being the second and final day of the Santa Barbara Open. Tommy would be playing on the beach circuit next summer but for now he was still on scholarship and the UCLA coaches wanted him to focus on his indoor game. They probably wouldn't like it if they knew that Tommy was at Sorrento nearly every day. Rightly or wrongly, the coaches felt that the movement and technique of the beach game was so different from indoor volleyball, that playing on the beach too much would be detrimental to your indoor game. Tommy said the more he played, the better he got, whether it was indoors, grass, or beach. I didn't know enough about indoor volleyball to have an opinion one way or the other, but if you watched Tommy Ruderman play indoors, it was hard to argue with him.

Marlowe had phoned Scott Rodgers from Santa Barbara earlier and said that he and Andrew were playing in the semifinals of the winner's bracket that morning. If they were to win the tournament, this would be the thirteenth straight event they had won, the last six from last year and the first seven of this year. They already held the record for most consecutive victories and this was just adding to it. It was history in the making.

I took off my shirt and threw it next to my backpack up against the wall. In addition to a PB and J sandwich, the pack contained my best corduroy shorts and an aloha shirt I carefully selected to wear to Jennifer Ryan's later that day. I sat on the sand with my back resting against the wall. It hit me that in a few short hours I would be on the other side of the wall being entertained by one of the most famous and beautiful actresses in the world. *Jennifer Ryan!* Doug Williams interrupted my daydream, yelling from Court Two that he needed a partner. I jogged out there and started bouncing the ball around with him. Normally a chatterbox, always smiling and upbeat, Doug wasn't his usual self. He hadn't said a word except to say "hey" in a sullen monotone when I got to the court. Something was amiss—his shoulders slumped and he moved slowly.

"LJ, you alright man? You look like your dog just died," I said, as we began passing the ball back and forth.

"Actually, I'm not doing real well. Last night my wife told me she wanted a divorce. Said she wants a separation right now ... wants me to move out."

I caught the ball, stopping our warm-up. "Jeez Doug, that's terrible. Did she say why?"

"Just that she felt we were drifting apart. Didn't feel like I cared anymore. Said she still loved me, that she would always love me, but that we might be better off living separately. I'm gonna miss my boy, I'll tell you that."

Going from being a "just out of high school" kid to a Viet Nam soldier ended Doug's youth prematurely, thrusting manhood upon him, ready or not. Then he got married, two years after returning from the war, to his high school sweetheart, Marissa. It was my humble opinion, and I had noticed this pretty much as long as I'd known him, that LJ had been on a quest to become, at thirty-two years old, a teenager once again. The teenager that disappeared so abruptly when the Army called. Doug Williams was a good man, but a reluctant father and husband.

I set the ball to him, starting our warm-up again. "What are you gonna do? You gonna try to talk her out of it?"

"Her mind seems pretty set right now. I'm going to get an apartment close to my house. She's agreed to go with me to a marriage counselor. Hopefully we can work it out."

"Well, good luck. I'm really sorry."

LJ gave a half-hearted chuckle and said, "So that's my excuse if I play bad. I'm tired as hell. Didn't sleep hardly at all and when I did, I had nightmares about Nam. Seems like whenever I get stressed out about something I have more nightmares than usual."

I stopped our rally again and held the ball. "What happens in the nightmares?"

"Oh man, you really want to know?" He cocked his head sideways and had a pained expression as he began to explain. "About three months into my tour, our platoon was ordered on a day long march to God knows where, for God knows what reason. A couple hours into it, we got ambushed outta nowhere. For the next half hour or so we were up to our necks in the most brutal close-up firefight."

I sat down on the volleyball and looked up at him as he spoke, feeling his emotion.

"The VC were everywhere, mixed in with our guys, close range shooting, using bayonets. A couple of my best buddies didn't make it. Half our platoon went down. But the part that haunts me more than anything ..." He paused for a few seconds and ran all ten fingers through his thick hair, from front to back. He took a deep breath and continued. "I had to bayonet this kid. Looked like he was about fourteen. The look in his eyes, the terror in his eyes ... as I stabbed him. That's what I have nightmares about."

Not knowing what to say, I didn't say anything. I felt horrible for LJ, but he seemed willing and almost eager to talk about it. Probably did him good to talk about it. Finally I muttered softly, "Nobody should have to experience anything like that."

"You're right, nobody should."

WE PLAYED against Rabbit and Scott, normally a pretty good matchup for LJ and me. But we had a tough time with them today, losing 15-8. Neither of us played very well. I hit a couple balls out that I wouldn't normally and LJ was erratic with his passing. But it was a gorgeous warm day, not too hot, and playing that game was the perfect tonic for LJ and for me. The tension of the last few days had been building, starting with the disappearance of Jack, then the incident with the paparazzo, almost getting arrested at the police station, and the ongoing frustration of not knowing what to do next to find Jack. And now this news from LJ. I really felt for him.

After the game finished, we jogged to the water and jumped into the surf. The cool salt water washed over my body, erasing the sweat and sand, and more than that, clearing my mind.

LJ popped out of the water a few feet away from me and said, "There's something else I didn't tell you."

"Yeah?"

"The other night at TT's, when I took Michelle home ..."

"Yeah?"

"Well, she invited me in ... one thing led to another ..."

"No! Really?" *Lucky dog!* I saw his grave look and changed my expression accordingly. "Did your wife find out? Is that why she asked you to leave?"

"No, she doesn't know. It was just coincidence that it happened the day before. Maybe it was God's way of punishing me. It was the first time I've ever done anything like that. All those months I'm away working ... never even considered cheating on her."

A cameraman in the film industry, Doug worked television and feature films sometimes seven days a week, and occasionally a lengthy movie job out of town.

"But at least we're going to get counseling. I just hope it's not too late."

A large wave formed behind us and we both took off, getting a good ride almost to the shoreline. I stood up and wiped the salt from my eyes, the foaming whitewater up to my waist. I moved to shallower water, then jogged a few yards to catch up with LJ, who had ridden the wave further and waited on the hard packed wet sand.

I put my arm around his shoulder after reaching him. "It'll work out for you—it's gotta work out."

I detected a trace of a smile for the first time today as he looked down at the sand shaking his head. "It was a lot of fun—that night with Michelle."

"I'll bet," I said.

"But you know what?" Now his expression turned serious once more. "I wish that night had never happened."

The shower at Sorrento was your standard basic beach shower—cold water only—with a push button good for about five seconds of water flow. Hold your thumb on the button to keep the water flowing and you only had one hand left to wash yourself. I usually did a combination, sometimes holding the button and sometimes going with two hands. A while ago, somebody wrapped a bungie cord around the shower pole such that you could slide the tightly wrapped stretchy cord on top of the button for a constant flow of water *and* two hands to wash yourself. But the cord disappeared and now we were back to the old method. We kept a bar of soap on the top of the metal pole, so if you were at least about six foot tall, you qualified to get yourself a little cleaner than those who couldn't reach the top. Today I stayed in the shower longer than usual, used the soap all over my body, getting presentable for my date.

After the shower, I grabbed my backpack and headed to the bathroom to change. Out of habit, I took a deep breath before entering, although I could never hold it long enough to escape the variety of odors. I stepped lightly across the soaking wet cement floor puddled with ocean water and urine, both of which had dripped off of people in one fashion or another. I could only hope that the mixture did not include ingredients from the overflowing toilet in the corner stall.

Getting dressed in the beach bathroom was an acquired skill. The challenge was to get dressed without letting your clothes touch the floor. Plus, I wanted to get out of there as quickly as possible. I worried that if I stayed too long, I would walk into Jennifer Ryan's smelling like eau de toilet.

At four o'clock I exited the bathroom and rubbed my feet in the sand to rid them of whatever might be on the bottom. I walked straight through the parking lot and around to the front of Jennifer Ryan's house. Dressed up in my good shorts and best aloha shirt, I purposely avoided the group at the courts. I didn't want the questions, since I knew I would have to lie about it. It would be disaster if they knew where I was going. They would be peeking over the wall and worse, probably verbally harassing me. I intended to tell the whole story, but not until it was in the past.

A call button and speaker box protruded from the stuccoed block wall facing Pacific Coast Highway. A video camera sat high on the wall facing the speaker box. Butterflies gathered in my stomach as I pushed the button and waited for an answer. About thirty seconds passed and no answer. I pushed the button again and this time a male voice responded, "May I help you?"

"Yes, this is Paul Townsend and I am here to see Miss Ryan."

"One moment, please." After another thirty seconds or so the gate buzzed, which was my permission to enter the hallowed grounds. I opened the gate and walked through a small garden area to the front door. Standing at the door, my knees weak, my stomach felt like it did when I approached Janelle Newman's house on my first date. I suddenly had a panicked feeling that I was woefully underdressed, that I should have taken the time to go home, shower, shave, put some cologne on, wear some nice khaki pants and real shoes instead of the flip flops I was wearing.

But, too late now. I reached to ring the bell. Before my finger even touched the button, the door opened and there stood Jennifer Ryan, answering her own door. I figured it would be the butler or manservant, or whatever you wanted to call the male voice that answered the buzzer at the front gate. In my mind, I thought I would have time to enter the house and gather myself a bit before she made her appearance.

"My hero! Thanks so much for coming, Paul. Come on in," she said as she reached her hand out to shake mine. Her hand felt soft and small and wonderful as my large, calloused hand embraced it. My hands bore the marks of a racket stringer, including thick skinned fingertips from the weaving of the strings.

She was shorter than I remembered from Buck's, and certainly a lot shorter than I imagined after seeing her on television and in the movies. Then I looked down and saw that she was barefoot. The top of her head was about even with my chest, about five foot four I estimated.

"Where's my racket? I thought you were going to bring my new racket," she said, her aqua blue eyes looking up at me inquiringly.

My heart sank like it does when you're at the airport to fly overseas and realize you forgot your passport at home. "Oh, I'm so sorry. I totally forgot. Let me run up right now and get it." I turned and took a step toward the front door. Preoccupied with what I would say and how I would act, I had completely forgotten about her new racket, strung yesterday and hanging on the completed rackets peg in the Tennis Department.

"No, don't worry about it. I can send somebody to pick it up. I was just excited to see it." She tucked a few errant strands of her shoulder-length, sun-bleached, light brown hair behind her ear.

I turned back toward her. "I feel like an idiot. I'm really sorry."

"Stop it. It's not a big deal. Come in, come in. What can I get you? Glass of wine, beer, mixed drink?"

I felt better about my wardrobe. Jennifer was dressed casually, wearing a pair of white cotton shorts and a tank top. Through the thin, white, tank top material I could see she was wearing a pink bikini underneath.

Conscious of trying to act older and more sophisticated, I passed on my first choice, beer, and answered, "A glass of wine would be great."

She pressed her palms together, holding them just below her face. "Do you have a favorite?"

I was going to show my colors if I answered that question, so instead said, "Whatever you're having is fine with me."

"I took a trip up to the Santa Ynez Valley last weekend and stopped at the Sanford and Benedict Winery. They had the most wonderful Pinot and I brought home a case. How about that?"

Not even sure what Pinot was, but again, not wanting to show my ignorance, I eagerly agreed. She led me through the Spanish style house to the backyard area where a patio table with a big umbrella stood near the pool. Sitting down on the large, heavily cushioned chairs, it occurred to me that we were only a few feet away from the lounge chair where she had been sunbathing only three days before. *Long lean legs, perfectly shaped ....*

"So Paul, tell me about yourself and how you came to be a paparazzi killer."

The image of her in the lounge chair was still in my mind, and I was desperately afraid my thoughts showed on my face. I chuckled nervously. "Well, Miss Ryan..."

Jennifer interrupted, "Paul, please, you're making me feel old. Call me Jennifer."

"Okay ... Jennifer. I'm in my final year at UCLA, majoring in Economics. You pretty much know the rest of my life— stringing rackets at Buck's Sporting Goods and hanging out behind your back wall there. As for how I became a paparazzi killer, well, it just kind of happened. Hasn't happened before and may not ever happen again."

She leaned back in the chair and rested her clasped hands on her lap. "Where are you from? Where'd you grow up?"

"Kansas. Beautiful Kansas."

She leaned forward and her eyes widened. "You're kidding. My aunt lives in Wellington. We used to go there all the time when I was a kid."

"I grew up in Winfield, about forty miles east of there."

"What a small world—just down the road from my auntie." Then she smiled at me and nodded her head. "A Kansas boy."

A tall, darkly complected man with a neatly trimmed black moustache and long black hair pulled into a ponytail, approached. He appeared to be in his late forties or early fifties. He set down two large wine glasses, each half full of red wine, and a platter of jumbo shrimp resting on crushed ice, with a cup of red cocktail sauce in the center.

"Paul, this is Edward," Jennifer said.

I stood up and we shook hands.

He said, "I'll be right back with a selection of crackers and cheeses to go with the Pinot Noir."

"Thank you, Edward. This looks delicious," Jennifer said. "Yeah, you boys sure do hang out on the beach a lot. It seems like sunup to sundown every day. But you know what? I really like having you back there. Makes me feel like I'm being watched after."

Once again, I flashed back on the three of us standing on our logs, peeping over the fence. She was being watched after alright.

"I do love coming to the beach here, Miss ... I mean Jennifer. I started playing volleyball a couple years ago and just fell in love with the game. I come here every spare moment I have. All my best friends are here. It's more than a game really. It's a whole way of life." I took a sip of the wine. "Mmm ... that's really good." I held the glass up high, looking at the burgundy colored liquid. "The sun, sand, friends, competition, and the feeling you get after a really good workout—then the ocean and cold beer afterwards. I can't imagine anything better. You should try playing sometime." The wine was loosening me up. Here I was inviting Jennifer Ryan to play volleyball. I would have never imagined it.

"It looks like so much fun. I would love to learn how to play. Is it hard?"

"It takes a little practice. I could teach you." I picked up a piece of shrimp and dipped it in the sauce.

"Well, I'll look for you out there. Maybe I'll sneak out and you can give me a lesson," she said.

"You would love it so much. And I would be honored," I said, then took a big bite of the shrimp.

Edward came back with a tray of several types of crackers and three different types of cheese. I smiled and nodded my thanks to Edward, then looked back at Jennifer. "Can I ask you a stupid question?"

"Sure, go ahead. I think I've already been asked every stupid question in existence, so fire away," she replied.

"Do you like being famous?"

"Ha! You want the short answer or the long answer?"

I sipped my wine and leaned back in the cushy chair. "I've got time."

"Then I'll give you both answers. The short answer is: Who wouldn't love being famous? You're adored by everyone. You've got money to do whatever you want. What's not to like?" Holding her wine glass in her left hand, she lifted her right, palm up and fingers spread. "But the real answer is a little more complex. Sometimes I love it and sometimes I hate it. I love the satisfaction of knowing that I've given a great performance. It's wonderful for my ego when people want my autograph or want my picture. And I truly do love the luxuries I am able to indulge in… this house, fantastic food, the finest hotels everywhere I go."

She reached for the cracker and cheese plate and picked out a couple of each to place on her dish, then scooted the plate to my side of the table. I grabbed a couple crackers and made a sandwich with some soft, white cheese.

"But the bad part is that I can't do many of the simple, ordinary things most people take for granted. I can't just run out and grab a bite to eat somewhere. I can't go to the grocery store, at least not without everybody staring at me, making me feel uncomfortable. Although I went to Buck's the other day, it's usually pretty difficult for me to go shopping anywhere. It's difficult to be spontaneous. Everything has to be planned in advance, and I hate that. I'm so envious of you being able to go to the beach whenever you want and just hang with your friends. I would give anything to be able to do that." She scooted her chair back and crossed her legs at the knee.

As she spoke I flashed to a scene from one of her movies, I can't remember which. She was enjoying a dinner conversation at a fancy restaurant, then got up to go to the restroom and kissed her date on the way. What I wouldn't give for one, good long kiss from Jennifer Ryan.

"Being famous tends to isolate you. It's difficult to have relationships." She looked away for a second, toward the beach, trying to gather a thought. "I feel sorry for the guy. If he isn't well known himself, he instantly is once he starts dating me. It is really hard on the guy. And my work schedule doesn't make it any easier. I'm married to my work. Are you sorry you asked?"

"No, no," I chuckled. "I admire you. I don't think I could do it. Don't think I'd wanna do it. Be famous I mean."

She hesitated and seemed to be studying my face. "I think you're the first person to ever say that to me ... that you would choose not to be a star."

"Probably just the crowd you're hanging out with. It just wouldn't be for me, I don't think. But you must love what you do."

Still looking at me intently, a smile began to form. "You're right—I do love acting. If I could do it all over again, I wouldn't change a thing."

"It certainly has its benefits," I said, motioning to the yard and the house. "And you're so talented. I love everything you do. I've seen every movie, some of 'em twice."

"Oh, you're so sweet. Thank you," she said.

Slowly but surely, she was becoming a real person to me. She wasn't the woman in the movies that I had idolized for so long. She was just a regular person, a real life human being. Granted, she was an extraordinarily beautiful, real life human being.

"What's your favorite role you've ever played?"

She paused and looked down at her clasped hands resting on the table. "The one role that was so different for me, but that I loved more than any of the others, was when I played a special undercover agent for the NYPD. I got to chase bad guys, use some karate, shoot 'em up. They let me do a lot of my own stunts, and I loved it!" Her eyes got big and I could sense her excitement. "They even trained me how to use a gun, which I had never even held in my hand before. It was … empowering."

WE HAD MADE a good dent in the crackers and finished off most of the shrimp. Edward returned again to refill the wine glasses. My tension was gone. The wine had done the trick. I flashed back on a poster I had of her on my bedroom wall in Winfield. I found myself noticing things about her I had never paid attention to on any other woman. The smooth skin on her bare shoulders … the delicate nape of her neck.

"By the way, I love the rocks and the waterfall—really cool."

"Thanks, I wish I could take the credit. When I bought the place, I hired a landscape architect to completely re-do the backyard. But the house is a different story. I'll take credit for that. Can I give you the grand tour?"

"Sure, I'd love it."

For the next twenty minutes, Jennifer led me from room to room through the 6,500 square foot hacienda. She had decorated the entire house herself and was justifiably proud of it. We walked through the formal living room into a large adjoining room that looked like a super deluxe miniature movie theater. A dozen plush leather reclining chairs set on three levels faced an eight foot by fourteen foot screen. A dark red, mahogany bar, about ten feet long, occupied the rear of the room. An antique popcorn machine sat on one end of it. The room was carpeted and wallpapered in earth tones and four framed movie posters hung on the walls. The posters were collector's items from classic films: Wizard of Oz, Gone with the Wind, North by Northwest, and Rebel Without a Cause.

Upstairs were five bedrooms, all of them large enough to be master bedrooms in any normal house. One of the rooms was Edward's and another was used by a live-in housekeeper who I had not met. Two were guest rooms and the largest, the real master suite, was Jennifer's. Beautiful Spanish tile was utilized throughout the house and large colorful area rugs added warmth in the bedrooms. Jennifer's room had large side windows and glass double doors leading to a balcony with a view of the Pacific Ocean. Volleyball games were in progress, but I was a world away. A colorful quilt with Aztec Indian designs covered her king sized bed. Several pieces of Aztec artwork adorned the walls.

I picked up a corner of the quilt to take a closer look. "Beautiful, just beautiful. Now can I tell all my friends that you asked me into your bedroom?" The alcohol said that, not me.

She giggled and said, "Yes, I guess that would be accurate."

AFTER THE HOUSE TOUR, we walked back outside. "Feel like taking a dip in the pool? We've got some time before dinner. I keep the water warm."

"That sounds really good. I've even got my trunks in my pack since I came straight from the beach."

"Okay, why don't you go upstairs and get changed and I'll meet you in the pool."

She pulled her tank top over her head to reveal the bright pink bikini top that had been teasing me. Stealing glances at her as I moved, I grabbed my pack and raced up to one of the guest bedrooms to change back into the board shorts I had started out the day in. I thought of all my friends back in Winfield, and how there was absolutely nothing I could ever say or do that would convince them that I was really here.

"OH, MAN, you weren't kidding when you said you keep the water warm. This feels awesome."

The late afternoon air had a chill to it which made the water feel even better. Jennifer glided slowly, taking lazy strokes to make her way the length of the pool, her slender legs just below the surface kicking gently. Then I said something I probably would never have imagined saying without the wine in me. "Jennifer, I've got to tell you … you look amazing."

Her face flushed. "Why, thank you. You look terrific yourself."

"Thanks," I said, then felt awkward, wishing I hadn't said it.

She dove under and swam the length of the pool underwater. It occurred to me that we were in full view of the Sorrento crowd should they look over the wall. From then on, I made a conscious effort to speak at a lower volume. The last thing I needed was a bunch of guys poking their heads over the wall hootin' and hollerin'.

She surfaced at the opposite end and said, "Thanks for coming over. I need to relax like this more often. You're great company."

I said, "You know, I think we should do this every day. It would be really good for you."

She laughed out loud, pulled her wet hair back out of her face and off to one side. I was having a hard time not staring at her. I kept thinking somebody was going to wake me up from this dream I was having. I pushed off from the wall of the pool, turned on my back, drifting across the water, taking easy back-strokes and heading for the waterfall. I stopped underneath the flow coming down from the rocks, tilted my head forward and closed my eyes, the warm water pelting down, massaging my neck and shoulders. The combination of the Pinot Noir and the waterfall had me on the road to deep relaxation. I exhaled a deep, moaning sigh as the water beat down on me, releasing tension in my shoulders.

Then, something grabbed at my ankle. *What the hell?* Jennifer had quietly swum underneath and devised a shark attack. She surfaced near to me, laughing hard at the startled look on my face. Aiming to retaliate, I dove under, grabbed her by both ankles, and pulled her along the surface.

"Okay, I give, I give," she said as I released her. She continued to giggle, her face only inches from mine. I resisted the urge to wrap her in my arms and kiss her. Edward broke the spell by coming to the edge of the pool and declaring that dinner would be served in five minutes. We both made our way to the pool steps, climbed out, and wrapped ourselves in the large plush towels which had been set there for us. I walked into the house and up the staircase, Jennifer right behind.

"C'mon, move it buddy," she said, and gave me a pat on the behind as we reached the top. "Meet you in the dining room." Then she skipped off to her room and I went to mine.

I slipped out of my suit, dried myself, then paused for a moment, examining my image in the mirror. I flexed my pectoral muscles, twisted my lean body back and forth, then spoke to my reflection. "What's going on here, Townie? Are you misreading this?"

EDWARD GREETED me at the bottom of the stairs, inviting me to follow him to the dining room where he showed me to my seat.

"What would you like to drink with your dinner, sir?" Edward asked.

"Same thing we were drinking earlier is fine with me. Thanks."

A minute later he came with the bottle and filled the smaller wine glass on the dinner table. I sipped on the wine as I waited for Jennifer. She appeared with a big smile on her face, her blue eyes sparkling, and her wet hair tied into a ponytail. She had slipped into a loose fitting, lavender colored summer dress. As she approached, my eyes looked downward to her bare feet, to the same crimson colored toenail polish that had caught my attention a few days before in her backyard.

"More Pinot? I'm going to have to keep my eye on you," she said.

"Don't worry, I'm a trustworthy drunk." Smiling broadly, I held the wine glass up in a toast, "Here's to the paparazzo that made all this possible."

Suddenly realizing her glass was empty, I poured half of my wine into her glass, probably not proper etiquette, but she didn't seem to mind. We clinked our glasses and drank to Carl Sedgewick.

First was a green salad with candied pecans and crumbled gorgonzola cheese, followed by freshly made tortellini pasta with pesto sauce and pine nuts. The main course was sautéed halibut stuffed with crab and covered with a white sauce. Rich, creamy, white chocolate gelato was the finishing touch to a grand meal, the best I could ever remember having. After savoring the last few bites of gelato, we remained at the table for close to an hour, chatting about the fantastic meal, her tennis game, the shark attack, and future volleyball lessons.

"Shall we move to the living room?" she said.

I stood up, then drained the last bit of wine from my glass before following her to the sectional sofa in the living room. Moments later, Edward entered, holding a tray with two small drinks.

"Do you like brandy?" Jennifer asked. "I love a bit after a meal like that."

Again, not wanting to reveal my simple, uncultured background, I readily agreed and took the glass from Edward's tray.

I raised the small glass for another toast. "Edward." I got his attention before he left the room. "Here's to you! What a great meal."

"Thank you, Mr. Townsend. I'm so glad you enjoyed it." Then he continued out of the room.

"Isn't he the best? It's a wonder I'm not a big fatso."

DURING DINNER, feelings of guilt had entered my consciousness, not able to erase the image of Tommy, Andrew, and me spying on Jennifer three days before. I remembered how upset she had been. *Get ... out! Get out! Oh God!* We had violated her privacy. We had violated *her*. I had to come clean and confess everything. It may be one of the dumbest inclinations I have ever had, but my conscience was in overdrive and I had no choice.

I had yet to say a word, but Jennifer must have seen the anguished look on my face. She said, "What's the matter? What are you thinking about?"

I think I audibly groaned. I envisioned her and Edward picking me up and tossing me in the street, like they used to do out of the swinging saloon door in the Wild West. "Oh jeez, there's something I gotta tell you."

"What? What is it?" A look of concern replaced her smile.

"Do you remember three days ago when you were in your backyard lying out by the pool and you heard the guys on the other side of your fence?"

Jennifer's face turned blank and she did not answer.

"That was me and two other guys. We snuck back there to get a closer look at you with no clothes on. And I'm so sorry." I hung my head, looked down at my lap, then glanced up at her.

Still no words from Jennifer—her expression didn't alter. I nervously rambled on. "I feel terrible. It was such an invasion of your privacy. But once I started looking at you, I couldn't stop. You are just so incredibly beautiful and it was like I couldn't help myself."

Her look softened and she thankfully interrupted me. "You, the paparazzi killer, spying on me? Isn't *that* ironic?"

I gave a half-hearted laugh. "Yeah, it kinda is."

Jennifer stood up, took a step towards me and motioned for me to stand up. She draped her arms across my shoulders, moved her body close to mine, and reached up to give me a kiss on the cheek. Then she moved her lips around to meet mine. After a brief, but luscious kiss, she expertly traced the outline of my lips with her tongue, before I pressed my mouth against hers, drinking her in, my fantasy a reality. My hands moved up and down the back of her dress, pulling her closer.

Ending the kiss and moving back a few inches, her eyes looked downward as she played with the top button of my shirt. "So you liked what you saw?"

"Oh, my God."

She looked deeply into my eyes and said softly, almost in a whisper, "I think you need to do a little closer examination."

Holding my hand, she led me up the stairs, down the hall and into her bedroom. She closed the door.

Toto, I have a feeling we're not in Kansas anymore.

The alarm woke me out of a dead sleep at five-thirty Monday morning. After slapping at the clock a few times trying to quiet the loud, irritating buzz, I finally picked it up, took a close look, methodically found the switch, and flipped it to "off". Through all of this, Tommy remained asleep in his bed, only a few feet from mine. I swung my legs over the side of the bed and sat up, rubbing my eyes, still not fully awake. I pulled open the curtains and the darkness outside reminded me this was the earliest I had been up since our occasional before-school basketball practices at Rosedale High.

Today we would stake out Jerry Moberg's house in hopes of following him to work, or wherever he might go. We needed to find out what he knew. We wanted to see if anyone would visit his house, or if anyone else lived with him.

"Hey! Tom! Wake up!" Tommy finally began to stir. "C'mon, you got ten minutes. We gotta get going." The last thing I wanted to happen was to drive all the way to Manhattan Beach and find out he had already left the house.

"Ugh, I changed my mind. You can handle it, man," Tommy mumbled.

"Bullshit. Get your ass out of bed."

With that encouragement, Tommy accepted the inevitable and sat up. He made his way over to the closet, picked up a t-shirt off the closet floor and sniffed at the armpits to see if it was wearable. He had a habit of throwing his dirty clothes in the bottom of his closet, where they stayed, waiting for laundry day. This, in and of itself, was not unusual. The problem arose when he would do his laundry, because he was too lazy to fold the clothes and put them in the dresser or to hang them up in the closet. So the clean load of clothes would get tossed into the bottom of the closet. After a few days of tossing dirty clothes into the same pile, he had no idea what was dirty and what was clean, so he would have to put them to the sniff test. And since he had no way of keeping track, sometimes he would be completely out of clean smelling clothes. On more than one occasion, he took a can of Right Guard and sprayed the armpits of a shirt so he could wear it for the day.

Within a few minutes he found a shirt which passed the test, threw on some beach trunks, and we were on our way, walking out of the apartment and down the stairs to the parking garage.

AMAZING that so many people in Los Angeles were up, out of the house, and on the freeways, and it wasn't even six o'clock. But although it was crowded, traffic moved well, and it only took us twenty minutes on the 405 to arrive at the Rosecrans

Avenue exit. Shortly thereafter we arrived at the 29th Street walkstreet where Jerry Moberg lived. We pulled around to the rear alleyway and parked about half a block down the hill from his house, gambling that Jerry was parked in his garage and would exit that way, as opposed to walking out his front door. With no parking allowed in the alley, we parked illegally, blocking his neighbor's garage door. It was six-thirty and the sky was finally turning a lighter shade of blue.

Ten minutes, twenty minutes, thirty minutes passed with no activity whatsoever on the entire block. At about seven-fifteen, an older woman, maybe in her early sixties, opened a gate leading into the alley on the opposite side of Jerry's house and headed toward us, walking her dachshund. As she passed, she peered suspiciously into the car. We smiled and waved.

Tommy said, "You know, we probably can't stay here too long. People are gonna think we're child molesters or something."

"Yeah, hopefully Moberg will show his face soon," I said.

But there was no sign of him, and by eight-thirty it seemed like we had smiled and waved at every one of his neighbors. The garage door next to our car began to open, so we drove uphill to the top of the alley and around the block, before parking on Highland, half a block below Moberg's house. We were less conspicuous there and still confident we could follow him when, and if, he left.

I ended up parking in a red zone so that we could have a clear view straight up the alley to his garage. We hadn't been there more than five minutes when Tommy said, "Hey! That's his door, isn't it?"

I started up my car as Moberg backed out his shiny, black Mercedes sedan. Driving to the bottom of the alleyway, he put his left blinker on, waiting for a break in the traffic. Tommy and I slouched down in the seats hoping to avoid notice, since we were directly across the street from where Moberg waited. He was making a left turn, which was fortunate, since we faced that direction. Otherwise, we would have had to make a U turn, and with the heavy morning traffic, we could very well have lost him. Moberg finally got an opening and proceeded south on Highland. Quickly we left our space, cutting in front of somebody who gave us an angry horn. One car separated us as we moved forward.

"Great job, Townie! We're on him like white on rice," Tommy said.

We easily followed the black sedan into downtown Manhattan Beach and into the left hand turn lane at Manhattan Beach Boulevard. He proceeded east, away from the ocean, for a couple miles, before signaling to turn left into the TRW complex. He parked and walked into one of the many nondescript two-story office buildings which filled the TRW campus. Neither Tommy nor I knew what TRW stood for, or what the company did.

"Okay, now what?" Tommy asked as we sat in our car, parked in the TRW lot.

"I have no idea."

More people arrived to work and entered the same building that Moberg had entered a few minutes before. We silently watched until finally I said, "Let's just go inside and ask to see him."

"And say what to him?" Tom asked.

"I don't know. Just make him nervous that we know where he works." Putting pressure on Jerry Moberg seemed like the only way we would get any information out of him.

So Tommy and I, completely out of place in our shorts, t-shirts, and sandals, walked into Building R2. We were surprised by the armed security guard at the entrance checking employee badges as people arrived.

"We're here to see Jerry Moberg," I said to the guard.

"What is the purpose of your visit?" he asked.

"We're friends of Jerry's, haven't seen him in a while, and wanted to say hello." I answered truthfully, except for the "friends" part. The guard told us to sign the visitor's log as he dialed Moberg's extension.

"Hello, Mr. Moberg?" the guard said, reaching for the log book to read our names. "You've got a Mr. Paul Townsend and Mr. Tom Ruderman here to see you." There was a pause and then he said, "They say that they are friends of yours and just wanted to say hello." Another pause and then, "Okay sir, thank you. I'll tell them." The guard hung up the phone and turned to us. "He says he'll be right down."

"Yes!" I thought to myself, then looked at Tommy and shook my fist in triumph.

A few minutes later Jerry Moberg walked down the stairs and into the lobby. Recognizing us immediately, the color drained from his face. He motioned for us to come to the opposite side of the room, out of earshot of the guard. A small pulse beat rapidly at the base of his throat. Moberg struggled to keep his voice down. "What are you doing here? How did you know I worked here?"

I said, "We followed you here from your house this morning. We need to talk with you and we're *not* going to give up. You either talk to us or you can talk to the police, cause that's where we're headed right after we leave here."

"No! No police!" Moberg spoke louder than he intended and the security guard looked at us suspiciously. Then, moving closer to us and lowering his voice again, he said, "Okay, we'll talk. But for God's sake, not here. Come to my house tomorrow night at six." And without so much as a goodbye, Moberg walked up the stairs and left us in the lobby. We thanked the guard, who looked at us quizzically as we left.

Walking out the glass doors of Building R2, I patted my roommate on the shoulder. "Well Tom, cancel whatever you were planning for tomorrow night. Looks like we've got a hot date in Manhattan Beach."

21

In order to qualify for membership in the prestigious Letterman's Club of Rosedale High, you had to have earned a varsity letter in football, basketball, baseball, wrestling, track & field, swimming, or tennis. Almost every boy at Rosedale who received a letter ended up joining the club, as it was considered an honor. And everyone in the club wore their Letterman's jackets proudly, with embroidered patches for each sport that you played sewed on to the large letter "R". Some of us, myself included, went a step further and attached medals we had won at track meets or various other tournaments. I looked like a highly decorated military hero jangling down the halls of Rosedale High.

Toward the end of the school year, the Letterman's Club held a party at the Holiday Inn in downtown Winfield. It was a dance, not quite as formal as the prom, but you were expected to wear a tie and bring a date. Ever since the night of the Alpha Theta basketball practice when I had walked Lori to her car, I had been working up the courage to ask her to go with me. The week before the big Alpha Theta—Delta Delta Delta basketball game and a full month before the Letterman's Club party, I abandoned all good sense, walked up to her between classes while she was opening her locker, felt a little dizzy, but stuttered out the question. As remarkable as the fact that I had asked her, was the fact that she had said yes. *She said yes!* This would be the second date I had ever been on, the first one being so traumatic that I was not eager to try again.

The big game could not have gone better. For the first time in three years, Alpha Theta beat the Tri-Delts. I received accolades for the victory, even though once the game started everything I taught them over the course of the previous month was forgotten in a mad scramble. But great players make great coaches, and I had Cynthia Fernandez, who scored fourteen points. The final score ... 22–16.

But now the game was history, and it was time for a more important night in my life, the Letterman's Club party. I drove to Lori's house to meet her parents and pick her up. The expected drilling from Lori's dad went something like this: "Have you figured out where you're going to college yet?" and then, "So what do you think you want to major in?" Since my answers to the first two questions were barely adequate, he moved on to a tougher subject. "What do you think you want to do when you get out of college?" And then of course there was, "How late is this dance going to last?" and, "We expect you to have her home by eleven," and, "You're a good driver, right Paul?"

After ten minutes that seemed like thirty, Lori and I said goodbye and drove to the Holiday Inn, a couple miles from her house. From the parking lot, we walked directly to the banquet hall, a separate building adjacent to the hotel. There were over sixty members of the Letterman's Club and most everyone was at the dance. Counting dates, nearly one hundred and twenty high schoolers filled the hall. After passing through the front door, I noticed large, rectangular tables to the far left side of the room filled with bowls of potato chips, French onion dip, and trays of carrots, celery and ranch dressing. Two large bowls of red punch and stacks of white styrofoam cups were on the next table. Several attendees carried small bottles of gin or vodka in the inside pocket of their jacket to give the punch a little punch.

Green tablecloths covered several round tables in the back half of the room, and centerpieces of yellow roses adorned each table. Green and gold crepe paper hung from the walls, draped in semi-circles around the perimeter of the room. The front half of the hall was cleared for dancing, and a DJ on a raised platform played the Beach Boys, Beatles, Rolling Stones, and Credence Clearwater Revival. He kept things moving by giving us a good mix of maybe five or six fast songs and then a slow one.

We sat on two of the metal folding chairs which lined the side of the dance floor. "Hey Lori, they just put out some chocolate chip cookies. You want me to get you one?"

She rested her hand on my forearm. "Sure." Moving closer to my ear in the loud din, she said, "How come you won't slow dance with me?"

All night I had avoided the slow dances, not wanting Lori to know I was an awkward idiot. "I dunno. I never really learned how to do it," I said, looking away, toward the dance floor.

She gave my shoulder a little shove with the palm of her hand. "Don't be silly. There's nothing to learn. You just put your arms around me and move your feet around."

"Okay, next slow song," I said with trepidation, and then went to get the cookies, stopping on the way back for a shot of courage from one of my basketball teammates.

"OW! THAT'S OKAY, I walk on 'em too," Lori said, as I smashed her toes one more time. "Just shuffle your feet. That way you'll bump into my shoes, instead of stepping on top of them."

And that seemed to work for me. I made it through the rest of *Don't Worry Baby* without abusing my date any further. By the time ten-thirty rolled around and the music stopped, I had a couple more slow ones under my belt and felt like an expert. After a little more milling about, the chaperones started to shoo us out the front door. I was thinking that Lori's dad would be happy as I pulled into her driveway at ten forty-five, a full fifteen minutes before our curfew.

"I had such a fun time. I'm so glad you asked me to go. C'mon, walk me to the front door." Lori prompted me, although I had already told myself ahead of time that I was not going to repeat the fiasco of my first date, when I dropped off Janelle Newman and said "see ya" without even turning off the car engine. Lori hopped up on the first of two stairs that led up to the porch and turned around to face me. "You stay down there," she said.

With Lori on the first step, we were very nearly the same height. She clasped her hands behind my neck and I put my arms around her waist, drawing her closer to me. I was more confident since the slow dancing. Our faces only inches apart, I lurched forward and kissed her awkwardly on her lower lip. After my first attempt, she expertly moved forward and kissed my lips gently.

Then she whispered, "Can I ask you a personal question?"
"Sure, what?"

"And promise it won't hurt your feelings?" she asked, as I prepared for the worst.

"What?"

"Have you ever kissed a girl before?"

My charade was over. I had been found out. But she wasn't mocking, laughing, or even smiling. She was asking seriously. And I trusted her.

"No, not really," I said.

"What do you mean, not really?"

"Never on the lips," I said, wincing at the words.

"Well, this is a big night for you ... slow dancing, kissing. Okay if I give you a little lesson?" I didn't say anything but nodded in response. She moved her hands from behind my head to my shoulders and became my teacher.

"The first thing to know is that you tilt your head a little to the right so you don't bump noses." She demonstrated by tilting her head slightly to the right. I did the same.

"Okay, good. Now, as you move your face closer to mine you want to part your lips, not so your mouth is wide open, but just a bit. Then run your tongue along your lips to moisten them." Again she showed me what she meant by parting her lips and wetting them with her tongue. She moved her mouth closer to mine and said, "Now, the most important thing. Relax your lips."

Our faces inches apart, I asked, "How do you relax your lips?"

"I know it sounds weird, but if you think about it, you can do it. And if you do it well, it'll make you a great kisser," she said. "Now the fun part ..." she whispered as she drew me to her and kissed me gently.

With Lori still on the first step and me standing on the grass, we kissed each other again and again. I didn't want to let go of her. I wanted to keep holding her and kissing her all night.

"Well, Mr. Townsend, I think you've made great strides. You're a fast learner." She playfully tapped my nose with the tip of her finger.

"Oh, I don't know. I think I need lots more practice," I said, with a big grin on my face.

"Well then, I think you should come right back here tomorrow night so we can do just that."

With that, I kissed her once more, said good night, and drove away feeling like I could have conquered the world.

22

Tom and I made our way back to Westwood after our early morning adventure with Mr. Moberg in Manhattan Beach, discovering that Monday morning at nine was not the time to be traveling the 405 Freeway. The K-Earth disc jockey announced that it was ten o'clock just as we pulled into our apartment's underground parking garage. The trip was a success. We had frightened Moberg with our persistence. He didn't like that we knew where he worked, and was obviously nervous about us being there. He was ready to talk. I was sure of it. What he had to say, I had no clue, but I was eager to hear it, and could hardly wait until tomorrow night.

"SO, HOW'S it going with Nancy? You seeing her tonight? Want me to get lost or anything?" I shouted out to Tommy from the bathroom, toweling myself off after a belated morning shower.

Tom sat at the living room table reading the Los Angeles Times and munching on a piece of wheat bread with peanut butter and honey. "No, I think we may be toast. I'm kinda getting tired of her."

"You have *got* to be kidding me. You met her one week ago! And she's beautiful!" I came around the corner into the living room, a white towel wrapped around my waist.

He looked up at me from his paper, then out the window. "I don't know, I thought she was pretty cool in the beginning ..." His voice trailed off as he shook his head.

This happened over and over again with Tom. He had no trouble meeting girls, would go out with them two, three, four weeks, and then lose interest. I'm no psychologist, but I think Tom was afraid of getting close to someone, afraid of how vulnerable it made him, afraid of the commitment. No doubt his fear stemmed from being an intimate participant in his parents ugly relationship. He was a little down about it, but not so much that I couldn't continue to harass him a bit.

"What, did she have a blemish on her elbow? A freckle on her toe? You prefer Curly and she likes Shemp? I don't blame you man, definitely grounds for a break-up."

"Oh, screw you, Townie. You're just a sex deprived, jealous old man."

I laughed and agreed with him as I entered the kitchen, a pair of gym shorts having replaced the towel, scrounging for something to eat. I settled for the heel of the loaf of wheat bread, then, with no peanut butter left, I unwrapped a slice of American cheese to put on top.

I carried my epicurean delight into the living room and joined Tom at the table. "When are you heading down to the beach?" I said.

"Pretty soon, I think. Just wanna take a shower. You gotta work, right?"

"Yeah, today's the first day of the big clearance sale. Everybody has to work it. It'll be crazy busy. No beach time for me. I'll be at Buck's from noon to nine."

Tom got up to carry his plate into the kitchen. "Sounds like a blast."

"Hey, thanks for going with me this morning. I think we scared him into talking. Two of us were definitely better than one," I said, taking a bite of the cheese.

"I'm sure he thinks we're both a little psycho, following him to work like that," Tom said, turning the corner to go into the bathroom for his shower.

Speaking loudly, so he could hear me behind the closed door, I said, "Yep, that was the idea."

FIVE MINUTES before noon and I had to park two blocks away because of the bargain seekers filling up the front and rear lots. I made my way through the maze of people and sales racks to the back stairway which led up to the time clock. I looked down the row of timecards and found mine. There was a note attached with a paper clip. It read simply, "Call me," and was signed, "Jennifer" with a phone number written beneath her name. I shivered with desire recalling last night. I hadn't been sure what to expect of Jennifer after the events of yesterday. It would have been presumptuous of me to get back in touch with her by ringing the bell at her front gate. I didn't have her phone number, until now. I figured a woman like her would just move on, leaving a trail of guys like me in her wake. And who was I kidding? Her at thirty-two and me at twenty-one? It was a one night romp for her and that was it. I had convinced myself of all this in the span of twelve hours since I had left her house. And I *was* convinced ... until I saw the note.

On the other hand, maybe I was reading way too much into the two word note. Maybe she just wants me to bring the new tennis racket to her house. Maybe she wants to make it clear never to expect anything like last night ever to happen again. Maybe she wants to hire me as a bodyguard to take care of all the paparazzi.

"Hey, Paul, come on man, we need you down here." Ernie Nichols' voice roused me from my fruitless meditations. He had seen me go upstairs several minutes ago and had three customers waiting for help.

"Sorry Ern, coming right now." I stuffed the note in my pocket, inserted my timecard down the slot on the top of the clock, and pressed the bar which imprinted my card with 12:04.

THERE IS ONE thing to be said for being super busy at work—time flies by. Before I knew it, it was five-thirty, time for my dinner break. Walking through the Ski Department on my way to clock out, I saw Renee for the first time all day.

"Are we having fun yet?" I asked her.

"Oh my God, this is nuts. Are you going on your dinner break? Can I come with you?"

"Sure. I'm walking to Pinocchio's. Let's go."

Renee found Stacy and got permission to take her break. After we clocked out, we made our way through the chaos and escaped through the rear door without having anybody snag us for help along the way.

Moving through the parking lot towards the sidewalk, Renee skipped ahead, then turned around to face me, walking backwards as she spoke. "Didja miss me? Huh? Huh? Didja?"

I admit to being a novice in the ways of women, but I was not stupid. So I answered, "Of course I missed you."

"Yeah right, that's why you called me so many times." Renee waited for me to catch up, then walked alongside me. "Okay, time for you to fess up. How was your *hero's* dinner?"

I took a deep breath and said, "It was a good time. She is a very nice woman and the house is amazing."

I proceeded to tell Renee everything about my visit, leaving out the last few hours. I did my best to describe it as a platonic visit with an older actress who I was a fan of. And possibly because I gave her so many details about the food, the house, and the yard, she seemed to buy it. This was one of those times in life where one can rationalize not telling the whole truth in the name of sparing another's feelings. And saving my own skin too, of course.

We entered the front door to an onslaught of garlic, basil, and oregano. Trays full of various dishes, ready to be served, filled the steaming hot display behind the glass counter.

"Let's eat here, whadda ya think? It's too crazy at work. We won't be able to eat in peace," I said.

"Amen to that," she said.

I ordered my usual eggplant parmigiana and Renee got the ravioli. We carried our meals into the darkened dining area and sank into a comfortable booth with burgundy colored, cushioned vinyl seats.

"This is our second date and both times, Italian restaurants. Not very good planning if you're trying to impress me," she said.

"Well, I got a little lucky the first time. I thought maybe it was the Italian food."

She extended her leg under the table and I felt her toes on my knee. My pulse quickened as her bare foot traveled up and down my calf. "Next time try sushi, maybe you'll get even luckier."

Ever since we had kissed in the parking lot behind La Barbera's, something had been nagging at me about our budding relationship. She was intelligent, fun to be with, beautiful ... but I kept coming back to her age. It didn't feel right. I was falling for this girl and falling fast. But my moral compass was pointing the opposite direction of my heart and there was nothing I could do about it. I hadn't planned on bringing up these feelings until that very minute.

But the next words out of my mouth were, "Renee, there's something I need to talk to you about."

"Yes?" she said cautiously, shifting forward in her seat.

"I realize I've only known you a couple weeks, but I feel a connection and I'm starting to have strong feelings for you," I started.

She reached across the table and put her hand on mine. "I feel the same way about you."

I looked down at my plate and withdrew my hand. "But it's not right. A twenty-one year old man should not be involved with a seventeen year old girl. It's just not right and I can't do it."

Renee stared at me, stunned, looking as if somebody had slugged her in the stomach. She stammered, "W-what? Why not?"

"I can't explain it any other way. Something is telling me I shouldn't be doing this. Like I said, I really, really like you and it's starting to scare me."

"People our ages go out all the time. I can't believe you're saying this to me." I could hear the anger in her voice.

My confidence was evaporating and my voice went up an octave. "I can't believe I'm saying it either, but I had to do something now before we got more involved."

Her disbelieving eyes locked onto my face, silently pleading with me, but I couldn't meet her gaze. Tears began to roll down her cheeks. "You're really serious about this, aren't you?"

"Yep," I said, barely above a whisper.

Sobbing, she got up from the table and jogged unsteadily toward the exit door.

"Renee, wait. Don't leave."

But the door had already closed behind her. She was a half block away, running towards Buck's, by the time I'd opened the door to follow.

WHEN I RETURNED to work, Stacy asked if I knew what was wrong with Renee. Renee had told her she didn't feel well, and needed to go home. Stacy said it looked like she had been crying.

"I don't know, it may have been my fault. I'm sure she'll be fine tomorrow."

I felt a little ill myself. Seeing Renee upset like that, especially knowing that I was the cause ... made my stomach hurt. And the worst part was that I was beginning to doubt myself. *Is twenty-one really too old to be going out with a seventeen year old? I wasn't so sure anymore.*

After closing at nine o'clock, all employees were required to stay an extra half hour to clean up and organize stock after the wild day. More craziness was in store for tomorrow and Buck wanted everything back in its place before we left. Tennis was not as bad as the rest of the store and Ernie and I were able to get everything looking good by nine-fifteen. Buck gave us permission to leave a few minutes early, so we clocked out and walked toward the back exit together.

"You go on ahead, Ern. I forgot I need to make a phone call. I'll be in Wednesday. Probably see you then," I said, as he continued out the door into the back parking lot and I retreated into Tennis.

"Okay man, have a good night," he said.

By myself in the Tennis Department, I reached in my pocket for the note from Jennifer. I decided I should call her now, since if I waited until I got home, it would be impolitely late.

"Hello?" a male voice answered. I thought I recognized it as Edward's, but did not ask.

I leaned up against the workbench, stretching the phone cord to its maximum length. "Hello, this is Paul Townsend calling for Jennifer."

"Just a moment please, Mr. Townsend. I'll see if she is available."

After a few seconds, Jennifer came to the phone. "Hi Paul, how are you? I see you got my love note."

I stood up straight and moved closer to the phone base. "Yeah, were you in the store?" I felt my heart begin to pound.

"No, no. I just called and had one of the girls there write it for me. Would it be too much to ask of you to bring my new racket over tonight? I've got a game planned for the morning and would like to try it out."

As tired as I was from the long day, it did not even cross my mind to say no. The thought of seeing her again exhilarated me. "Sure, be happy to. I'm just leaving here now and can be there in a few minutes.

"Great. I'll have Edward open the gate so you can pull your car in. Thanks so much. I'll see you in a few."

I hung up the phone and found Jennifer's new Wilson Ultra hanging on the peg where we kept all the finished rackets. I went to the shelf below where the rackets were displayed and found the Wilson cover, zipped it around the racket head, and headed toward the back door. In the parking lot on the way to my car, I noticed Ernie had pulled back into the parking lot and was getting out of his Corvette.

"Just couldn't bear to leave us, huh?"

He chuckled. "No, I can guarantee you it's not that. I forgot my rackets and I've got a lesson tomorrow morning," He jogged past me, heading back into the store. "Hey isn't that Jennifer Ryan's racket?" he asked, stopping and looking back.

I tapped the covered racket head against the palm of my hand. "Yeah, she wants me to drop it off at her house."

His face twisted in agony. "Why, you lucky little ... what, you guys are best buddies now?"

I knew he was kidding but I also knew he was jealous. He had quizzed me relentlessly about my dinner and grimaced at most of my responses. It would probably kill him if I told him what had happened after dinner.

Leaving the Buck's parking lot, I proceeded towards the beach, made a right on Ocean Avenue and then drove down the long incline that led to Pacific Coast Highway. After reaching the bottom of the ramp it was only a few hundred yards on the Highway to Jennifer's house. As promised, the gate was open, awaiting my arrival. Turning left into her driveway, the electric gate began to close behind me. I sat in my car for a minute before getting out, closed my eyes and took several deep breaths to calm myself. The memory of last night came back in full force, now that I was on the property and about to see her again. The tiredness of a few moments earlier had disappeared, erased by a rush of adrenaline. I walked up to the front door and rang the bell. Would Jennifer be the one to answer, like yesterday? I didn't have to wonder for long because the door opened almost immediately and there she stood, a big smile on her face, wearing a pair of yellow, nylon running shorts, a white cotton tank top, and, as I was learning was her custom, nothing on her feet.

"Come in, come in," she greeted me. I took a couple steps into the foyer and she closed the door. "Thanks so much for coming over. I have something to confess. I don't really have a tennis game in the morning." She smiled mischievously.

She stepped towards me, got on her tiptoes, stretched her five foot four frame, and gave me a quick kiss on the lips. Then she pressed her body up against me, her soft, moist lips met mine, and she melted me with a long, passionate kiss.

"I was just looking for an excuse to have you come over," she whispered into my ear.

I pulled my head back and looked at her. "Jennifer, let me explain something to you. You don't need an excuse to invite me over. You just say to me, 'Paul, I'd like you to come over.'"

She giggled and said, "Okay, you've got a deal."

I realized I still had the racket in my hand and gave it to her. "Here you go, custom strung by yours truly, guaranteed never to hit a bad shot."

She unzipped the cover, eased the racket out and took a couple of swings. "Feels perfect." Then she put the cover back on and set the racket down on one of the antique looking chairs in the entryway. Holding my hand, she led me into a room I had not been in the day before. I guess I would call it the TV room, or a family room.

"What can I get you to drink? The house specialty tonight is a Mojito—Caribbean rum with fresh lime juice. What do you think?"

"You haven't steered me wrong yet."

Jennifer left to retrieve the drinks, and I sank into the luxurious leather couch, leaned my head back and gazed at the ceiling fan above. I literally pinched myself in my right thigh, then laughed out loud for doing so. The couch and two adjacent love seats, also made of the same dark brown leather, were arranged in a semicircle facing a large black television screen in the dimly lit room. The stereo tuner and tape deck to my right glowed with a soft, amber light. Soft melodic jazz emanated from the speakers. The music lulled me as I sank deeper into the couch. I closed my eyes and my mind drifted to yesterday evening, to the dreamlike image of Jennifer removing her clothes and slipping underneath the plush comforter on her bed, as I lay waiting.

"Here you go, señor." Jennifer handed me my drink and woke me from my brief daydream. She sat next to me on the couch, facing me, one leg folded beneath her. "How was your day?"

"Long. I was up at five-thirty for something I had to do in Manhattan Beach, then worked nine hours at Buck's ... which was crazy because it was the first day of our big clearance sale." I took a sip of my drink. "Mmm ... did you make these?"

"I did. All by my lonesome. No help from Edward," she said proudly.

"Well, here's to you then." I reached up and clinked my glass with hers. We both took a long drink of the lime and rum concoction. "How about you? What'd you do today?"

"Pretty lazy day, really. Never even left the house. My agent came by with a couple scripts he's looking at, so I read through those a little bit. When he left, I laid out by the pool for a while, worked on my full-body tan ... *with no onlookers this time.*" She gave me a playful, evil eye.

I still felt guilty about our voyeurism, but I smiled at her jibe. "What about Edward? Where is he when you're gallivantin' around with no clothes on?"

"I just let him know ahead of time and he makes himself scarce. But I don't even think he cares," she said, with a dismissive wave of her hand.

"Do you think he's interested in women? Has he ever been married?"

"Nope, never married. I'm pretty sure he's gay, but I've never asked him about it. He's got a guy friend that he usually hangs out with on his days off."

I raised my eyebrows and nodded, then rested my hand on her knee. "How about you? You wanna get married someday—have kids?"

A smile formed at the corners of her mouth, then disappeared, replaced by a thoughtful expression. "I would ... yeah, I would. And the clock's tickin', huh? It's just so hard in my business. But pretty soon I'll stop working so much and get serious about it. Kinda made it sound like a big chore there, didn't I?" Her smile returned.

It seemed to me that she was wrestling with the idea even as she spoke.

"You know what I mean? It's a life changing decision, and once you make it, you have to go for it." She reached over and gave my knee a little shove. "What are you doing the next few years? You want to help me out? Have some little volleyball players and racket stringers running around?"

"Well, I *was* kind of wondering what to do after I graduate." I smiled, raised my eyebrows and looked to the ceiling. "But I don't know, you might just be a little old," I said, with a giggle, then covered up as the expected blows started my way.

"I ... am ... not ... old. You're just young," she said sternly. She began to pelt me with her tiny fists.

I protected myself by moving in closer and wrapping my arms around her. She hit me half-heartedly a couple times on the back, then I moved my face to hers, kissed her, and the battle was over. As we kissed, I moved my hand slowly along the outside of her thigh all the way up underneath her nylon shorts, exploring the baby soft texture of her bare behind.

"So much for the shy young man I knew yesterday," she said in a low, sexy whisper.

"It's your fault. Look at you. How's a guy supposed to act like a gentleman?" I replied softly.

"Now that's the way you're supposed to talk to a woman, Mr. Townsend. Maybe the beating taught you a lesson."

"That's right. I learned never to talk about how old you are," I said, then put my hands in front of my face, palms out, in self-defense. "Just kidding! Just kidding!"

Jennifer did her best to make a mean face and raised both her fists. Then I lowered my arms and collapsed backward on the couch, laughing out loud. Jennifer climbed on top of me and rested her head on my chest. We both giggled softly.

I finally whispered to her, "I keep thinking about your tanning project, and I'm worried about the tan lines. I think I need to do a thorough search. Just wanna make sure you've gotten rid of all of 'em."

She laughed and stood up stiffly from the couch, putting her hand to her forehead in a salute. "Private Ryan, reporting for inspection, sir." She turned and gallantly pointed to the backyard. "To the jacuzzi!"

She grabbed my hand and pulled me up from my seat. She headed for the door, beckoning me with her forefinger to follow. Obediently I pursued ... out the door, then out the double doors to the soothingly hot water of the small pool embedded in the cliffside. We both wore our birthday suits into the water and I completed the tan line inspection.

AFTERWARDS, we made our way upstairs, but unlike yesterday, this time I did not emerge from her room until the following morning. Jennifer was still asleep as I got dressed. I softly kissed her on the cheek and tiptoed out, closing the door behind me, another night for the ages. But as I passed through the gate and drove onto Pacific Coast Highway, all I could think about was a certain seventeen year old high school girl.

24

Tommy stood cooking scrambled eggs in our tiny kitchen upon my return from Jennifer's. Eggs were one of several dishes I had taught him to cook since we moved into the apartment. I had some training at home from my mom, but Tommy had been clueless. Now his repertoire included scrambled and fried eggs, pancakes, hamburgers, hot dogs, grilled cheese, and tacos. He wore a long, white apron as he cooked, the kind that looped over your neck, went down to your knees, and tied with a string in the back. I'm not sure where he got it or why he had it, but he liked wearing it. Maybe it made him feel like a real chef. The alluring smell of bacon drew me to the kitchen. Approaching the counter to grab a slice, my eyes widened, startled to see Tommy's bare behind in plain view out the back of the apron.

"What the hell? Where's your shorts man? You're grossing me out."

"Oh, sorry. I'm doing my wash." Tom began taking the bacon strips out of the pan, laying them on a napkin.

"And you couldn't save one pair of boxers to wear? Jeez."

Tommy looked apologetic. "Could've I guess. I just wanted to wash everything."

I reached to grab a slice of bacon. "How'd you get to the laundry room and back?"

"I was wearing this apron and went pretty quickly. Blue Whale One and Blue Whale Two were hootin' and hollerin', but nobody else saw me."

I just shook my head, went to grab a pair of my boxers out of the bedroom, and tossed them at Tommy as he cracked eggs and emptied them into the frying pan. "Put those on so I don't have to keep looking at that big old crack."

"Ah, you're just jealous of the beauty of my posterior. By the way, where were *you* all night, big guy?" he said, as he used the pancake turner to scramble the eggs.

I had no choice but to fess up about my night with Jennifer, since he knew I had been missing all night. Once again, I swore him to secrecy.

Tom set down the pancake turner and put on the boxers. "My God! She could have any guy practically in the world, and she's with you. What are you doin', giving her drugs or something? You're just a fuckin' stud!"

I leaned against the kitchen doorway, smiling from the kudos. "Stop it, Tom. It's not like that. We enjoy talking and spending time together. She's interesting, intelligent, and we get along really well."

"I'll say you do. Man!"

I made toast for the two of us, shared Tommy's eggs, and poured orange juice. After eating, I showered and changed into my beach trunks. I had the day off from Buck's so the two of us were going to drive to the beach together. Our plan was to come back to the apartment after the beach, clean up, then travel south to have our discussion with Mr. Moberg at six o'clock. I had high hopes of learning something which would get us past the dead end that we seemed to be at in our search for Jack.

IT WAS TEN-THIRTY when our feet touched the sand at Sorrento. Unlike the previous week, the skies had turned overcast. The fog rolled in last night, lifted somewhat this morning, but still completely blocked the sun. For most people, not a good beach day. But it was actually the perfect weather for beach volleyball—no wind, no sun to get in your eyes, and the air comfortably cool. Three games were already in progress as we walked toward the wall.

Just as we sat down, we heard the almost daily cry, "HELLOOO … BEACH!" Scott Rodgers came around the corner from the parking lot and made his way to where we sat. Early in the morning he would sort the mail to be delivered on his route, then come to the beach. Delivery of the mail could wait—he had his priorities.

Doug Williams got up from his beach chair, came over, and sat cross legged in front of us. "Any news on Jack?"

Scott dropped his bag on the sand and sat down heavily, his legs stretched out in front of him. I reached over and greeted him, gripping his right hand with my left. Then I looked back at LJ. "Funny you should ask. I checked in with the police yesterday and they've got a whole lotta nothing. But Tommy and I got a live one."

I spent a few minutes telling Scott and LJ of how we had gone to Jack's house and had to hide under the bed when the guys broke in and ransacked the place. I told them we found Jack's address book, started calling everyone, and got a strange reaction from this guy named Jerry Moberg. I told them how we had followed him to work, scared him a bit, and now we were going to meet him tonight.

"Where does he work?" Scott asked.

"A place called TRW. It's a big campus of several buildings near Manhattan Beach," I said.

Scott nodded and said, "Oh, I know TRW. I have a cousin who used to work there a few years ago."

"What kind of company is it?" LJ asked.

Scott reached into his bag, pulled out a volleyball, and began tossing it up in the air to himself. "They're into all sorts of things. They've got one division that just does credit reporting."

"Oh, yeah, I've heard of that," LJ said. He reached over and snatched the ball while it was on its way down into Scott's hands.

Scott continued, "They do a lot of work for the government, like building satellites and other military stuff. My cousin worked in the division that built the engine for the Lunar Descent Module, you know, the spacecraft that was used to land on the moon."

"Hmmm … I wonder how Jack knows this Jerry Moberg guy?" LJ questioned to no one in particular.

"I don't know, but I suppose we'll find out tonight," I said. "You guys ready for a game?"

Tommy, Scott, Doug and I all got up together, walked through the cool, damp sand to one of the outer courts and started to warm up. We agreed that the most fair teams would be for me to play with Scott and Tommy with LJ. Tom would have to play on the left, his off side, but he was so much better than all of us, it evened things out. I enjoyed playing with Scott, a natural right-sider. I did much better on the left, so we played well together.

SOAKED WITH perspiration, I dove headlong for a short shot by Tommy, popped it up with my left fist, then slammed home a nice set from my partner. I ended the point caked with sand, then did my best to brush it off my arms and hands so I would be able to play the next point without sand flying into my eyes. The last play scored us a point. It was now 7-4, we were up. I had the ball and readied myself to serve for a second time. But Tommy and LJ stood together with their backs to us, conferring, apparently discussing strategy for the next point.

Suddenly LJ yelled out, "What?! You've *got* to be kidding me!"

Tommy put his hand over LJ's mouth, trying to quiet him, but he continued, "Alright, Townie, out with it. I want details!"Holding all that juicy gossip inside had been too much for Tommy to handle. Right in the middle of our game he had let it slip.

Scott shrugged his shoulders and furrowed his brow. "What? Details about what?" he asked, feeling like he was the only one who didn't know what we were talking about.

LJ said, "Your partner over there has spent the last two nights with Miss Jennifer Ryan. I'm talking … *in bed* … *with* … Jennifer Ryan!"

Scott looked incredulous. "Yeah, right. Paul? What the hell is he talking about?"

"Jesus, Tom, nice job keeping that secret," I said, as I glared over at Tommy.

Tom raised his hands and shrugged. "Sorry, man, I tried. I really tried. It was like a powerful force within me that had to come out. Kinda like when you eat some bad fish or something."

Resigning myself to the inevitable, I said, "Alright boys, gather 'round. You might as well hear the whole story." LJ hurried over to our side of the court and he and Scott sat down in front of me like kindergartners at story time. I recounted how Jennifer had come into Buck's, recognized me from the picture in the paper, and invited me over for dinner. I even told them how I had confessed to her that I was one of the Peeping Toms. I explained that the second visit was to deliver the racket and that one thing led to another. They listened intently with their mouths half open. I had no intention of giving any more detail than I had already. Jennifer deserved that much from me.

LJ slammed his hands down on the sand. "Oh, man, you owe me big time. I'm the one who gave the Outlook your picture."

"Yeah, yeah. I'll buy you a beer next time we go to TT's. Now can we continue our game?" I signaled I was done talking by standing up, grabbing the volleyball from Tommy, and moving to the back line to serve.

"Alright, alright. But I still think you're holding out on us. We'll get the rest out of you eventually," LJ said, as he moved back to his side of the court.

I raised my open palms in the air and laughed. "There's nothing more to tell. You got the whole story."

Before I served the ball, Scott looked back at me shaking his head. "That is one fucking unbelievable story."

Then, as I started to serve the ball, I heard him mutter one more time, "Un ... fucking ... believable."

25

Against my better judgment, we drove the Death Trap to Jerry Moberg's house. Tom insisted, saying he felt bad that I was always driving. I told him there was a good reason I was always driving, like that I wanted to stay alive. The Falcon came through, and we arrived a few minutes early. Parking was an adventure near his house because of the walkstreet, but we found a metered spot about a block away.

We rang the bell, Moberg answered the door with a grim expression, and unlike the last time we were here, he immediately motioned for us to come in. He directed us up the stairs to the living room, where large picture windows looked out at the crashing white water of the Pacific Ocean meeting the sand. Houses in this part of Manhattan Beach had an upside-down design to take advantage of the views. The kitchen, living room, and family room were all upstairs and the bedrooms were downstairs, the opposite of what you normally find in a two story house. As we stood at the window admiring the view, he brought two glasses of ice water and invited us to sit on the long couch while he took a seat opposite us in an armchair.

"I'm sorry boys. I don't remember your names," he said, setting the ice waters in front of us on the coffee table.

"I'm Paul and this is Tom," I replied.

"And how is it that you know Jack?"

"We know him from the beach. He goes to the same beach to play volleyball that we do up in Santa Monica," I said.

Moberg brushed back some of the few strands of hair he had left and tucked them behind his ear. "And please tell me again what happened to Jack?"

"Well, we don't know. That's what we're trying to figure out. We were at the beach playing a volleyball game last Thursday when a man in a suit and tie came walking up to the court and said he needed to speak with Jack in private. They walked to the parking lot and around the corner out of our view. And we haven't seen him since. We reported him as missing to the police. We went to his house to see if he had been home and while we were there two men broke in through the window, came in and ransacked the place, looking for something. We're not sure what."

"And you got my name out of Jack's address book?"

"That's right. We got it at his house before the crooks arrived, then we called everyone in the book to see if anybody might know something," I said, then took a sip of the water.

Moberg leaned forward in his chair, his forearms resting on his knees, hands clasped, looking down at the burgundy shag carpet. He paused for a moment and then started in. "Jack and I have known each other over thirty years. We met in a mechanical engineering class at UCLA and became friends. The next quarter we moved into an apartment together in Santa Monica. We were roommates for nearly two years and we've been in close touch ever since. Has Jack told you boys about his past?"

Tom and I answered simultaneously, "No, not really."

Moberg took off his wire rimmed glasses, fogged them with his breath, then wiped them clean with his shirt. "Well, Jack grew up in Germany and, as you can imagine, it was not an easy thing being Jewish in Germany in the thirties and for- ties. And that's probably the biggest understatement you'll ever hear. His father was a real hero, moving their family from the city to the country to avoid being shipped off to one of the death camps."

He put his glasses back on, carefully adjusting them on his nose. "Of course, no one knew they were death camps at the time. Everyone was told they were internment work camps, but Jack's parents were smart enough to realize they were some- thing to be avoided. They fled to the countryside, moving in with Jack's aunt and uncle on a farm about an hour outside of Muncheberg, their hometown."

Moberg paused and looked down. When he started speak- ing again, I could sense the pain in his voice. "A few weeks before the end of the war, the Russian army was marching towards Berlin, raping and murdering innocent German civil- ians along the way. They stopped at Jack's uncle's farm and killed his mother, father, aunt, and uncle. They also killed his wife and seven year old son."

"Oh, my God, he never said anything about ever having a wife or a son," I said.

Moberg leaned back in the armchair and sighed heavily. "Yes, he married at a very young age ... eighteen I believe it was. He always told me she was the only woman he has ever loved."

"I guess I understand why he didn't want to discuss it," I said, glancing over at Tommy who nodded in agreement.

"Shortly after the end of the war, Jack came by himself to Southern California to try to start anew, escape from the painful memories that haunted him. And over time he was able to do that for the most part. He even changed his name when he came over. For the first twenty-six years of his life, he was Isaiah Rosenberg. As you probably know, he has done some acting and has the car business. He has people he knows in Germany who are constantly looking for older models of Mercedes that are in good condition. Jack buys them from his German friends, gets them over here to California, modifies them to meet California standards, and sells them for a profit. It doesn't make him rich because he only handles about ten to fifteen cars per year, but it's easy and doesn't take up too much time."

"Do you think this guy who came to the beach had something to do with the car business? He did have an accent, might have been German," Tommy said, moving forward on the couch.

"No, I doubt that it had to do with his cars." Moberg appeared as if he wanted to keep speaking, but stopped, looked at us directly in the eyes, first at Tom, then at me. He had the tired, haggard look of a man who hadn't slept well in a while, with dark circles under his eyes. The skin on top of his nearly bald head glistened with perspiration.

"Before I continue, I need to have your promise that you will not repeat what I am about to tell you, especially not to the police. I've thought long and hard since you came to my workplace yesterday morning about whether I should be telling you this. Since Jack's life may be in danger, I felt like I had no choice." He shifted again in the chair, edging closer to us. "About three years ago Jack approached me with an idea. You see, he has never really gotten over his hatred of the Russians for what they did to his family. He wanted to know if I would be willing to provide him with some type of data or information from TRW that the Russians might be interested in. His idea was to insert inaccuracies into information we were providing, so that whatever they were using it for would be compromised. In a small way, this would serve as a bit of revenge for Jack."

My mouth went dry and I reached for the water. "What was in it for you?"

"Dinero ... moolah," he said, rubbing thumb and forefingers together.

"Did you do it?"

"Yes. Jack made contact with the Russian Consulate in Munich on one of his trips to Germany. The Russians were excited to get information on the project I was working on at the time, and still am working on, by the way. And they paid us well."

"What's the project?" Tom asked.

"Well, I'm an optical engineer in the Applied Technology Division. We have a contract with DARPA."

"What's DARPA?" I interrupted.

"Stands for Defense Advanced Research Projects Agency. Their charter is to develop the technologies of the future, really try to get out in front of it, be on the cutting edge. And one of the things that DARPA is very excited about is the idea of developing a laser beam with enough power so that it could be used as a military weapon."

Raising my eyebrows, I put a hand to my forehead. "Wow, a laser? Sounds like science fiction."

"Yeah, it does. We're just in the infancy of the technology, but DARPA is devoting a lot of money to it and TRW has some of their top scientists trying to advance the science."

"And the Russians are doing the same?" Tom asked.

"The intelligence we have is that the Russians are also trying to develop this technology but are way behind where we are."

I said, "Just out of curiosity, what would our military do with a high powered laser? Don't we already have guided missiles and bombs that do everything a laser could do?

It was apparent that Jerry Moberg was excited about his work. His shoulders were no longer slumped, he held his head higher, and his eyes were alive again. "The laser would have lots of advantages for some applications and wouldn't be intended to replace our other systems, just complement them. Imagine a high energy laser placed on an airplane that could automatically track enemy aircraft, stay focused on the target with no possibility of human error, and disable the enemy plane within seconds. Or place one on a ship and have the ability to strike an enemy ship in a fraction of the time it would take for a torpedo to arrive.

Tom's mouth was agape, a look of awe on his face.

"I see what you mean. Pretty cool stuff," I said.

With new excitement in his voice, he continued, "But the most exciting possible application that we've recently started discussing is in space."

"As in outer space?" I asked.

"Yes, outer space. Say another country, Russia for instance, launches several nuclear warheads on missiles towards the United States. The United States could have a series of satellites in orbit, each of which has on board a system to detect the missile in flight, lock onto it with a high energy beam, and incapacitate it before it can cause any damage. It would be the ultimate defense system, effectively eliminating the long range missile before it gets anywhere near the United States. And this could be done effectively in space because, with the lack of atmosphere, the laser beam can travel great distances without much diminishment of its power."

"But the enemy missiles would be in the earth's atmosphere wouldn't they?" Tommy asked.

"Yes indeed, but the laser could travel from the satellite to the entry point of the earth's atmosphere with little loss of power, intercept the incoming missile at its apex, and therefore still have plenty of power to disable it."

"What is it you're selling to the Russians?" I asked.

"Let me give you a quick layman's version of how the high energy laser works." Moberg walked over to a desk in an alcove adjacent to the living room and brought back a pad of paper and a pencil. He began to sketch. "The laser cavity contains an energy source, highly reactive chemicals that release a great amount of energy when they are mixed together in the enclosed area. At each end of this enclosed area is a very large mirror." He drew large circles to represent the mirrors at each end of the cylindrical laser cavity. "The energy created, or you could think of it as a bright light like you would see with an explosion, bounces back and forth between the mirrors and amplifies in power. There is another mirror within the structure that diverts a portion of the light source away from the cavity, then through a series of large lenses, to focus the beam on the target."

I leaned back on the couch, clasping my fingers behind my head. "Okay, that makes sense. So my question still is ... what are you selling to the Russians?"

"I was getting to that. Being an optical engineer, my expertise is in developing the huge, heat resistant mirrors that are necessary to sustain enough energy within the laser cavity to make the resulting beam powerful enough to do some damage. Without a large enough, strong enough, and optically precise enough, set of mirrors, you end up with a big strong flashlight, but not much of a weapon. It is in the development of these mirrors that we are far ahead of the Russian scientists. So Jack and I have been feeding them critical information about how to build these mirrors."

I couldn't believe he was telling us all this stuff. We must have scared the crap out of him, I thought. Or maybe he was just really concerned for Jack, and felt like we were his best hope.

Moberg continued, "But with the wrong numbers I have been putting in just the right places, I'm sure our comrades over there have been plenty frustrated, spending months and months developing and constructing the mirror only to have it fail miserably when they test it. I believe our data has set them back at least a couple years from where they would have been if they had developed the technology on their own."

"So you would give the information to Jack and he would give it to the Russians?" Tommy asked.

"Exactly. I agreed to Jack's idea with one condition. I would remain completely anonymous. Jack would be their only contact and they were never to know where he was getting the information. I am able to photograph important documents while I am at work and then give the film to Jack who takes it to Germany for pickup by the Soviet agent."

"It sounds like maybe this was a Russian guy who took Jack. What would they want with him?" I asked.

Moberg got up from his chair and walked to the window, gazing out at the rolling waves. Then he turned to face us. "In the beginning, about two and a half years ago, I was giving them accurate information, but nothing very vital. It was old technology for mirrors we had developed years ago for lower powered lasers. The idea was to gain their trust and let them know we were legitimate. Well, they took the bait, and soon we were making regular deliveries and getting some major money in return. After about a year, following Jack's plan, I started to make some changes to the data before photographing the documents. My guess is that one of their scientists suspected that the data had been modified and they came to see Jack for an explanation."

"That certainly sounds plausible. The only problem is we still have no clue as to where they might be," I said.

He took a couple steps toward us and remained standing, our clue that he was ready for us to leave. "I'm afraid you're right about that, Paul. I wouldn't even know where to begin."

We rose from our seats, thanked him, and began walking out the door. But before we reached the step, he gripped my arm. The short, balding man looked up at me with intensity in his eyes. "This is a good thing Jack and I have been doing. I hope you understand that. But if you tell the police any of this, he and I will be going to prison for the rest of our lives."

We opened the gate and walked down the hill to our car in silence. I was amazed by the story, shocked might be a better word. An overwhelming sense of melancholy overtook me. What now? Was it hopeless?

We climbed in Tom's car and he started the engine.

"Hey Townie, can you get out and give that trunk a good slam shut? It's always popping open—looks like it's open now."

So I got out and, sure enough, the trunk was not latched. I lifted it all the way up and was about to slam it down when I stopped. Jack's beach chair, cooler, and umbrella were right where Tommy had put them nine days before. I stared at that old umbrella with all the writing on it, and the smell of Jack's cigars wafted up. *Where are you, Pops? Where are you?*

On the drive home, and after we got back to the apartment, Tommy and I discussed Jerry Moberg's revelations. We agreed that he and Jack were doing a good thing for our country. The Russians were well behind us in optics technology and misleading them with false data was using up the time and energy of their top scientists, delaying their advancement in this field. But having said all this, we understood why Moberg wanted to keep it quiet. The fact that they were receiving a lot of money made it look bad ... like they were doing it for the wrong reasons. It almost certainly meant that, if they were exposed, they would be convicted. Baffled as to what to do with this newfound information, we now knew one thing with certainty—Jack was in real danger. We surmised what Jerry Moberg did not explicitly say, which is that they were likely pressuring Jack, or worse, to give them his source at TRW. They would have no use for Jack once they found out who and where Jerry Moberg was. All of this was interesting enough, but we went to bed around midnight not knowing if we were going to be able to do anything at all to help Jack.

THE OBNOXIOUSLY loud ring of our telephone awakened us. "Hello?" I mumbled.

"Hello, is this Paul?" a female voice asked.

"Yeah, who's this?" I asked, still half asleep.

"This is Lori ... Lori Lewis."

"Lori? Holy cow, Lori. I haven't heard from you in ... "

"Paul, I'm sorry for calling so late but I just arrived here in Los Angeles. I drove for the last three days straight from Winfield."

"You're here!? Wow! You drove all the way from Kansas? You shoulda called me." I pulled the covers aside and sat on the edge of my bed.

"I wanted to surprise you. So ... *surprise*! Would it be okay if I came over and spent the night at your place? I'm practically out of money and can't afford a hotel."

"Gosh Lori, sure you can come over."

Tom rolled over, groaned, and with a dismissive wave of his hand, motioned for me to use the other phone.

"Hold on a sec. I'm gonna switch phones." I moved into the living room and Tom hung up the bedroom phone. "Okay, I'm back. Where are you now?"

"I'm at a pay phone on Gayley and ... Le Conte Avenue. I figured if I just drove to UCLA you couldn't be too far away."

"Just head up the hill on Gayley. We're at the top of the hill on the corner of Gayley and Kelton. Look for me standing on Gayley and I'll show you where to go."

Tom poked his head into the living room, squinting at the light. "Okay, you got me curious. Who was that?"

"Lori Lewis. First girl I ever dated. She just drove all the way from Kansas."

"Sounds like she wants you, Townie, driving all that way. You want me to get lost so you can have the place to yourselves? I can sleep on the balcony. Promise I won't peek." Tom let out a loud yawn and leaned against the wall, propping up his sleepy body.

"No, no. It's not like that. We ended it a long time ago. I'm not sure why she's here, but it's not to see me. We haven't even talked in two years," I said.

He moved back into the bedroom and climbed in bed, speaking louder now so I could still hear him. "Let me see here … an ex-girlfriend drives half way across the country and then calls at midnight asking to spend the night with you. I'm sorry, but that tells me she wants you, wants you bad."

I just shook my head and rolled my eyes as I left the apartment to go meet Lori. Standing in my sleepwear on the dirt path running along Gayley Avenue, I saw Lori's tiny red Honda Civic slowly climbing the hill. She pulled over to where I stood and I hopped into the passenger seat. I leaned over and gave her a quick hug and a kiss on the cheek. "I can't believe you're here. You look great! It's good to see you. Why'd you come all the way out here? I know it wasn't just to see me."

Her thick, dark brown hair hung just below her shoulders, shorter and wavier than I remembered. In contrast to the dark hair, her smooth skin was creamy white, and she wore bright red lipstick on full lips, the ones that had taught me so well.

She didn't answer, but turned to me, her large brown eyes moist with happiness, leaned across the console and wrapped her arms around my neck, hugging me tightly. Still embracing me, she said, "It is *so* good to see you." Then she wiped a tear away and straightened in her seat. "Okay, where to?"

After driving around the block and up Veteran Avenue, we found a parking space two blocks down on Kelton. I pretended not to struggle with her suitcase as we walked toward the apartment building, but it must have weighed a hundred pounds. Lori Lewis had been my first girlfriend. We were together the summer after I graduated from Rosedale High. When I left for UCLA in September, we didn't exactly break up, but we knew in our hearts it was over. Plus, I began to change as a person almost the minute I arrived in Southern California. By the time I returned to Winfield for the summer after my freshman year, it wasn't the same with Lori. That was nearly three years ago and I had only seen her once since then, when I went home for Christmas during my sophomore year.

As we entered the front door of the apartment, I said, "You don't have to worry about being quiet. My roommate's awake. Some crazy person just called and woke us both up."

Lori gave me a little slug on the shoulder. Right on cue, Tommy emerged from the bedroom to meet our visitor.

"Lori, meet my roommate, Tom. Tom, this is Lori Lewis."

Lori said, "Pleasure to meet you. I'm sorry to barge in on you like this."

I'm not sure if it was the sleepiness or the hypnotic beauty of Lori, but Tom suddenly became a stutterer. "N-n-nice to … m-m-meet you."

He had a big, goofy grin on his face and after they shook hands he forgot to let go. Lori finally had to ask for her hand back. I saved my roommate from making a complete idiot of himself by interrupting their introduction. "So Lori, you were about to tell me what brings you to LA."

Still looking at Tommy, she said, "Oh, yeah ... right. I just had to get away from Winfield. I graduated from City College and thought I might transfer to a school out here somewhere."

Tommy, his smile firmly in place and seemingly recovered, said, "Well, you are certainly welcome to stay here as long as you want."

"Why thank you, Tommy. How sweet of you," Lori said, touching her hand to his arm. "To be honest with you guys, the most important reason I left Winfield was because I just broke up with my boyfriend. He was acting strange and I wanted to get away from him."

I dragged her suitcase into the living room and let it fall over with a thud. "Who was your boyfriend? Anybody I know?"

"It was that same guy I went out with before we started going out."

"Mad Max?! You've got to be kidding. Why in the world did you get back together with that weirdo?" As I spoke, our neighbors below us pounded on their ceiling, upset about the fallen suitcase. "Sorry," I yelled.

"Oh c'mon, he's not that bad. When you left to come out here, Max and I drifted back together. When you're with some-one for as long as we were, you really want to work it out, you know? We had so much time invested, so much history."

I nodded in agreement, mostly to be polite. Lori had so much going for her, it boggled my mind that she was with a psycho like that for so long.

"But I finally gave up. He loves me so much, but he's just not the right guy for me. And when I broke it off with him, he started following me around like he did the first time we broke up. I got weirded out and had to get out of there."

"Well, that was smart of you. Like Tommy said, you can stay here as long as you want."

THE THREE OF US chatted for another half hour before we agreed to hit the sack. Tommy dragged in the mattress from the balcony while I brought out my sleeping bag from the bedroom closet. We didn't have an extra pillow so I gave her mine and pretended like it was a spare. Tommy and I said good night to her and headed back to the bedroom.

"Oh my God, Townie. You didn't tell me she was hot!" Tommy loudly whispered.

"Shhh, not so loud," I whispered. "Yeah, she's cute. You should go for it." I grabbed a sweatshirt from the drawer to use as a pillow and climbed into bed.

"What about you? She's your ex. You got dibs."

"No, no. That was a long time ago. We're just friends now."

I folded my sweatshirt neatly, put it under my head, then closed my eyes and drifted to sleep with visions of Rosedale High and Lori Lewis dancing in my head.

27

My eyelids opened, but the rest of my body remained motionless, still sleeping. Without moving my head, my eyes rotated to look at the digits on the clock: 9:28. Gears in my brain began to turn, weighing the pros and cons, finally making the decision to leave the comfort of my bed. Odiferous Right Guard aerosol filled the air. Tom must have been out of clean shirts. Venturing out of the bedroom, I left the deodorant smell behind and my senses were slammed by the wonderful aroma of link sausage. Tommy had cooked pancakes and sausage for our houseguest and in a further effort to impress Lori, about half an hour ago, had leaped out of the window into the pool below. Lori was still in her sleeping bag, but fully awake and talking with Tommy when I walked in.

"Top of the morning, Townie!" Tommy exclaimed, a little too cheerfully for first thing in the morning.

"Mornin' Tom, morning' Lori," I mumbled.

"Lori and I saved you some breakfast, cause we love you so much."

"Yeah? I am pretty loveable." I went into the kitchen and turned on the stove to reheat the pancakes. I threw the sausage into the frying pan with the pancakes and in a couple minutes, had a nice hot breakfast. After drenching everything in maple syrup, I brought my plate and a fork into the living room and sat on the couch. As I ate, I came to life. "So what's on the agenda today, guys?"

Tom was on the other end of the couch, setting the volley-ball to himself, occasionally hitting the ceiling, causing parti-cles of the cottage cheese insulation to rain down. "Well, unless you've got another idea, I figured I would show Lori around, give her a tour of the campus, maybe go down to the beach later. You wanna join us?"

"Probably not. I've gotta work from noon to six, and I'll probably just hang here until then." I shoved a forkful of pan-cakes in my mouth, but kept talking anyway. "How about you, Lori? Anything in particular you wanna do?"

"No, the grand tour sounds great. I'm supposed to meet up with some cousin I never knew I had, but that's not until tonight." She scooted herself out of the sleeping bag and stood up, raising her arms high toward the ceiling as she yawned. "Do you guys mind if I hop in the shower right now?"

"Not at all. In fact, I'll stand guard in case Paul tries to sneak a peek," Tom said, holding the volleyball now and grin-ning widely.

"Thanks, Tom. I feel safer already," she said, looking at me, smiling and shaking her head.

AFTER SHOWERING, Lori went into our bedroom to get dressed. It was Tom's turn to shower and I was in the kitchen doing the dishes, when I heard the knock on the door. Our kitchen had a small window looking out to the open air hallway and it was close enough to the front door for me to see Nancy Williams, waiting patiently.

"Hi, Nancy. What's going on? You just missed breakfast," I said, surprising her by greeting her through the kitchen window.

"Oh ... hey. Is Tom around?"

"He is indeed. Welcome to our humble abode," I said as I moved two steps out of the kitchen, opened the front door, and held my arm out in a sweeping gesture to welcome her in.

Just as Nancy stepped into the living room, Lori walked out of the bedroom, her hair still wrapped in a towel. A look of mild distress crossed Nancy's face, probably afraid of what she had walked in on.

"Lori, I'd like you to meet Nancy Williams. Nancy, Lori Lewis." They shook hands and I was just starting to explain to Nancy that Lori was visiting from Kansas when Tommy's voice shouted out from behind the closed bathroom door. "Hey Lori, how 'bout a little help in here? I've got a spot on my back I can't reach." Then he began guffawing.

The three of us blushed at once, all for different reasons. I excused myself, walked to the bathroom door, opened it and said, "Hey Tom, Nancy's here." And then, lowering my voice, said, "Thought you might want to know before you opened your mouth and stuck your foot in it again."

I went back to the girls in the living room and finished explaining to Nancy that Lori was a friend of mine and had come in last night. In damage control mode, I even told Nancy that Lori and I used to date in Kansas, and she was visibly relieved upon hearing that. A minute or two later, Tom entered the living room with a towel wrapped around his waist, looked at Lori, then at Nancy, hesitantly took a step toward Nancy and gave her a quick kiss hello.

"Well, what a nice surprise," he finally said to her.

"Sorry, I should've called. I just wanted to see what you were up to today," Nancy said.

Tom, now back in control of the situation, said, "Don't be silly. Stop by anytime. As a matter of fact I am touring Miss Lewis around the campus in a little bit and we would love to have you join us."

Then Lori, sensing that Tom still needed a little help, said, "That would be fun, Nancy. Please come with us."

"Okay, sure. I'd love to," she replied, the beginnings of a smile crossing her face.

I excused myself again and went back in the kitchen to finish the dishes. Lori followed me, and when we were around the corner and out of view, she tapped me on the shoulder and mouthed the words, "Is she his girlfriend?"

I furrowed my brow and shook my head, then whispered in her ear, "They've only known each other for a week."

She smiled, nodded, and strolled back to sit on the couch with Nancy while Tommy got dressed in the bedroom. Another half hour passed before they all said goodbye and began moving out the door. I pulled Tommy aside and wished him luck. After they left, I showered, got dressed in my tennis whites, and left to drive to Buck's.

THE MADHOUSE of the first day of the sale did not last. Although the event continued throughout the week, it was only slightly busier than a normal weekend now, it being a Wednesday, and the third day of the sale. I counted only a dozen or so customers in the Ski Department as I made my way through the thinned out racks of clothing towards the back stairs and up to the time clock. My eyes scanned down the row of timecards looking for mine. Not finding it, I noticed one card covered by a small white envelope. Lifting it out of the slot, I saw that the envelope had my name on it, written in feminine handwriting. I immediately thought of Jennifer, remembering the "call me" note from two days ago. It also crossed my mind that, although I had her phone number, she didn't have mine, and this was the only way she knew to reach me.

My pulse quickened as I opened the envelope. It was indeed from Jennifer. The note read:

Dearest Paul,
You don't call. You don't write. Just love me and
leave me. Ha-ha. Are you busy tonight?"
Love, Jennifer

I tried to imagine a time when I could possibly be too busy for Jennifer Ryan. I walked into Buck's empty office. He had gone out to the trailer for lunch. In my wallet, I had the slip of paper with Jennifer's phone number. I dialed the number and Edward picked up, told me Jennifer was not there, but that she had left instructions to invite me for dinner if I was available. I told him I could be there by six-fifteen. *Dinner with the possibility of extracurricular activity at Jennifer Ryan's! I must be living right.*

THE DAY PASSED in a slow crawl of anticipation. I was the only one working in Tennis, and once I finished the two rackets that needed stringing, I had to invent things to do. I organized the clothing racks, trying to find items which were out of place, straightened up the repair area where we installed leather grips and drilled out the wooden rackets. I inventoried the various types of nylon and gut string.

Renee was not working that day, making it easier to keep her out of my thoughts. The image in my mind of her crying at the restaurant put a knot in my stomach. I wanted to hold her tight, tell her I had made a big mistake and that I would never, ever hurt her again. But I wasn't sure I could do that. The other voice in my brain was telling me I had done the right thing, painful as it was.

SIX O'CLOCK, thank God, and I made a quick exit, pulled out of the parking lot and headed west towards Jennifer's house. I thought I would need to park in the Sorrento lot, but as I approached, the electronic gate began to open. They must have seen me coming with their security cameras. While waiting for a break in the oncoming traffic, I glanced over into the parking lot. Doug Williams was loading his umbrella and beach chair into the trunk of his car, calling it a day. I shrank in my seat, not wanting to be seen visiting Jennifer. But when he closed the trunk and walked up to the driver's side door, he looked up and recognized my car.

"Paul! Hey Paul!" he yelled, cupping his hands to his mouth.

I didn't answer him but looked his way and waved. A small break in the traffic developed and I pulled into the driveway, the gate closing behind me. LJ's voice resounded, "You da man, Paul! Go get 'em stud!" I reminded myself to give Tommy more shit about his big mouth.

I rang the bell and once again Jennifer answered it herself. My jaw dropped. She wore a formal black cocktail dress, sleek and silky. Hanging above the low cut neckline of the dress was a simple strand of white pearls. Her hair was pulled back tight into a bun with wisps of curls dancing on either side.

She smiled. "You've always seen me in shorts and tank tops. I wanted you to know I can clean up pretty well."

"I'll say you can. You look ... whew." I finally closed my mouth.

Prancing toward me like a model on a runway, she gave me a hello kiss on the cheek and said, "Just keep talkin' Paul, just keep talkin'. Flattery will get you everywhere."

THE EVENING AIR was warm and the sun still well above the wall, it being a good hour and a half before sunset. Jennifer gathered her dress, then sat down at the pool's edge, dangling her feet in the warm water. I kneeled to remove my tennis shoes, then joined her. Edward brought us glasses of white wine and a tray filled with crackers, cheeses, grapes, and big, deep red strawberries.

"So what have you been up to since I saw you last?" Jennifer asked.

"You wouldn't believe it if I told you."

She stopped moving her feet in the water and turned toward me. "What? Tell me."

I paused, breathed deeply, then started in. I told her the story of Jack's disappearance, how Tommy and I had tracked down Jerry Moberg, and how he and Jack were selling the faulty optics technology data to the Russians. I relayed as best I could the description of the high energy laser and the critical role the mirrors play. She was at first disbelieving, laughing it off as science fiction.

Finally, convinced I was telling the truth, she pressed her hand over her mouth as she gasped. "So what can we do? It seems like we should call the police or maybe the FBI."

"I promised Moberg I wouldn't do that. He and Jack would go to prison for a long, long time."

"Why don't you hire a private detective? I'm sure I could come up with someone good," she said.

I reached down with a cupped hand and dipped a fly out of the water. "I don't know about telling all this to a total stranger.

It's such a sensational story I'd be worried he would leak it to someone."

"Then just hire him to find Jack, but don't give him any of the background details."

I turned to look at her. "Maybe you're right. I'll have to think about it."

Edward appeared in the double doors and called us for dinner. The sun dipped under the wall and the sky was at its most beautiful, with burnt orange colors near the horizon, intermixed with a vibrant aqua blue higher in the sky, streaked with bright white clouds. We didn't want to leave it, so Jennifer suggested we eat outside. Edward brought us a Capresi salad, slices of fresh mozzarella alternated with juicy beefsteak tomato slices. The main course of filet mignon with blue cheese crumbles and grilled asparagus followed. For dessert, he had made a fresh fruit tart with blueberries, raspberries, kiwis, and strawberries. Being famous may not be high on my list, but being rich, and having someone like Edward cooking meals—that I could get used to.

After finishing dessert, the night air had cooled and we moved inside. We made our way to the TV room. The Righteous Brothers' *Unchained Melody* softly filled the room.

"May I have this dance?" I asked.

"Why, Mr. Townsend, there is nothing I would enjoy more."

We must have looked like an odd couple, Jennifer stunning in her black evening dress, and me in my country club tennis whites, slightly grubby from the day's work. We moved silently through the room for several minutes ... her soft, moist lips on mine as the song came to an end. I ran my hand down the smooth slickness of her silky dress.

"Penny for your thoughts," Jennifer whispered, her warm breath erotic on my ear.

"I've been thinking the same thing ever since I arrived and saw you in that dress. A penny for yours?"

"Oh, it's going to cost you a lot more than that," she said, laughing softly. "I was thinking that I've never made love to a tennis pro before." She reached back and undid the tightly wrapped bun, allowing her hair to fall freely about her shoulders.

We held each other close, her head under my chin. Even her hair smelled delicious. She moved her hand down the back of my shorts and gave a gentle squeeze to my behind. Then she broke from my embrace, drifted back a couple steps, turned and walked to the double doors that led to the foyer. She closed them slowly, turned around to face me, her back up against the doors. Moving towards me, she stopped a few feet short of where I stood. She unzipped the back of her dress and let it slide to the floor. A shy smile crossed her lips, contradicting the boldness in her eyes. She was a goddess in pearls. Michelangelo could not have done better.

I didn't bother to check the underground apartment parking space when I returned from Jennifer's. We were only allotted one space for our apartment and I was sure that Tommy had taken it. So, at one-thirty in the morning I combed the neighborhood for an open space, finally finding one about four blocks from our place. As I walked from my car, nearing our building, my eyes widened in surprise to see Lori moving towards the front entrance from the opposite direction.

"Isn't it a little late for a nice girl like you to be walking the streets?" I said loudly, from about thirty yards away.

Lori laughed. "Just looking for a kind person to take me in. How about you, kind person?"

We converged at the front stairs of the apartment building, hugged, and began walking up the steps. "Hey, you wanna sit down and chat for a few minutes? I'd rather stay out here so we don't wake up Tom."

We sat on the green, astroturf-covered stairs that led up to the front door from the Kelton Avenue sidewalk. "How was your night? What did you end up doing?" I asked.

"It was fun. I went to my cousin's in Encino. She and her husband took me to Hollywood to walk around, do the tourist thing—Graumann's Chinese Theater, all the stars on the sidewalk, dinner at Canter's Deli. We had a good time. Where were you?"

"Oh, I was in Santa Monica having dinner with this woman I've been seeing," I said, looking down at my shoes.

"This *woman*? You make it sound like she's fifty years old."

"Well, she *is* ten years older than me. But we're more friends than anything."

"Oh c'mon, that doesn't sound like you. Let's hear it. What's the scoop?" She nudged me with her shoulder.

"No, really. She came into the store I work at, we got to talking, and she asked me to dinner. We've only been out twice." I'm not sure why I was so reluctant to reveal Jennifer Ryan's identity. I guess I just didn't want the big reaction and all the questions.

A car drove by slowly, another late returnee fruitlessly looking for parking.

Lori's voice increased in volume a notch. "Ten years older and *she* asked *you* to dinner? Okay, fess up Townsend. I would surmise that she fairly attacked you when you took her home."

I smiled sheepishly. "Well maybe a minor frontal assault."

She giggled and said, "I knew it. I knew it." She leaned forward, elbows on her knees, hands clasped together, still grinning at my expense.

I reached over and put my hand on her arm. "Hey, I've never had a chance to tell you this, but I wanted to say thank you. Back when we were going out, I wasn't exactly Lance Romance. Thanks for being so patient with me."

"That's sweet of you to say. You were my little project. And I'll tell you something maybe you didn't know." She fiddled with her hair, twirling the ends with her finger. "I was devastated when you left me to go to college. I tried to be strong and pretend like it was no big deal, but I was in love with you, and it was very, very hard when you left."

I put my arm around her shoulders and pulled her close to me. "I'm sorry. I had no idea."

She turned her head away. "No, don't be sorry. You were always honest with me. I knew you had to leave Winfield."

Now I was wishing I hadn't brought up the subject in the first place. "Well, I'm still sorry. I hate to think that I hurt you."

Looking back at me, the moisture glistened in her eyes. "It's just the way life is sometimes. The only way to avoid getting hurt is to never fall in love in the first place."

I nodded in agreement. We sat there in silence, enjoying the cool night air. She rested her head on my shoulder and I breathed in the intoxicating fragrance of her perfume.

"Any idea where you want to go to school, what you want to do?" I asked.

"Not sure, but I was thinking about going to nursing school. I think it would be interesting and I really think I'd be good at it." She sniffed, the after-effect of the near tears.

I picked up a twig on the stair and tossed it on the street. "Oh man, you would be great at it. That sounds like a perfect thing for you to do. I remember you were always good at science and you're a very caring person. Plus, you'd look hot in a nurse's uniform. Just think of all the doctors you'd meet."

She smiled and pushed me away playfully. "I'm not sure I'd want to be with a doctor. They're a little too devoted to their jobs. I want someone devoted to me. Is that being selfish? I'm just hoping I can meet a nice guy and have a normal relationship for a change."

"Well, I can tell you one thing. There's a guy sleeping up in our apartment right now who seems to have the hots for you. I'm not sure how normal he is though."

Even in the darkness I could see her blushing. "I like Tommy. You've got good taste in friends." Then putting her hand on top of mine, she said, "What about us?"

I quickly turned my head to her. "You and me? You mean get back together?"

She nodded, biting her lip and looking down, avoiding my eyes. I found her hand and held it.

"You know I'll always love you. But to try to recapture that "first love" feeling we had … that would be unfair to both of us."

She had a faraway look in her eye, probably remembering another time and place. "It was really, really good, wasn't it?"

"It was great, but it wouldn't have lasted. We both had too much growing up to do, too many big changes ahead of us." I let go of her hand and began rubbing her back.

"As much as I'd like to disagree with you, I think you're right. I'm in love with the memory of what we had and what we felt. Trying to rekindle that could never work. I guess timing is everything, huh?"

"Yep. If we'd met when we were older instead of when we were seventeen …" My voice trailed off. "Well, whadda ya think? Time to get some sleep?"

We stood up from our streetside seat. I stretched my arms high in the air, let out a loud yawn, then turned to follow Lori up the stairs. I quietly unlocked the apartment door and we crept in, not wanting to wake Tommy. I said good night to Lori and slipped into the bedroom without turning on the lights. I tiptoed across the room, not to disturb him. Easing myself onto my bed, I started to untie my tennis shoes, then heard a low pitched, guttural, moaning coming from Tommy. It didn't sound quite human.

"Tom, are you awake?" I said softly. He did not answer me but the moaning became louder. It sounded like he was having a bad dream.

"Tom? *Tom.* Wake up, man." I said it louder, but still no response. I turned on the lights to rescue him from his nightmare.

"Tom? Tom?" His eyelids were halfway open but his eyes rolled upward, not seeing me. His face was drained of color. I couldn't wake him.

Then I noticed the blood. Just below his right shoulder, a large patch of bright red blood, wet on his t-shirt. I pulled down the sheet and blanket covering him. *Oh my God! Blood! Lots of blood!* "Lori! Lori! Come in here quick!" The entire lower half of his t-shirt and the bottom sheet below him were drenched in red.

Hearing the panic in my voice, Lori rushed through the door. She took one look at the semi-conscious Tommy covered in blood, gasped, then cried out, "Oh my God! Oh my God!"

I grabbed the phone on my nightstand and dialed 911. My eyes welled up with tears as I told the operator the situation. She assured me paramedics had been dispatched and would be there shortly.

Lori battled hyperventilation, her eyes flooded with tears. "What can we ... oh God! What do we do?"

Tommy was still not responding to us, weak from the loss of blood and barely holding onto consciousness.

"Grab some napkins out of the kitchen!" The only thing I could think to do was to find the wound and apply pressure to stem the flow of blood. Lori returned with the napkins and gently lifted his t-shirt as I attempted to locate the source of the bleeding. At least half a dozen places on his chest and stomach gushed blood. My hands trembled and teardrops fell on Tommy's chest as I pressed down on three of the holes using the white paper napkins. Lori covered two more.

"Stay with me, buddy. Stay with me. Help is coming. You're gonna be okay," I said to him, not knowing if he could hear. Minutes seemed like hours. Finally, we heard pounding on the front door and I got up to let the paramedics in. They quickly went into action, sealing off the wounds to stop the bleeding. Within a couple minutes, they had Tommy loaded on a stretcher and maneuvered him out of the bedroom. Several of our neighbors, hearing the siren of the paramedic truck, stood in the hallway or on their balconies. Tommy was silent and unconscious as they carried him past the people and down the stairs.

The captain of the team stayed behind to speak with us. "Any idea who did this?" he asked.

I wiped away the wetness from my cheek, unknowingly smearing blood on my face in the process. "No sir, I don't."

He looked at Lori. "And you, Miss?"

"No, I'm visiting … from out of town. We just met … yesterday," Lori managed to get out, fresh tears running down her face.

The captain said, "I've put a call into LAPD to have them send somebody over. They should be here within a few minutes. I'm required to stay with you until they arrive."

"Do you think he's going to be okay?" I asked.

"He lost a lot of blood," he said, exhaling loudly. They'll give him a transfusion when he arrives at the hospital. I can tell you that another few minutes and we would have been too late. What I don't know is the extent of internal damage. It looked like he was stabbed seven or eight times. We have to hope that no major organs were hit."

There was a knock on the door and two policemen entered. The captain briefed the officers, then wished us good luck before he left. The police detective noted no evidence of forced entry, although the balcony sliding door was unlocked and someone could have climbed up fairly easily. Nothing had been stolen. It appeared that whoever had done this had come specifically to get Tommy. One of the officers left our apartment to speak with the neighbors, who were almost all out now, milling in the hallway outside our front door. The remaining detective again asked us if we knew of anyone with a grudge against Tom. *The paparazzo!* I explained to the officer what had happened last week at the beach and that the photographer had vowed to get all of us. The detective put a call into the station to have them locate Carl Sedgewick for questioning. *If it is Sedgewick, it's probably me he was after. It just so happened that Tommy was here and I wasn't. Is this my fault? Sedgewick had been angry, very angry, but was he crazy enough to commit murder?*

Tom was still alive when he arrived at the emergency room at two-fifteen. They gave him three pints of blood, a dose of morphine, then took him into surgery. Three and a half hours later, we had no news. It was an awful, agonizing wait. After finishing with the police at the apartment, I had called Tom's mother and father in Santa Monica. They were now with us in the large lobby area of the hospital.

Karen Ruderman's eyes were puffy and red from crying on and off since she received my call. In spite of the hour and the circumstance, she was smartly dressed in a light green pantsuit. I had met Tommy's mother before on several occasions, but his dad, only once. Tom's father could have passed for one of the many homeless transients in Santa Monica, unshaven for several days, unkempt, scraggly hair, and bloodshot eyes. I hadn't noticed any tears, but he was definitely upset, pacing nervously in his two tone Quicksilver beach trunks, threadbare t-shirt, and flip flops. Karen confided in me when Rudy was out of earshot that she hadn't seen him in a year, although she was not surprised at his appearance. Divorced for seventeen years now, there was no more hostility between them, but it was hard for me to picture that they had once been together. Karen was so outgoing, friendly, and ... dignified. Rudy almost seemed anti-social, although maybe this wasn't the time for a fair assess-ment, given the circumstances. Tommy's earliest memories as a child were of his parents fighting, loud and sometimes physical arguments which scared the young boy. His father never hurt him but Tom remembered being frightened, because of what he witnessed him say and do to his mother.

A LITTLE AFTER SEVEN, a doctor wearing light blue scrubs approached the four of us in the waiting room. "Are you Tom Ruderman's parents?"

Tommy's parents stood up and took a step towards the doc-tor, searching his face trying to detect whether the news was good or bad. "Yes, that's us," Karen answered. Lori and I also stood up, Lori clutching my hand tightly.

"I'm Dr. Liebensohn. Your son has just come out of surgery. We didn't see any damage to the heart, lungs, liver, or kidneys. That's very good news. His stomach was punctured and we had to stitch it up, but there was no damage to the intestinal tract. He'll be staying here for several days since the biggest risk at this point is infection, and we'll have to monitor him closely. But all in all, I would venture to say that he is one very lucky young man."

"Oh, thank God. Bless you. Bless you, doctor." Tommy's mother, tears streaming, put her hands on the doctor's shoul-ders, and buried her head in his chest. The doctor hesitantly put his arms around her and patted her on the back. Pulling her head back, she asked, "When can we see him?"

"I would imagine it will be at least a couple hours in recovery before he is alert enough to visit with you, but keep in mind he will still be heavily medicated for the pain. Could be a little loopy for a while," Dr. Liebensohn said.

"We're used to that with Tommy," I said, and everybody gave a little chuckle.

Dr. Liebensohn walked away and Karen nearly collapsed in my arms, relieved and spent from the emotion. Then, as she shifted to give Lori a hug, I shook the cold, clammy hands of Rudy Ruderman.

"Paul, thank you for being there for Tom, for calling the paramedics and getting him here so quickly. If you hadn't been there, we might have lost him," Rudy said as Karen nodded in agreement.

The UCLA Medical Center, one of the top rated hospitals in the country, and therefore the world, was less than a mile from our apartment. From the time I dialed 911 to the time Tommy received treatment was a little over fifteen minutes, and this close proximity had likely saved him. Had Lori and I chatted a little longer on the steps last night, Tommy would have lost his life. That's what I kept thinking about.

"You're welcome. I'm just glad we got home when we did," I said.

We excused ourselves to walk to the hospital cafeteria to get a cup of coffee. When we returned, we sat with the Rudermans and explained the course of events once again, assuring them that their son had no enemies and was well liked by everyone.

"The only possibility we can think of is this guy at the beach the other day. He was a paparazzo trying to take photos of an actress that lives right there where we play volleyball. I got in a little scuffle with him and he said he would get back at me."

"Oh, that's right! I saw the article in the paper. I was going to ask you about that," Karen said.

"But why would that have anything to do with Tommy?" Rudy asked.

"We were just thinking if he was after me, maybe he got Tommy by mistake," I said, suddenly feeling very guilty.

"Oh ... I see," Rudy said. "Did you tell the police this?"

"Yes, they're going to track the guy down."

Tom's mother turned away without a word and sat heavily in one of the chairs.

Rudy just said, "Well, hopefully they find him."

TWO HOURS passed and the receptionist told us we still had to wait. Lori didn't hear because she was asleep on a couch in the waiting room. Finally, after another long hour, the receptionist motioned to us that we could see him. I woke Lori and we walked with the Rudermans down the long corridor that led to Post Operative Recovery. Although I had been with Tommy right after the attack, I was still shocked at how weak and frail he looked, when only twelve hours before, he had been the Southern California poster boy for good health and vitality.

A thin smile crossed Tommy's lips when he recognized us. "How ya doin'?" I asked.

He nodded that he was okay. I leaned close to his face and held his hand. "Who did this to you?"

Tom turned his head to look me in the eyes and whispered in a raspy voice, "It was too dark. I was sleeping and suddenly felt this terrible pain in my gut. I opened my eyes, saw the knife come at me again and again, but never saw his face."

I looked downward and buried my face in my free hand. "Oh, God. Oh, God. I'm sorry, man. I'm so sorry." Lifting my head from my shaking hand, I knew it would serve him better if I was strong. "They're gonna take good care of you here. You'll be outta here in no time." Then my smile returned. "I'm thinkin' this might work out pretty well for me. I should finally be able to beat you on the volleyball court now that you're handicapped."

Tommy smiled at me. "You just keep thinkin' Townie, that's what you're good at."

"Tom, I got vision and the rest of the world wears bifocals," I said.

"By the way, Townie?"

"Yeah?"

"It'll never happen," he said, his smile broadening.

Lori stepped in closer to Tommy, gave him a quick kiss on the lips and told him we would be back later in the day to check on him. Tommy motioned for Lori to come nearer him, then said something I couldn't hear. Lori laughed. Then we said goodbye to Tommy's parents, leaving them alone with their son.

"What did he whisper to you right before we left?" I asked Lori as we walked down the hall.

"He said when I come back later in the day, to leave you behind."

I just shook my head. "It seems the operation was a success—back to normal."

WE HAD BEEN FOREWARNED that the LAPD investigators would be at our apartment today and that we would have limited access. When we arrived, yellow crime scene tape blocked the front door, and several of the neighbors milled about in the exterior hallway outside the apartment, happy to see me when I appeared. Many of them had been questioned by the investigators about noticing anyone unfamiliar in the complex last night. Nobody had. Eight to ten of them gathered around me and I gave them the details of everything that had transpired the night before, and that Tommy survived the ordeal.

The detectives would not allow us to enter the apartment, but retrieved our swimsuits for us. We had decided to park ourselves in lounge chairs by the pool until they finished collecting evidence, expected to be later in the afternoon. Lori and I were close to collapsing from lack of sleep and withdrawal from the trauma of last night. Blue Whale One offered to let us use her apartment to change into our suits.

At poolside, I took a deep breath of the chlorine scented air and exhaled. It was a warm, cloudless day and the sun felt good on my skin. I had brought down one of our towels. I draped it over my face to provide coolness and darkness as I lay on the flattened lounge chair. Lori removed her t-shirt and busily applied sunscreen to her entire body, this being her first day in the Southern California sun and not wanting to get burned. Even in my exhausted state, I moved the towel from my eyes and offered my assistance, as much to see her in the bikini as to be helpful.

She tossed me the bottle of Coppertone. "If you could put some on my back that would be great."

With a grunt and a groan, I lifted my upper torso out of the lounge chair, swung my legs to the side, leaned over and squirt some of the lotion on her shoulders as she sat with her back to me. I spread the white, creamy liquid all over her back down to her bikini bottoms.

"You have beautiful skin, so smooth and soft."

"Bring back any memories there, Mr. Townsend?" She read my mind.

"Well actually, it's been so long ago now, and there have been so many women since then—the memories are a little fuzzy. What was your name again?"

She twisted around in her chair and gave me a good solid slug in the shoulder.

"Okay, now it's coming back to me. Who could forget that punch. By the way, that's about the third time you've punched me since you got here. You got some pent-up hostility or what?"

Just then, we heard the unmistakable vocal disharmony of Singin' Sammy belting out from the second floor balcony overlooking the pool ... *our* second floor balcony. "Open up the window, let some air into this room ..." He proceeded with the rest of the stanza from the *Credence* song, finishing with, "Mama told me not to come ..."

Then he leaped off the balcony into the pool below, not surprising anybody in the lounge chairs except for a wide-eyed Lori, her mouth agape, not having previously been introduced to our neighbor. One of the detectives came out on the balcony, probably curious where the Speedo clad intruder had appeared from. Although he lived several apartments south of our place, Sam had been known to climb over the low stucco walls which separated the balconies and make his way to our deck, before jumping into the pool. Sammy popped right out of the pool and headed toward the stairwell to continue his rounds, causing little more than a murmur amongst the pool patrons, who were accustomed to his act.

Peace restored, I finished rubbing the lotion onto Lori's back and lay down, putting the towel back over my eyes. Another deep breath and the muscles of my body began to go limp and heavy. Sleep came quickly after that, and although I was awakened a few times by people coming and going from the pool area, it felt good to get what sleep I did over the next few hours.

A LITTLE AFTER four o'clock we were permitted to re-enter the apartment. I involuntarily shivered at the sight of the bare mattress that was once Tommy's bed. They had taken the blankets and bloody sheets as evidence.

"I'm not sure I can sleep in there. It's kinda giving me the creeps," I said as I emerged from the bedroom.

"You're welcome to join me out here. I'll protect you," Lori said.

"If I slept out here, you might need someone to protect *you*," I said as I sank into the couch.

"Who says I want to be protected?" Lori sauntered toward me, newly tanned in her pale yellow bikini.

She stood facing me, then leaned over, straddling me, putting her hands on the back of the couch. "Do you remember the lessons I gave you?" Then she covered my lips with hers and kissed me, a soft delicate kiss. She relaxed her arms and eased her body onto mine.

I ran my fingers beneath the tight fabric of her bikini bottoms and pulled her close to me. "Do you really want to do this?" I whispered when our lips parted.

Breathing rapidly, she moved her face around, kissed my neck, then my shoulder and down to my chest. She looked up at me, her chin resting on my stomach.

"Whadda ya think—maybe just once for old time's sake?"

She lifted her head and leaned back, running her hands along my thighs, stopping at my knees. She stood up, pranced to the window overlooking the pool, and closed the curtains. Then she did the same at the sliding glass doors. I watched her every move, noticing that her bikini bottoms were pulled down an inch or so, revealing her new tan line, as well as the tiny birthmark in the shape of South America I remembered so well. I was mesmerized by the slender waist, the full hips, the muscular dancer's legs.

Then I came to my senses.

"I can't do this, Lori. Not with Tom suffering like he is. I know how much he likes you. It wouldn't be right."

She plopped down next to me, exhaling. "You sure your name is Paul Townsend? From Winfield, Kansas? Cause the Paul Townsend I know would no sooner turn down hanky panky than jump off a cliff."

"C'mon, you know what I mean," I said. She was actually correct. I think I had completely lost it.

With an air of resignation, she said, "Yes, I do. It could complicate things. Shame."

Then she put her hand on my knee and used it to push herself up off the couch. "To the showers for me. Think I'll take a cold one."

Watching her hips sway as she moved toward the bathroom, I think she was purposely teasing me. I made a mental note to inform my roommate of the supreme sacrifice I had just made.

AFTER LORI finished, I took a quick shower myself. We both dressed, then started the journey back to the Medical Center. It did us good to get some exercise, a different type than we were contemplating a few minutes before.

Tommy's parents were leaving through the front entrance as we approached.

"How's he doing?" I asked.

Rudy Ruderman, looking even more haggard than he had earlier, answered, "He's tired and pretty drugged up. He slept for a good part of the time since you left this morning, but the doctor is happy with how he is responding.

"Fantastic. That's awesome," I said.

We said goodbye and headed to the elevators to go to Tommy's fourth floor room. He was sleeping when we got to his room, so we sat there talking quietly to each other, careful not to wake him. After about twenty minutes he opened his eyes and said in a tired voice, "Hey, I thought I told you to leave him behind."

Lori laughed, got out of her chair and gave him a kiss, a little longer than the one she had given him in the morning when his parents were there.

I said, "Don't mind me. I like to watch. Just pretend I'm not here." I paused, enjoying the smile on Tommy's face. "How are you feeling, man?"

"I'd love to tell you I'm feeling like a million bucks, but it's more like a hundred," Tom said, his voice still raspy from being intubated during surgery. "But I'll bust outta this joint before too long."

The three of us talked for a few more minutes, then watched Gomer Pyle on the television in his room. I lay down on the unoccupied second bed in the room and Lori sat in the armchair trying to figure out why we thought Sergeant Carter was so funny. By the end of the episode, Tom needed to rest, so we said our goodbyes and departed the Medical Center.

We walked the short distance into Westwood and entered Mario's, one of my favorite Italian restaurants, to get some dinner.

"I don't know about you, but it's early to bed for me tonight," I said, as the hostess seated us.

"If I wasn't so hungry, I'd put my head down on my plate and fall asleep right here," Lori agreed.

We shared a large antipasto salad and a plate of ravioli, then set out for the hike up the hill, up Gayley Avenue, back to the apartment building. It was not yet eight-thirty when we trudged in. I brushed my teeth, washed my face, and changed into my standard sleepwear, a t-shirt and some gray cotton, UCLA Volleyball gym shorts that I had inherited from Tom. I apologized to Lori for conking out so early but the apology was unnecessary since she was already rolling her bag out on the mattress, preparing her bed. I gave her a hug goodnight, turned the corner into the bedroom, closed the door, and literally fell into bed. I was asleep within two minutes.

I SLEPT so soundly that I heard nothing of what happened in the next room. First, there was the knocking. It was so incessant that it eventually jolted Lori awake. It was a little after eleven. She unzipped the sleeping bag, climbed out, cleared the last bit of sleep from her head, then made her way through the dark to the door. She squinted through the peephole at the late night visitor. *Max!* She could not believe it. Anger quickly rose within her. After traveling all the way from Winfield to Los Angeles to rid herself of him, here he was, like a recurring nightmare.

She unlatched the door, opened it, and screamed at him, "What in the *hell* are you doing here!? How did you know I was here? *Are you crazy!?*"

She wanted to punch him. His eyes were glassed over, unfocused, not seeming to see her. He said nothing, just kicked the door, forcing it open wider. He violently pushed Lori in the chest with the palm of his hand, knocking her to the floor. He stepped over her and went straight for the bedroom. Looking up from the floor, she saw the flash of metal in his hand and instantly realized what was happening.

She screamed at the top of her lungs, *"Paul! Paul! He's trying to kill you! Paul!"*

Lori's scream made my heart skip a beat. I sat bolt upright in my bed. It didn't register what she had said, but I understood the panic in her voice. As Max entered the room, I threw off the covers and scrambled to my feet. *This is the person who attacked Tommy!* I stood in the darkness by my bed, my senses heightened by fear. *He has a knife!* Backlit by the open bedroom door, the figure moved slowly towards me. I took one step back, weighing my options.

"We'll see how much she likes you when you're dead," Max said.

The voice was easy to recognize, even after three years. In a flash, it all made sense.

"Max, take it easy man. Let's talk this over." I heard the shakiness in my voice.

There was no reply, only a grunt and a quick motion toward me. Backed up against the dresser, I had nowhere to go. I turned sideways and used the full length of my right leg to kick at his midsection, sending him reeling backwards. I used the opportunity to hop on my bed to get around him. But he recovered in time to cut off my path of escape and came toward me again, swinging the knife back and forth wildly. This time I kicked straight ahead, aiming for the body parts just below his midsection. He grabbed my foot, causing me to fall on the bed and then to the carpet. But the force of my kick made him lose his balance and fall to the floor next to me.

I churned my legs like a child having a tantrum, kicking him in the face and keeping my body away from the knife. Even in the darkness, I could see that he was rising from the floor, up on one knee now. I stopped kicking and rolled away from him. Just as I regained my footing, within my peripheral vision another figure entered the room. *Lori!?* Next, a loud metallic thud reverberated and Max yelped, then went limp. Then, another thud. Lori held the frying pan up high and was about to come down with a third blow when I grabbed her arm, stopping the downward motion.

"That's enough. He's out. Hopefully you didn't kill him," I said, gasping for breath.

"Hopefully I *did* kill him," Lori said.

Max did not regain consciousness until after the police arrived, much to my relief. Lori had kept the frying pan close at hand just in case. They handcuffed him and took him away within minutes. Two of the LAPD officers stayed behind to question us. These were different policemen than had been here the night before and they didn't know what had happened. We stood in the center of our living room, the two of us still in our sleepwear. For over an hour, we gave them the story of Lori's past relationship and how he had followed her here from Kansas. We explained that he had attacked Tommy last night, probably trying to get me.

"And where is Tommy now?" the officer asked.

"At the UCLA Medical Center, in intensive care," I said.

"We'll go over there tomorrow and get a statement from him. It doesn't seem like we'll have any trouble convicting this guy," he said, finishing up some notes on his clipboard.

I started to thank him, but Lori interrupted. "As long as they keep him locked up. I wouldn't be surprised if he came right back after us if they let him go."

The officer answered, "No need to worry. He won't be getting out. They won't offer bail to somebody who is mentally imbalanced."

At twelve-thirty we said goodbye to the police. After they left, Lori turned to me and fell into my arms. She buried her face in my chest and began weeping. I tried to comfort her, but the events of the past twenty-four hours had caught up with her.

"I'm so ... sorry. It's all m-my fault," she said between heaving sobs.

"Don't be silly. It's not your fault. The guy's a psycho."

She looked up at me with red, tear-laden eyes. "I should have never come here. If I hadn't come, then Max wouldn't have followed, and Tommy wouldn't be in the hospital right now."

I gave her a gentle kiss on the lips. "Lori, listen to me. Tommy and I both love that you are here. How could you have known that he would follow you? Stop beating yourself up. Heck, you may have just saved my life. Think about that." I continued to stroke her hair and hold her close to me.

"I did smack him a good one, didn't I?" she managed a smile in the midst of all the tears.

"You certainly did."

I took her hand, walked over, and sat down with her on the couch. We chatted for a few minutes and then both of us agreed we should try to get some sleep. The adrenaline coursing through my veins wouldn't make it easy. I kissed her good night and we went our separate ways. I lay in bed for a long time, staring at the ceiling, reliving the fight with Max. Eventually the lack of sleep of the past two days took its toll, exhaustion reigned, and I slept.

IT WAS SEVEN-FIFTEEN when I sat up in bed and rubbed my face. I had slept, but not well. I had woken up twice during the night, imagining that Lori was screaming. Both times I had raced into the living room, only to find her sound asleep.

I took creaky, wobbly, sleep-deprived steps toward the bathroom sink to brush my teeth. I peeked around the corner into the living room. Streaks of sunlight found their way through the balcony curtains. Lori lay curled into the fetal position on the edge of the mattress, the sleeping bag only covering her from the waist down. She probably had a rough night, too. I tiptoed to the kitchen. I opened the fridge and took out the bacon, laying several slices flat in the frying pan.

"You better be making enough for me too," Lori said, coming to life when the smell wafted into the living room.

"There might be a tiny bit left over." I tried my best to sound serious. "By the way, I want you to know that I am using your weapon to cook with. The frying pan that saved my life is back to frying up bacon."

Lori laughed. "Thank goodness you've got a good, heavy duty pan. It sure did the trick."

"In all seriousness, thanks for helping me out. I'm not sure what would have become of me if you hadn't jumped in," I said.

Lori got up from the mattress and walked over to the kitchen. She looked a little haggard, dark circles under her eyes. Her sleeping attire was an oversized t-shirt with a photograph of John, Paul, George and Ringo on the front. "Not that I didn't think you could take him. I just wanted to get in on the fun."

After the bacon was cooked, I made the milk and egg mixture for French toast. Then I took out a loaf of sourdough, dipped a slice of the bread into the liquid, thoroughly coating it, and began cooking it in the same pan the bacon was in. Lori stood to my side with her hand on my shoulder, looking into the pan. "Where did you learn how to cook?"

"Mom gave me survival training before I left home. Bacon, eggs, pancakes, French toast, I can handle. Beyond that, I'm in trouble."

"It looks terrific. I'm starving."

Clearing the Jack Rosen papers off the table, we sat down to eat.

"I was thinking of going to see Tommy," she said, as she cut up the French toast.

"You go ahead. I'm going to stay here and make some phone calls. Just keep your paws off him. Remember he's a sick man," I said, trying to hide my smile.

She pulled her fist back to give me another slug.

I scooted my chair away from the table, getting out of her range. "Okay, okay. I'm sorry. No more punches."

We made our peace and finished our breakfast.

TOMMY AND I had worked through about two-thirds of the names and numbers that we needed to call. Occasionally we would get a return call from the messages we left, but there were certainly a lot that we had not heard from. The gold mine that we struck with Jerry Moberg motivated me to continue calling, even without Tom's help.

After she showered and got dressed, I drew a little map to help Lori get back to the hospital. Then she started out on the fifteen minute walk. I settled at the table with the telephone and Jack's address book. The corner of the "R" page was folded over, indicating either Tommy or I had called everyone from A through R on the previous pages. Turning to 'S', I dialed the first number, Al Sorenson. As was typical, I had no idea who this was, and after several rings, an answering machine picked up. I spewed forth my reason for calling, leaving my name and number at the end of the message.

I began to dial the next number on the page—Ivan Sokolov, it read. I hung up the receiver when I saw the writing underneath. It said simply, "Ocean Plaza Hotel, Room 518", and then underneath, were written the words, "always stays in the same room". Next to his name were two phone numbers, one apparently an international number. I surmised it was a home number for wherever Ivan Sokolov was from. The second number had a Santa Monica prefix, and I guessed that was for the Ocean Plaza Hotel. After staring at the entry for a couple minutes, I picked up the phone and dialed the Santa Monica number.

"Hello, Ocean Plaza Hotel. May I help you?" the young female voice answered.

"Yes ... yes, hello," I said unevenly, collecting myself. "May I be connected to Mr. Ivan Sokolov?"

"Yes, certainly. Let me see. Yes, here he is ... Room 518. Please hold for a minute. I'll connect you."

31

The phone rang only once in Room 518 before I abruptly hung up on my end, not sure I was ready to speak with Ivan Sokolov. After a couple minutes, my mind racing, I picked up the phone again and dialed "O" to speak with the operator.

"Yes, operator, can you tell me where this number is located?" I read her the second number next to Sokolov's name.

"That would be Munich, Germany, sir. May I connect you?"

"No ... no. Thank you, operator." I hung up the phone, took a deep breath and put my hand to my forehead.

My gut told me Ivan Sokolov was mixed up in the business Jerry Moberg told us about. *He is here in Santa Monica. This must be the guy that took Jack from the beach. I'll go to his hotel room, knock on the door, tell him who I am and ask him what happened to Jack. No, too dangerous. Better if I stay anonymous. I'll try following him.*

Maybe he'll lead me to Jack. But I don't even know what he looks like. How do you follow somebody if you don't know what they look like?

I needed a plan. And right now my brain was mush from too little sleep. Scheduled to work from noon to six, I decided to call in sick. I needed time to sit down and think about this. I went into the bedroom and lay on my bed, staring at the ceiling. Who could I get to help me? Maybe it was time for the private detective, like Jennifer suggested. I imagined that before he got involved, he would want to know why he was tracking Sokolov and why Jack was kidnapped. I wasn't ready to reveal all this to a stranger. The information was too explosive. And telling the police would be the same as putting Jack behind bars for the rest of his life. *I wish Tommy was here. Boy, how I wish Tommy was here. I need to get into Room 518. Maybe Jack is in that room!*

I showered and shaved, then got dressed in my best pair of long pants, some dark blue polyester slacks, and a white dress shirt. I thought it might help me fit in better at the hotel to be dressed nicely. I became aware of Tommy's side of the closet, barren as usual, except for a few empty hangers and the pile of clothes below. A sudden sense of sadness overtook me, not rational since I knew he was going to be okay, but it enveloped me nonetheless. I had almost lost my best friend. And that stack of clothes just reminded me of it.

Minutes later I ventured out the front door, waved at Blue Whale Two, who was sitting on their living room couch with a bag of chips watching something on TV, and headed off to the Ocean Plaza Hotel.

I ARRIVED at the hotel, built in the late 1930's, a dramatic example of the Art Deco architecture of the time, and one of the poshest, most expensive hotels in Santa Monica. Seven stories tall, the structure sat on the eastern side of Ocean Avenue, right where Santa Monica Boulevard ended. The western side of Ocean Avenue had no development because of the unstable nature of the bluffs, and was occupied by a pedestrian parkway overlooking the Pacific Ocean. The views from the hotel were therefore unobstructed and magnificent. I drove into the entrance, skipped the valet parking and parked in one of several visitor's spots which surrounded a large fountain in the center of the circular driveway.

I couldn't bring myself to get out of the car, the reality of being there weighing on me. I slouched in my seat, fingers tapping the steering wheel. How to get in the room? And what would I find once I got in? My first thought was to follow the maids to see when they would be cleaning his room. Then I could just walk in and pretend it was my room. Odds are the maids wouldn't know Sokolov. Or would they? Since he stayed there so often? It was worth a shot. I got out of the car and walked to the circular revolving doors at the entrance. Passing under an elaborate chandelier and across a colorful Persian rug, I made my way to the elevators, stepped in, and pushed the button for the fifth floor.

After exiting the elevator, I moved a few steps to my left and saw the black, acrylic sign with gold painted numbers "Rooms 502—528" and an arrow. I looked down the long corridor of rooms. *The maid cart!* Toward the end of the hall a maid picked up folded towels from the cart and carried them into a room. Were they finished with Room 518 or yet to get there? As I approached, the maid closed the door of the room she had been working in, and moved the cart further down the hall. Disappointed, I realized this probably meant they were already finished with 518. Arriving at the room, I looked down to see a Do Not Disturb sign hanging from the doorknob. The

maids hadn't even gone into Sokolov's room. He was probably
in there.

Blame it on lack of sleep or just a lack of common sense,
but, impulsively and angrily, I knocked on the door. I stood
there, leaning forward with one hand on the door frame, staring
at the closed door, tired and ready to have it out with him. I
waited. Cursing under my breath, I pounded with my fist, loud
enough for the maid at the cart to stop in her tracks and look
my way. But still no answer. I decided to go to Plan B.

It occurred to me that I might convince the front desk to
give me a room key if I identified myself as Ivan Sokolov. I
would say that I had accidentally left the key in the room. I got
back on the elevator to return to the lobby. My mind churned
with all the possibilities of what I might find if I successfully
gained entry. Even though I had pounded on the door, Sokolov
himself might be in the room. If he were, I would apologize
and blame it on the front desk for giving me an occupied room.
Secondly, I figured Jack might be in the room. Maybe Sokolov
was using his hotel room to hold him hostage. The third possibility was that nobody would be in the room, in which case
I would go through his belongings and see if I could discover
some clues as to where Jack might be.

I left the elevator and began the walk to the reception desk,
which faced the antique-filled sitting area. There were two
people working behind the counter: an older, blonde haired
woman, probably in her forties, and a younger man, maybe
just a little older than me. Since the woman seemed busy with
paperwork and the man was smiling as I approached, I went to
him.

"Hello, I am in Room 518 and I seem to have locked my
key in the room. Do you have a spare I could borrow?" I said,
happy that the lie came out so smoothly.

"Certainly sir, not a problem." He turned to the cubbyhole marked 518, retrieved a key, and slapped it down on the counter. As I reached for it, the man said, "Sorry, what was your name, sir?" His hand covered the key.

"Sokolov ... Ivan Sokolov," I said.

The young man's expression instantly changed to a frown as he retracted his hand, gripping the key firmly. "I'm sorry, sir. You are not Mr. Sokolov. Who are you? What is your business here?"

"Oh ... I, uh. Sorry ... I, uh. I'm actually a friend of his. I needed to get something out of his room and figured it would be easier to just pretend I was him. Sorry. Sorry."

The last sorry was spoken as I backpedaled away from the counter. Then I turned and half walked, half jogged to the revolving doors, continuing straight to my car. I quickly started my car and left the parking lot, glancing behind me to see if anyone followed.

32

After the debacle at the hotel, still shaken, I decided to go to work. Waiting at the red light on Wilshire and Lincoln, on my way to Buck's, I made the decision to go back to the hotel later in the day in hopes of somebody different being at the reception desk—somebody that didn't know Ivan Sokolov. Even though he stayed there often, I couldn't imagine that every employee knew him. With a new plan in place, I calmed down. I would go back to the hotel after work.

A little before noon, I parked in the rear lot, and entered the back door.

"Hey, I thought you were sick," Buck said as I reached the top of the stairs.

"Oh ... yeah. I was a little hung over this morning, but started feeling better so I thought I would come in," I lied.

Buck chuckled. "Don't you think you're a little over-dressed? You come straight from the party or what?"

I looked down at my clothes as if they were someone else's and had strangely landed on my body. It hadn't even occurred to me that I was wearing the slacks and dress shirt until Buck said something. "Oh, jeez. Yeah ... I, uh, had to do something else before I came here. I need some new tennis things anyway, so I'm going to pick some stuff out and change downstairs."

Buck looked back down at the desk and continued his writing that I had interrupted. He spoke as he wrote. "Well, I'm glad you're here. Ernie's off today and there's a mess o' rackets to do. Afraid I was going to have to go down there and do 'em myself."

SIX RACKETS waited to be strung. Hopefully it wouldn't be too busy with customers, since I would be hard pressed to get all of the rackets strung with too many interruptions. Being at Buck's, my thoughts turned to Renee. I wanted to apologize to her, just for the fact that I had made her so upset. I hadn't changed my opinion about her being too young, and as conflicted as I had been, I was still convinced I had made the right decision. She was an extraordinary girl, and that's what made it so difficult. But just because she's beautiful, intelligent, and fun to be with, doesn't change her age.

My mind swam with thoughts of Renee, Tommy, Jack, and Ivan Sokolov as I finished with the vertical strings in a Head Master aluminum racket. I pulled the next string taut to the specified calibration of sixty-two pounds and the entire racket head began to bend out of shape. I had forgotten to secure the throat of the racket properly in the stringing machine, allowing the entire frame to bend as the vertical strings, minus the coun-terbalancing horizontal strings, exerted their force. A rookie mistake—the last time I had done this was over a year ago. My stomach sank like when you see a parking ticket on your windshield, knowing I would have to pay for the ruined racket. Luckily, we had an identical frame with the same four and five-eighths inch grip in stock, so I was able to start over and get the racket done for the customer.

I PUT THE FINISHED racket up on the peg for pickup, stretched my arms high in the air, and yawned loudly. I moved to the window that looked out over the front parking lot and noticed Ken and Renee walking across Wilshire, probably having gone to All American Burger for lunch. They strolled across the parking lot, then Ken veered away from her towards his car, apparently going somewhere, maybe home for the day. Just as he was about to open his car door, Renee trotted over, put her hands on his shoulders, stretched up and gave him a kiss. Then she skipped away toward the front door of the store. *Are you kidding me?* I blinked my eyes and shook my head, not believing what I had just seen. *She acted heartbroken over me two days ago!* I calmed myself and thought maybe there was an explanation.

She entered the store and I almost marched straight into the Ski Department to confront her, but thought better of it. *It isn't as if she has any obligation to me. We were never boyfriend—girlfriend. I cut the relationship off before it ever started. Then why am I so upset?* She was with Ken so quickly. I felt betrayed. The dinner at La Barbera's, the words and kisses we exchanged. Was it all a lie?

I clocked out for lunch, walked through the Ski Department without seeing her, and continued out the back door to my car. I drove the short distance to Bay Cities Italian Delicatessen and picked up a turkey and cheese sandwich to go. When I returned, she stood near the back entrance at one of the circular racks for ski pants, straightening, re-hanging, and organizing the sizes.

"Hi Paul, what's for lunch?" she said, her voice hollow and detached.

Eyeing her closely, I couldn't detect much from her expression. "Turkey and cheese from Bay Cities. Hey, can you come back with me for a second? I want to ask you a question," I said.

Renee followed me into the supply room. "So what's the deal with you and Ken?" I asked, bluntly.

"Wow, news travels fast around this place. What do you want to know? He asked me out about a week ago. After our little chat, I went back to him and told him okay, so we went to a movie last night. Did I act properly? Does that course of events meet your approval?" I detected more than a hint of bitterness.

I felt numb. I couldn't be angry with her. "Yes, of course. You didn't do anything wrong."

"Well, thank goodness I didn't upset you."

"I'm sorry, Renee. I'm really sorry for the way this turned out."

She looked at me, started to say something, but then just shook her head and walked out.

I clocked out at precisely six o'clock and went straight back to the Ocean Plaza Hotel, ready to try my Plan B all over again. I brushed my hair before leaving the car, grabbed two tennis rackets I had brought with me from Buck's, took a deep breath, and walked into the lobby. I immediately looked to the reception desk to see if either the man or the woman who had been there earlier were still there. Neither was—only one girl was behind the counter. Given that I was already dressed in tennis clothes, I thought it would be a nice touch to carry a couple rackets, make it look as if I had just finished playing a match, and was returning to my room.

I stood at the dark mahogany counter, opened my mouth to commence my script, but the beguiling beauty and friendly smile of the young Asian girl temporarily rendered me speechless.

"May I help you with something?" she said.

"Yes, um … my name is, uh … Ivan Sokolov, and I'm in Room 518. I rushed out to play tennis earlier and forgot the key in my room. Do you have a spare I can use?"

She smiled at me and said, "Not a problem Mr. Sokolov." Then she turned around, found the box marked 518, took a key out and handed it to me. "How was your game?"

"What's that? Oh, my game. Very good, thank you. Could've served better, but overall very good. Thank you for the key." I hurried away, excited that my scheme had worked this time.

"Uh, Mr. Sokolov?" she called at me.

"Yes?"

"The elevators are that way," she said, pointing the opposite way I had been headed.

"Oh yes, of course," I said as I turned around. "Must be a little light headed from all that exercise." I gave her a quick smile and hoped she didn't notice the deep shade I had blushed.

"Have a good night, Mr. Sokolov."

I rode the elevator to the fifth floor and walked quickly down the hall to Room 518, my heart pounding like a drum, fearing that I would barge in on Ivan Sokolov. I listened with my ear to the door for a few seconds to see if I could detect anyone inside. The Do Not Disturb sign still hung on the knob. "Well, it's now or never," I said audibly as I inserted the key, opened the door a crack, fully expecting to hear someone yell: Who's there?! What do you think you're doing coming in my room without knocking!

But all I heard was the ticking of the clock on the nightstand. I stepped into the room and exhaled, relieved that Sokolov was not there. My relief was quickly replaced by disappointment, the glimmer of hope that Jack would be in the room, now extinguished. The large picture window attracted me like a magnet, momentarily distracting me from the task at hand. The sun was low on the horizon, still a couple hours from sunset, the uneven waters of the Pacific Ocean sparkled like silver glitter. Looking a bit to the north, I could make out the volleyball courts at Sorrento and see that a couple of games were going on. I tore myself away from the mesmerizing view and felt a new fear that had not occurred to me as I was devising my plan. *What if Sokolov arrives now, while I am in his room?* I couldn't claim that I had been given the wrong key by mistake. What could I say? That I was Room Service sent here by mistake? No, the tennis clothes wouldn't work for that one. I'd be up Shit Creek without a paddle. Slightly panicked at the thought, I hurriedly began looking through all of his stuff.

His suitcase lay open on the floor, but I found nothing but clothes and toiletries. The large cherrywood desk near the window had several pieces of paper scattered on top of it. One was the hotel reservation, indicating he had been here since last Friday, the day before Jack disappeared, and that he had reserved the room for a total of ten nights. *Sokolov could be the guy that came to the beach on Saturday, but his name is in the address book, so Jack must know him. And Jack didn't seem to know the guy at the beach.*

Next to the reservation slip sat a folded up dinner receipt from the hotel restaurant. The only other thing on the desk was a flyer listing all the events taking place in the Los Angeles area that week. I searched the closet, dresser drawers, and bathroom, but saw nothing of significance. Anxious to leave, I stepped back into the hallway, locking the door behind me, relieved that I hadn't been found out, but disappointed that I was empty handed. It was time for Plan B number two.

I WAS NOT LOOKING forward to my second Plan B. It would be a little risky, and I would need to get lucky. Since

I didn't know what Sokolov looked like, I couldn't just hang out in the hotel lobby and watch for him. I needed to wait in this fifth floor hallway until he came back to his room, so I could get a look at him. I figured I could read the paper in the lobby until he left the hotel, then try to follow him to wherever he was going. *But when is he coming back? An hour from now? Midnight? Tomorrow night? And once he gets back, how long will I have to wait for him to leave again? And will he lead me to Jack?*

I took a seat on the carpet near the fifth floor elevator doors. I'm sure I looked pretty silly sitting there in my tennis whites, rackets by my side. An older couple looked at me quizzically after they exited the elevator. A few minutes later a man in his mid-forties, dressed in a business suit and carrying a brown leather briefcase, got off the elevator, glanced at me with no reaction, and moved down the hallway towards Room 518. I watched with anticipation as he reached into his pocket for the room key. But he continued past 518 and entered a room further down the hall. Five minutes passed and a couple, appearing to be in their early thirties, the man wearing a dark suit and tie, and the woman a burgundy cocktail dress, emerged from the room opposite 518 and walked towards me. I picked up one of the tennis rackets and pretended to be adjusting the strings, avoiding their look. I was not interested in engaging anyone in a conversation. I hadn't thought of a good story to tell about why I was there.

Another twenty minutes passed, nobody came or left, and I began to question the intelligence of my plan. It had been about forty-five minutes and I was tired of sitting there. It might be hours before he came back to the hotel. And I was getting hungry, not having eaten since the turkey sandwich at two o'clock. Not quite sure what I was going to do later, but knowing that I had to eat, I stood up from my floor seat and pushed the "down" call button. I stepped into the empty elevator and rode it non-stop to the lobby. The doors opened and as I exited, I nearly ran into a man in his mid-fifties, well dressed in tan slacks and a white dress shirt, in an apparent rush to get on the elevator.

As the elevator doors closed, I stood motionless for a second or two. *Could it be him?* The door leading to the stairwell was about ten feet to the left of the second set of elevator doors. I dashed to the door, set the rackets down on the carpet, and raced up five flights of stairs. I came out of the door leading from the stairwell to the fifth floor breathing hard and walked a few steps so that I could look around the corner and down the hallway. The same man I had almost bumped into, hurried down the corridor. Edging back behind the corner to keep my body out of sight, I poked my head out and watched him as he stopped to put his key into a room door. My heart pounded and my forehead was wet with perspiration, perhaps from my sprint up the stairs, but more likely it was nerves. The man stood in the vicinity of Room 518, but I couldn't tell definitely from where I stood. The door closed and I ran down the hall to check it out. *It is 518! I have found Ivan Sokolov!*

It being a little before eight, he could be in his room for the rest of the night. But my instincts told me that since he had been in such a big rush, he would be going out again that night. I calmed my nerves, rode the elevator back down to the lobby, grabbed my rackets which were still lying on the carpet by the stairwell door, and plopped myself down in one of the lobby sofas that afforded me a view of the elevator doors.

"Hello, Mr. Sokolov. Going out for another game?" I had forgotten about the girl at the front desk.

"No ... no, just waiting for a friend. He wanted to borrow the rackets," I said, proud of myself that I had thought of something plausible.

"Oh, I see," she said, seemingly satisfied.

In the opposite direction of the elevators was the hotel bar and restaurant. After about twenty minutes of trying to make up my mind, I took the chance and left my post to order some food. I rationalized it, knowing I might be there a few hours waiting for Sokolov to leave, if he left at all. If I didn't eat, a couple hours from now they might have to drag my hunger ravaged corpse from the lobby couch.

I jogged the short distance to enter the busy restaurant and picked up a menu from the hostess. Two couples sat nearby, waiting for their tables. In a separate room off to the right, the bar was also packed, but I wedged past several patrons to get the bartender's attention and order potato skins. I told him I was waiting for a friend in the lobby and he said that he could serve them to me out there. Ten minutes later, I nervously munched on the appetizer, complete with melted cheddar cheese and bacon bits. I kept a wary eye on the elevator doors, hoping that I hadn't missed him in the five minutes I had been gone.

IVAN SOKOLOV stepped off the elevator as I finished my fourth skin, and his sudden appearance startled me to the extent that a small piece of potato must have gone down the wrong pipe, causing me to start coughing.

"Are you okay, Mr. Sokolov?" the girl at the reception desk called over to me.

But the real Ivan Sokolov thought the question was for him and he turned around with a puzzled look on his face, and said, "I'm fine."

Luckily he was still in a big hurry and pushed the revolving doors to let himself out without engaging the receptionist in any further conversation. I picked up my rackets, waved to the bewildered girl, and followed him out. In a stroke of luck, he had valet parked his car, allowing me time to get in my car and prepare to follow him. The visitor's parking where I parked was only a few yards from where his car would be delivered. Sitting in my car, I watched Sokolov wait for the valet, pacing back and forth, checking his watch, looking like a nervous businessman late for a meeting. I gripped the steering wheel tightly with both hands, tense with the understanding that I was about to get more deeply involved in something that might be out of my league. I worried about losing track of him. I had never attempted to follow someone surreptitiously. I was more concerned about keeping him in sight than being discreet, imagining that he would not be suspecting anyone to follow him.

The valet arrived with a new, navy blue Olds Cutlass, with rental car license plates. Sokolov handed the valet a bill, then climbed in the car as I started up my VW and backed out of my space. He drove halfway around the fountain, passing me in the process, and pulled onto Ocean heading north. Directly behind him, I rapped my fist softly against the wheel. He continued past Arizona Avenue to Wilshire, where he turned right and headed east. Several blocks later we were approaching Buck's Sporting Goods on the right hand side. *His turn signal is on! He's going to Buck's?!* I followed him into the rear parking lot and parked my car in exactly the same spot I had left nearly three hours before.

Staying in my car, my mouth grew dry as Ivan Sokolov got out of the Cutlass and headed straight for Buck's trailer. He paused momentarily at the entrance and Buck poked his head out, smiling broadly. They shook hands, Ivan climbed the two steps, ducked his head as he passed through the tiny door, then disappeared into a meeting with a man I thought I knew.

34

How does Buck know Ivan Sokolov? Why is he meeting with a Russian agent? Or is Sokolov just a German car dealer? I had a sick feeling in the pit of my stomach that I shouldn't have confided in him about Jack's disappearance. Waiting anxiously in the car, I tossed around the idea of marching into Buck's trailer and demanding that Sokolov tell me what had happened to Jack.

Whether it be from a lack of bravery or an abundance of common sense, I ultimately decided not to make an appearance in the trailer. I chose instead to wait until Sokolov left and follow him again. Staying incognito seemed like a better idea, at least while there was hope that he would lead me to Jack, although more than likely he would return to the hotel and I'd be right back where I started. For now, I was just going to sit in my car and wait ... wait until they were done with their meeting.

The store closed and employees began to trickle out. Hopefully they would not pay me any attention. I was trying to come up with a story that would explain my presence when Ken Slater's car pulled into the parking lot. He parked in the space directly facing me and I slumped down in my seat, hoping I would avoid notice. No such luck. He got out of his car and walked over to mine. I rolled down the window as he approached.

Leaning his forearm on the top of the door, he bent over to look in the window. "What are you doing here?" he asked.

"I was gonna ask you the same question," I said flatly, still slouching.

"Oh, I'm picking up Renee. We're gonna go grab something to eat. By the way, no hard feelings right? I mean … what happened with you guys? First she said she didn't want to go out with me because of you, then the very next day she says she's not seeing you anymore."

I turned my head and looked at him coldly. *He's two years older than me!* "I thought she was a little young."

Oblivious to my point, Ken answered cheerfully, "Well, that's good for me I guess."

Staring out the front windshield, I took a deep breath and flexed my fingers several times, until the urge to strangle him had passed. "Yeah, good for you."

Ken straightened and tucked in a part of his shirt. "You never answered my first question. What are you doing here?"

"I'm waiting to talk to Buck about something. He's got someone in there right now."

"Oh. Who's in there?"

"Dunno."

"Hmm … well, see you around," he said, and strolled away towards the rear entrance of the store. A few minutes later he emerged with Renee. As Ken unlocked the passenger side door,

Renee turned toward me and our eyes met briefly. I raised my hand to wave to her, but she quickly looked away, then climbed into Ken's car.

I SPENT the next half hour fidgeting in my car, alternately turning the radio on to distract myself, and then turning it off to quietly think about what Buck and Sokolov could be discussing. Angry with Buck and frustrated at not being able to do anything but wait, I became a little bolder. I left my car and tiptoed over to the trailer. Although the door was closed, the window on the end of the trailer was open. Nearing the trailer, I moved to the back and crouched beneath the window. If Sokolov were to have left right then, I could probably have moved to the other side to stay out of his sight. But getting back to my car without him noticing me, would be next to impossible, which meant I would likely lose the opportunity to follow him.

The voices were audible, but the whirring of the fan inside made it difficult to understand much. Sokolov did most of the talking. He spoke of wanting to go home and something about being almost done with the building. I could only guess that maybe the building he spoke of had to do with Jack. After a few minutes of careful listening, I gave up and crept quietly back to my car, wanting to avert the disaster of him leaving the trailer while I was eavesdropping.

It was now nine forty-five and the parking lot had emptied except for our three cars and the trailer. With the lot this empty, I stuck out like a sore thumb. He would certainly notice me if I followed him right out of the lot. So I drove my car into a spot on the street, in front of the store. I couldn't see the door to Buck's trailer since it faced south, away from me, but I had a clear view of the Olds Cutlass, and that was all that mattered.

A LITTLE AFTER ten o'clock Ivan Sokolov opened his car door, got in, and accelerated out of the lot, heading east on Wilshire. *Okay, here we go. Don't lose him!* I floored the gas pedal, shifting quickly from first to second to third gear, trying to keep up. One car separated us, and my adrenaline kicked in, excited that he was going the opposite direction of the Ocean Plaza Hotel. He continued on Wilshire until Barry Avenue where he made a right turn.

Approaching the intersection at Olympic Boulevard, Sokolov stopped as the light turned red. No cars separated us, so I had no choice but to pull up directly behind him. Shortly after we stopped, his car suddenly lurched forward. The screeching squeal of rubber on asphalt resonated as the Cutlass jetted across the intersection through the red light. Horns blared as he narrowly missed two cars. My mouth hung half open, stunned, watching as he sped off northbound. *I've got to follow, and now!* Unlike Sokolov, I inched forward, waiting for a safe opening across the heavily trafficked street. Every time a small gap developed in the westbound traffic, the eastbound lanes were clogged. Seconds ticked by. I could still see the taillights of his car about a block away, but they were rapidly getting smaller. I had to go now or he would be lost.

There was no real opening, but I stepped on the gas pedal anyway. Brakes squealed and a car skidded to a stop a few feet from my driver's side door. Halfway across now, I continued into the eastbound lanes, my eyes darting to the right. My foot pushed heavily on the gas, willing my gutless car to spurt across. I closed my eyes and said a brief prayer. Then came the jolt … a staggering, numbing jolt. The sickening crunch of collapsing metal surrounded me.

I cupped my face in my hands. I wiggled my toes, moved my right, and then my left leg, up and down. I raised my arms and rotated both shoulders. Nothing hurt. As far as I could tell, I was unscathed. I didn't exactly feel like I had won the lottery, but I said a prayer of thanks nonetheless. I lifted my head and looked out the window. My car faced west in the eastbound lane.

My Squareback got the worst of it. After examining the damage to my car, I made my way over to the light blue Mustang. Cars filed by slowly in the right lane, everybody taking their turn at viewing the damage. I glanced down Barry Avenue hoping for a glimpse of Sokolov's car. But he was long gone. The Mustang smashed the right rear fender of my car, spinning me around. The Ford, being heavier than my Volkswagon, incurred little damage, just a broken headlight and a small dent in the chrome bumper.

The older, gray haired, black woman remained in her car, her forehead resting on the steering wheel.

I knocked on the window. "Are you okay?"

She raised her head to look at me, her eyes more frightened than angry. She cranked down the window. "What's the matter with you, boy?! Are you crazy? Tryin' to kill an old woman like that."

"Sorry, ma'am. I'm really sorry," I said. "We should move our cars out of the street."

Luckily, my car seemed to drive okay. I pulled to the side of the street and we both got out of our cars. She moved slowly and I noticed her hands shaking. Now she was angry, and probably convinced I didn't have all my marbles.

"Ma'am, are you sure you're okay? Why don't you let me call an ambulance—let the doctor check you out."

She was hunched over, leaning against her car. She looked at me sideways with a sneer. "I'm just fine. You're the one that needs checkin'."

I went back to my car and found an old envelope and a pencil to write down my insurance information. I tore the envelope in half and gave it to her with the pencil so she could do the same. She searched through her purse, muttering to herself, finally locating her insurance card.

A police squad car arrived and two officers got out. One spoke to me while the other spoke to the woman. The four of us grouped together on the sidewalk next to my car. After the cops were satisfied we were okay, and that no alcohol was involved, they wrote me a ticket for running the red light, then left. The lady drove away without saying good-bye. I stood by my car, hanging my head, the door open, one foot on the running board. *What now?*

How had Sokolov known I was following? I got in my car and drove slowly down Barry, searching for the Cutlass. But it was hopeless. After two blocks, I stopped the car in the middle of the street and slammed my palms against the steering wheel. Damn it! *Damn it! DAMN IT!*

I stared up at the beige, vinyl material with a gaping tear that lined the ceiling of my car. I flashed back to Sokolov climbing into Buck's trailer, shaking his hand and smiling. I jammed down the pedal and sped away. I needed to have a little discussion with Mr. Braddock.

THE WINDOW of Buck's trailer glowed dimly, indicating he was still there. I parked my car, got out and slammed the door shut. I marched straight to the doorway, and didn't stop to knock. I blasted into the small space like a tidal wave had carried me in.

"Well, what would be bringin' you back here so late, young man?" Buck greeted me, his ruddy, red face showing the effects of a day's worth of whiskey and waters.

My jaw muscles tightened, my mouth a thin line, as I stared at Buck. "Why did Ivan Sokolov come to see you?"

Buck's smile disappeared. "How'd you know that? And how would you be knowin' Ivan Sokolov?"

"God damn it, Buck. I told you all about that business with the guy coming to the beach and taking my friend away. And Sokolov is mixed up with it. Now, what in the hell was he doing here?!"

Buck extended his arms, a burning cigarette tucked between two fingers, palms facing down. "Calm down, son. Sit yourself down." He motioned to the vinyl bench seat opposite him.

I crossed my arms tightly against my chest. "Sorry, I don't feel like sitting."

"Okay, suit yourself. Sokolov is a movie producer from Germany. He's got a big ol' production goin' on and they hired me to find 'em an old warehouse for one of their scenes. That's why you was drivin' me around the other day. Tonight's the first time I've set eyes on him. He came by to pay me."

Dizziness set in. I felt disoriented. Was I totally on the wrong track? Did Jack know Sokolov because of his acting work? I asked, "So you found him a warehouse?"

"Yep—over there on Barry near the freeway. I hooked him up with the property owner and they commenced workin' there the very next day."

I unfolded my arms and looked pleadingly at him. "Shit, Buck. You swear you're telling me the truth?"

He put the glass to his lips and tilted it all the way back, draining the last drops. "Paul, listen here. I don't know this feller from Adam. He tracked *me* down—got my name from a director friend of mine. Everybody in the business knows, if'n you need a spot to shoot in Santa Monica, call ol' Buck. He calls me and says he needs a small empty warehouse. Paid me five grand, all cash. When he came by tonight I figured I'd be neighborly and give him some whiskey. He ended up staying quite a spell. Musta gone through half a pack of cigarettes chatting about how he couldn't wait to get home. Said he's originally from Russia, but lives in Munich now."

I finally took a seat at the table across from Buck. "Hmm … what kind of movie is he working on?"

"Couldn't tell ya. He didn't really talk much about that and I didn't ask." He took a long draw on his cigarette, then snuffed it out in the crowded ashtray in the middle of the table.

"Well, can you give me the address of the warehouse? I gotta go pay him a visit."

He took a manila folder off the shelf next to the table and opened it. "2742 Barry Avenue. Right between Olympic and the freeway. But listen here, son. It's time to call the law. You could be gettin' yourself into a mess o' trouble."

"I know, I know. But I gotta at least see if Jack's there first. There's no reason to call the cops if they're making a movie. I'll be careful. I just need to look in a window or something to see if he's there."

"Then how 'bout I go with you? We can poke around a bit, then come back here and call the police if we need to." He reached for his cowboy hat and held it on the table in front of him, readying himself to go.

"Thanks for the offer, but you really don't need to do that. I'll be very careful, I promise."

I grabbed the sheet of paper with the address and said good night. Grimacing as I looked again at the crushed right rear panel of my car, I got in and began the drive back to the industrial neighborhood.

THE OUTLINES of the hulking brick and metal structures were barely visible, lit by the dim yellow glow of the well-spaced streetlights. The buildings were home to manufacturers and warehousers of a variety of goods, from furniture to food products to clothing, but at this time of night it may as well have been a ghost town.

I was the only car on Barry as far as I could tell, so I slowed to a crawl and squinted in the poor lighting trying to make out the addresses. On a dilapidated, corrugated metal building, I saw the numbers "2742" spray painted sloppily in the upper right hand corner. My fingers tightly gripped the steering wheel as I continued past the building for another block before stopping to park. I slowly opened the car door, got out, then closed it quietly before starting back towards the warehouse.

There were two windows on the front side of the building, one on each side of the front door. I cupped my hands up to the window to shield the reflection from the streetlamps as I peered in. Through the slits of the open blinds I could make out a couple barren desks, wooden chairs, and metal file cabinets. It didn't look like anybody had worked there for a while, as best as I could tell in the darkness. I put my hand on the doorknob and surprisingly was able to twist it counterclockwise. But although the doorknob itself was not locked, the deadbolt above it held the door firmly in place. I let out a deep breath, almost thankful that the door didn't open. The last thing I wanted to do was go inside that building.

Realizing I could learn nothing further from the front of the building, I walked down the driveway on the side of the building. I tiptoed along the southern wall, not seeing the Olds, but increasingly certain that this is where Sokolov had been headed. Moving away from the street, and away from the streetlights, I edged into darkness, magnified by a night thick with clouds blocking out the moon and the stars. About twenty-five yards from the sidewalk, maybe halfway to the rear parking lot, I froze in place. I remembered Sokolov bolting through the red light, obviously aware that he was being followed. My heart beat like the wings of a caged bird, the magnitude of the task before me crushing my confidence. *What am I going to do? I'm following some guy who's probably a Russian agent into a pitch dark alleyway.* I turned right around and started taking long strides back towards my car. The walk turned into a jog until I thankfully arrived at my car and got inside, breathing rapidly and perspiring freely in the cool night air.

Secure in my car, I tried to gather my thoughts. I swallowed hard, licking my lips. My heart returned to slightly above a normal pace. No cars were in sight and not a soul roamed about, the street deathly quiet and still. After several minutes, I regained my confidence and convinced myself to at least get to the rear of the building and see if there was a window. If I could just confirm Jack was in there, then I could call the police and have them take over. I remembered that Jerry Moberg had made me promise not to contact the police, but maybe the police wouldn't find out about the sale of the data to the Russians. Jack certainly wouldn't volunteer it. Ivan Sokolov wouldn't talk. They might do investigation into Sokolov's background and find something, or if they researched Jack's bank account, they would get suspicious. So, there was a risk, but it was a necessary one if the alternative was Jack's life. I just needed to find out if he was in there.

I thought it might be best to drive down the alley to the rear of the building. At least if I accidentally confronted someone as I proceeded to the back, I could speed away to safety. But then I realized, they would be able to hear my car from inside the building. After ten minutes of sitting in my car analyzing the situation, I had come full circle. The best thing to do was exactly what I had started out to do when I first got there. I took a long, quivering breath and clamped my lips tightly together. *Oh how I wish Tommy was here!* My courage would increase dramatically if it was the two of us.

I hurried down the deserted street, nervously glancing to my left, right, and behind, checking for onlookers. I took a right turn at the building and proceeded the same way I had gone before. I felt less frightened this time, carefully making my way in the darkness to the rear of the property, moving with admirable stealth. The side wall, which extended about twenty feet up to the roof, was solid, uninterrupted, corrugated metal. There were no windows and therefore no hope of learning anything about what was going on inside.

I reached the end of the building, and the rear parking lot. *The Olds Cutlass!* And next to it, a newer model Chevy Malibu and a Ford Fairlane. The back wall of the building, like the side, did not have any windows. It did however, have a large loading door, looking to be about fifteen feet wide and fifteen feet high. Built into the metal loading door was a standard size pedestrian door. From this closed door I detected signs of life, white light from within, escaping into the outside darkness, tracing the outline of the smaller door frame. In addition to the perimeter, a jagged crack in the lower half of the door looked like a bolt of lightning, the light peeking out there as well. I moved slowly, now on tiptoes, to the loading door. Any weariness from the lack of sleep of the previous two nights was completely forgotten. My heart thumped in my throat. *Was Jack in there?* I wiped perspiration from my brow with my shirt sleeve.

Once at the door, I lowered myself to my hands and knees onto the fine gravel of the parking lot, hoping to see something through the split in the metal. I put my right eye up to the one-eighth inch crack and squinted, trying to steady myself as my body trembled. *Somebody moved! And I hear voices! But what are they saying?!*

WHAM! THE CRUSHING blow came without warning. Pain plunged daggers through my head and neck. At once, my cheek pressed into sharp edged gravel, the foot on top of my head not allowing me to move. Blackness filled my consciousness. *Where am I?*

The voice snapped me out of it. "So, tennis boy, first hotel, then follow me, now peeking in building. I guess it's time for you to join party."

He kicked me twice in rapid succession, first to my ribs and then to the side of my head, raking my raw, bloodied face across the gravel. I became aware of a door opening. I was being held by my ankles, dragged into a brightly lit room. Then ... nothing but darkness.

I awoke to bright sunshine coming through a skylight in the roof, lying on my back on the cold cement floor. My wrists were taped together uncomfortably behind me. My ankles and even my knees were tightly wrapped. Gray metallic duct tape covered my mouth, wrapping all the way around the back of my head, connecting in a full circle. To my right, securely fastened upright to a heavy wooden chair, was a man, who even in my hazy state of consciousness, I realized was Jack Rosen.

The man didn't look much like Jack, his bloodied head hung forward and slightly to the right, making it more difficult for me to get a good look at him. But I did have a clear look at his bare feet, legs, and the same beach trunks he had worn the day he disappeared. *Is he asleep? Unconscious? Dead?*

The warehouse was as lifeless as the offices had appeared the night before. There were several pieces of heavy machinery, possibly metalworking machinery, partially covered with tarps and looking like they had not been used for a while. The lower half of the walls were covered with spatters of dark brown grease, presumably from the machinery when the factory was operating.

As far as I could tell, there was nobody in the building but me and Jack. The more alert I became, the more I felt the pain from the beating I had received. *It hurts when I breathe … possibly broken ribs.* My entire head throbbed, not just a headache, but it hurt on the outside as well as the inside. I rolled over on my side to relieve the pain in my wrists and hands, from an entire night of my body weight pressing them against the concrete floor.

At first I detected no movement from Jack, but after watching carefully I was relieved to see his chest rise and fall as he took regular breaths. I made as loud a sound as I could without being able to open my mouth, but got no response from him. Trying to think of what I could do, the answer was painfully obvious … absolutely nothing. The duct tape was firmly in place. I could barely move my fingers. They had wrapped the tape all the way from my wrists to my knuckles.

A strong smell of urine, from Jack no doubt, permeated my senses. I realized quickly that I was about to add my own contribution to the stink. After a few more minutes of pointlessly holding it, I had no choice but to relieve myself, soaking my tennis shorts. Tears streamed from my eyes, rolling off my cheeks to the warehouse floor. Then I heard a muffled grunt from Jack's direction. I lifted my head to see him looking down on me, his eyes glazed with terror. No words were possible, but his eyes communicated volumes. They were the eyes of a panicked parent. Before, it was just *his* life he had to worry about. Now *my* life was in danger and he was feeling responsible.

Jack was barely recognizable. His formerly round puffy face was now gaunt with sunken cheeks. It had been two weeks since he had gone missing, and who knows if he had been given any food. His left eye was swollen half shut and dried blood covered the majority of his face, obscuring numerous cuts and bruises.

THE METAL warehouse man-door creaked open, and I lifted my head to see four men enter the building. As they approached, I recognized one as being Ivan Sokolov and another as the man who had taken Jack from the beach. The other two men I did not know.

Sokolov said, "Good morning, my stinky friends." He kicked me softly in the leg, then turned toward Jack. "Mr. Rosen, are you glad to have company? Who is this tennis boy, so eager to save you?"

The four men stood in a circle, speaking amongst themselves, presumably in Russian. Two of the four lit up cigarettes. After an extended conversation, the man in the suit from the beach, who Sokolov referred to as Viktor, spoke to Jack in a heavy accent. "In spite our gentle persuasion, you unwilling to share name and location of your partner. We hope you to now reconsider."

They dragged me a few feet so that I was directly in Jack's line of sight. One of the men kneeled next to me and yanked my shirt up around my neck. He inhaled deeply on his cigarette, then lowered the glowing embers slowly, stopping an inch short of my bare chest. He tapped the smoldering stick and hot ashes landed on my nipple. I squeezed my eyes shut, the pain intense. The smell of burning chest hair wafted up to my nostrils. Then he lowered it again and pressed the fiery end between two of my ribs, holding it there until the cigarette was extinguished. "Aaugh!" My involuntary, muffled scream was followed by fresh tears flooding my eyes. Sokolov went to Jack and removed the duct tape from his mouth.

"You bastards! You *fucking* bastards!" The rage filled, raspy voice didn't sound like Jack.

"Why, Mr. Rosen, such language. You might guess what we planning for your friend. Has this improved your memory at all?" Sokolov said.

His jaw muscles taut and teeth clenched, Jack said, "Let ... him ... go. He has nothing to do with any of this. Let him go and I'll tell you what you want to know."

"Well, well. I'm glad you come to your senses. And many thank yous to you, tennis boy. You just what we needed." Sokolov bent down and patted me on the head.

One of the men came up to me, unwrapped the duct tape on my wrists, then removed the tape from my mouth.

"Okay, Mr. Rosen, we unwrap your friend's knees and ankles and he walk out of here, soon as you tell what we need to know."

Listening to the conversation, I came to the conclusion that they had been trying to get Jack to tell them the name and whereabouts of Jerry Moberg. Moberg had been feeding them false information for nearly two years and having discovered that, they needed to have a word with him. I am sure that their objective was to "convince" Jerry Moberg that it was in his best interests to begin giving them accurate information.

"Unwrap his legs. You stay here with me. Let him walk out the door ... then I'll give you a name and an address," Jack said.

The men laughed at Jack's boldness. Sokolov said, "Mr. Jack Rosen, I'm afraid we know you too well. You are stubborn man. Once the boy gone, you will not help us. You must tell us first what we need to know, then we release him. You have my word."

"Fuck you," Jack said.

Again, the men laughed. Two of them came and held my arms to the ground. A new cigarette was lit and this time Sokolov kneeled next to me and slowly lowered the burning embers to my face, directing it straight for my left eye.

I screamed, "Stop! Stop! I know the name of the person you are looking for! And I can direct you to his house."

Sokolov pulled the cigarette away, raised his eyebrows and said, "Is this the truth? How could you possibly know about this?"

Jack stared at me with a look of amazement, but said nothing.

Breathing rapidly and grimacing from the pain in my side, I said, "When Jack went missing, I went to his house and searched through all of his things. I was there when you broke into the house, hiding under the bed." I paused to catch my breath. Everyone stared at me, waiting for me to continue. "I found his address book and called everybody in it. Eventually I found the guy you're looking for. I went to his house and he told me the whole story."

Jack slowly shook his head. "Paul, don't you tell them. Don't do it, Paul."

I strained my neck to lift my head and meet his eyes. "It's the only way Jack ... the only way out of this."

"You wiser than Mr. Rosen, tennis boy. The name and address please? Or would you prefer another cigarette?" Sokolov said, planting his foot on my chest.

"I can give you the name, but I'll have to take you to the house. I know where he lives but don't know the address," I said.

"Don't, Paul ..." Before Jack could finish, one of the men pressed a fresh strip of tape across his mouth.

After a brief discussion in Russian, Sokolov decided that two of them would stay with Jack while he and Viktor would go with me.

"How do I know no harm will come to Jack?" I said, trying to sound strong, but the words coming out weakly.

"We have no interest to harm Mr. Rosen. We only want find his partner. We must hold him here to guarantee your cooperation. And I assure you, if you not lead us where we want go, harm *will* come to Mr. Jack Rosen," Sokolov said, gently slapping Jack on the cheek.

And with that, Viktor took the tape off my knees and ankles, and the three of us walked out the door.

Ivan Sokolov sat with me in the backseat of the tobacco scented rental car while Viktor drove. I directed them north on Barry back to Wilshire, and then west towards the ocean. Although Viktor did not seem to be in a rush, he inexplicably rolled through a light at 14th Street that had turned red a couple seconds earlier. I heard the abbreviated siren of a police squad car and turned to see him right behind us with the rooftop lights flashing red. *They're pulling us over!* Viktor steered the car over to the right hand curb and stopped. Sokolov reached into his inside suit pocket and pulled out a revolver no bigger than the length of his hand.

I flinched in pain as he jammed the gun into my sore ribs and said, "You say nothing. Understand? Nothing. And don't even look to him. Keep your eyes straight ahead."

The officer approached along the driver's side as Viktor rolled down the window. "License and registration, please."

Viktor spoke rapidly in Russian to the officer and then said, "No English."

Upon hearing this, the policeman peered into the back seat at me and Sokolov. "How about you two? Anybody speak English?"

Sokolov pressed the gun a little harder into my ribs and said something in Russian as he shook his head. As tempted as I was to try to alert the cop, I said nothing and shook my head also.

"Let me see your passport then. You understand passport?" the officer asked Viktor.

He reached into his pocket and handed his passport to the cop, who spent a couple minutes looking at it, then handed it back and motioned to us that we could leave. Viktor edged back into traffic and Sokolov thankfully put the revolver back in his pocket.

"Well done, Mr. Tennis. You smarter than I thought," Sokolov said.

Arriving at Ocean Avenue, I directed them to turn right, and after a couple blocks to veer left down the California Incline. Once on PCH, I had them enter the Sorrento Beach parking lot.

"What you trying to do? This where we picked up Rosen at beach." Sokolov, who had been quiet since the episode with the policeman, was suddenly irritated.

"The person you want lives in that house right there," I said, pointing north. "We can't get into his driveway unless he is notified in advance. We can park here and walk over to the gate. His name is Jerry ... Jerry Norbert. He knows me and will let me in."

I knew I was taking a big chance. I had told Jennifer the whole story about Jerry Moberg and Jack's disappearance but had no idea if she would realize what was happening right now. *Is she even home?* My hope was that she would sense the danger of the situation and call the police. The heavy Saturday traffic of Pacific Coast Highway whizzed past us as we walked from the parking lot to the front gate. I pressed the intercom buzzer. A few seconds passed with no response, so I pushed the button again.

This time Edward answered, "Yes, may I help you?"

I silently thanked God. "Hello, Edward, this is Paul Townsend."

"Yes, Mr. Townsend, how are you? Come right in," he said. The gate opened and we crossed the short path to the front door. I rang the bell and within a few seconds, Jennifer opened the door with a big smile, quickly turning to a look of puzzlement.

"Hello, Paul. Who are these people?" she asked, probably a little annoyed that I would arrive unannounced with two additional visitors.

"Hello, Mrs. *Norbert*. These are a couple friends of mine. We are all here to see your husband. Is Jerry at home by any chance?" I spoke slowly, hoping to give Jennifer a little longer to figure out what was going on. Her baffled expression remained and she said nothing in response for several seconds.

Then, her eyes widened. She placed her hand flush over her mouth, then lowered it, and said, "Oh, yes ... of course. Please come in. I'll go get him."

We stepped inside the foyer and waited as Jennifer moved quickly up the staircase. Sokolov looked around wide eyed and whispered something to his friend. I imagined they were thinking that they were paying this guy too much if he could afford a house like this. Feeling more confident of my plan now, I assumed Jennifer had gone upstairs to call 911. *What are these guys gonna do when the police show up? Will they shoot it out with the cops? Will they try to take us hostage?*

A little sooner than I would have expected, Jennifer reemerged and came down the stairs. "My husband will be with you shortly. May I offer you something to drink?"

"No, thank you. We are in quite a hurry. We wait here for Mr. Norbert," Sokolov said.

Suddenly Jennifer reached behind her, pulled a gun from her waistband, and held it with both hands, pointed at the Russians. "Put your hands in the air, *now*!"

Sokolov and Viktor didn't react to her words, just stared at her, disbelieving, frozen in shock.

Jennifer took two steps toward them, her arms extended and muscles taut, the gun unwavering. "I said *now*! Don't think I won't use this thing!"

This time they did as they were told, put their hands in the air, still with a startled look on their faces.

"Jennifer, they've got guns. I'll get 'em," I said.

She continued to point the gun at first one and then the other. I went behind and frisked them, taking a small pistol out of each of their suit pockets. After taking the guns I frisked each of them again, wanting to be sure they had no other weapons. Satisfied they were clean, I stepped away, put one of the pistols in my pocket, and pointed the other directly at Sokolov.

"Hey Edward!" I shouted, not knowing where in the house he might be. He heard me and entered from the backyard, oblivious to all that had taken place. He stopped short after passing through the double doors and arched his eyebrows.

"Oh, my. Miss Warren, should I contact the police?" he asked.

"No, don't do that," I answered for Jennifer. "I was just wondering if you had some duct tape I could borrow."

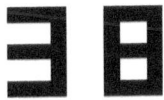

Santa Monica, California
Saturday morning
July 30, 1977

Edward did indeed have duct tape and I'm afraid I overdid it a bit, almost making living mummies out of both of them. After I related the situation to Jennifer, she insisted on calling her bodyguard, Jake Morris, who she rightly said would be very helpful when we returned to the warehouse. Jennifer hired Jake on a job by job basis, whenever she attended an event with lots of people. At times, she had him accompany her on location for filming, knowing that once people found her, the crowds would gather, and there was the potential for crazies. I was thinking it would have been nice to have him a couple nights ago when Mad Max paid his visit.

The original structure of Jennifer Ryan's house dated to the 1920's and although it had been remodeled several times, the current footprint of the house was the same as the original, with one exception, the garage. Jennifer had lengthened the small two car garage to accommodate her limousine. It was one of two cars she used in Los Angeles, and depending on the occasion, would either have Edward drive or a driver she hired on an hourly basis. The other car, squeezed into the garage alongside the limo, was a cream colored Porsche 912. She drove that herself for most of her everyday errands.

I finished putting one additional strip of tape around Viktor's ankles, then stood over them admiring my work. Jennifer came back into the foyer from the kitchen.

"If it's okay with you, when Jake gets here, we'll load these guys in their rental car and take them back to the warehouse," I said. I originally thought about taking the limo, but decided it was a dumb idea. It was too recognizable, and the Santa Monica Police knew it as Jennifer's. While I was busy getting the guys tied up, I had been going over in my mind a plan to overtake the other two guys once we returned to the warehouse. Entering the building quietly without them noticing us would be the key to a successful surprise attack.

"Sure, as long as we can fit. Edward will stay here. What kind of car is it?" she said.

"We? Uh, no, I don't want you going. There's no reason for you to get more involved in this thing," I said.

Jennifer looked at me like my Border Collie used to look at me when I tried to feed her a grape. "Paul, really. Don't you think I'm already about as involved as one could possibly be? I'm the reason these guys are taped up. You might just need my help. Did you think about that?"

"Yeah … but."

She stood in front of me with her hands on her hips, her delicate mouth set like a steel trap. "But what? I *am* going. What kind of car is it?"

"It's an Olds Cutlass. We'll fit, no problem. When Jake gets here, we'll discuss our strategy. Hopefully we'll be able to surprise the other two guys, get them tied up and get Jack out of there. Beyond that I'm not sure what the next step should be."

In the middle of my conversation with Jennifer, it occurred to me that I still wore the urine soaked tennis shorts. I sidled up to Edward and asked if he had something I could change in to. He took me up to his room where I inspected an array of pants, all about six inches too short for me. He was not big on wearing shorts, but luckily had one pair of khaki hiking shorts that fit reasonably well when I put on a belt to hold them up. After changing in the bathroom, I spent several minutes removing tiny pieces of gravel still embedded in my face. I washed the raw wounds with soap and water. It hurt like hell. Returning downstairs, I found Jennifer in the TV room, away from the Russians, who were noisy in spite of the tape over their mouths. I got out one of the two small pistols I had confiscated, looked it over cautiously, not familiar with guns and nervous just to be holding it. I went over and sat next to Jennifer on the couch.

"Here, let me take a look at that," she said.

I handed the pistol to her and watched as she examined it, impressed by her apparent confidence in handling the firearm. She had the somewhat larger gun from her bedroom lying next to her. Looking over the Russian gun carefully she said, "I'm not familiar with it, but it's loaded, I know that much. Why don't you leave them on the coffee table and we'll have Jake look at them when he gets here. We don't want any accidents.

I leaned forward with my elbows on my knees, hands clenched together. "Where did you learn so much about guns?"

"Remember I told you about that part I played? Well, they had to teach me how to shoot and get me comfortable using it so I looked like I knew what the heck I was doing in the film.

After we finished the movie, I got myself a gun for the house, in case of an intruder or something."

"That was so awesome how you whipped it out after you came down the stairs. Those guys didn't know what hit 'em." I smiled and shook my head.

THE GATE BUZZER announced Jake's arrival. Jennifer had told him ahead of time to park in the Sorrento lot. Jake Morris looked the way you would expect a bodyguard to look. He was not tall, maybe five-nine or ten, I would say. But he was thick with muscles, his neck only slightly less in diameter than his head. He wore a tight fitting black t-shirt, but then again I suppose when you are built the way Jake was built, every t-shirt is tight fitting. He had on denim pants, also black, and also rather tight fitting. Jake smiled when Jennifer introduced us, and it occurred to me that I was glad he was on my side. His greased, slicked back hair matched his black clothing, as did his eyes, which immediately shifted to the prone bodies of the two Russians.

"So what have we here?" Jake asked to no one in particular, tapping his shoe lightly on Sokolov's shoulder. I filled in Jake on most of the details. Jennifer had not told him much of anything on the phone, just that she needed him to come over immediately.

"That's the whole story and that's the reason we don't want to call the police," I said.

"And what happens to these guys?" Jake asked, taking a slow circular walk around them.

"I think we should take them back over there and leave 'em. We can't keep them here and we can't turn 'em over to the cops. Let me worry about that later," I said to Jake as Jennifer and Edward stood by listening.

Jennifer said, "Before we go, Jake, come look at these."

We walked into the TV room and Jake picked up one of the pistols on the coffee table. "These what those guys were carrying?"

"Yep," I answered.

Jake confirmed they were loaded and said they were German made. He engaged the safety on both weapons and handed them to me, explaining how to disengage the safety if needed. "You should take these with you. One, we don't want any evidence left here. And two, they might come in handy once we get to the warehouse. By the way, Edward, could you get me some Windex and a few paper towels? We're gonna want to erase fingerprints after we're done."

I found the keys to the Olds in Sokolov's pocket and left to retrieve the car from the beach parking lot. Edward opened the gate and the garage door. I backed up their car as close to the limo as possible and opened the trunk. We were hidden from anybody who might be looking from the Highway or from the palisades above by being far enough inside the garage. Jake helped me drag the squirming bodies out of the foyer and dump them into the trunk of the Cutlass, which was large enough for the two Russians to fit with room to spare. I slammed the trunk shut and pulled the car forward a bit so that Edward could close the garage door. Jennifer climbed in front with me and Jake got in back.

WAITING AT A STOPLIGHT, I twisted in my seat to face Jennifer and Jake. I described the layout of the manufacturing building, told him about the empty offices in the front and that they were holding Jack further to the rear of the building, near the back loading door.

"I should be able to get us into that front door," Jake said. "I've picked many a lock and those older deadbolts are usually pretty simple."

This was music to my ears. If we could get into the front office area undetected, it would be much easier to take them by surprise. "That would be so cool if you could do that. That's the ideal way to surprise them, I think. Start out in the front and sneak up on them using the machinery as cover."

I made a right turn on Barry. Being Saturday, the industrial neighborhood was mostly deserted. There were a few cars traveling the street and a couple people coming out of a building two doors down from our destination. I parked about a block past the building, right behind my car. Jake agreed that it would be best to approach the building on foot.

Jennifer walked in front of me on the sidewalk, her revolver tucked into the back waistband of her stretchy blue denim jeans, just as she had carried it when she brought it down the staircase from her bedroom. Next to me, Jake carried his handgun, a good bit larger than Jennifer's, in a brown leather shoulder holster on the outside of his t-shirt. My weapons were the two German pistols, small enough to carry both in my front left pants pocket. I looked up the street, turned to look behind, then, not seeing anyone, pulled out one of the weapons, disengaged the safety, and placed it by itself in my right front pocket. I felt strangely confident as our team of three arrived at the building. I had Jake on one side of me, Jennifer on the other, and a loaded gun at my disposal.

TRUE TO HIS WORD, within five minutes Jake had successfully picked the lock and opened the front door to the building. The three of us tiptoed into the office area. The building had no power, but sunshine coming through the front windows was enough for us to find our way. Jake stopped, turned to me, and mouthed the words, "Which way?"

I shrugged my shoulders and motioned to the left. The short hallway led to a large conference room, a dead end. Jennifer led the way back to the front door and continued down the darkened corridor to the right. Moving away from the windows, it got very dark, and I held my arms straight in front of me to feel the way. We could tell that the hallway made a left hand turn, presumably towards the back warehouse area. Sticking close together, we moved carefully and silently. Caught off guard by the closed door at the end of the hallway, we all ran into each other like a three car pileup in thick fog. I flashed quickly on the Three Stooges and stifled a nervous laugh. I whispered first to Jake and then to Jennifer that this door could be the end of the offices—beyond it, the manufacturing area.

"Let me take a look. I want to see if they're still in the same place as before," I said softly as I edged past Jake towards the door.

Gently and slowly turning the doorknob, I eased the door open a crack. Jack was in the same place as before and the two Russians were about ten yards away, leaning against the metal wall of the building, conversing and smoking cigarettes. I moved back from the door and Jake took my spot. He quickly appraised the situation, then let Jennifer to the front so she could have a look. Jake tapped me on the back and motioned for us to follow him back to the reception area, where we could talk more freely.

Back near the front entrance, Jake gathered us close to him. He placed one hand on my shoulder and the other on Jennifer's as he spoke. "We should all go separately into the warehouse. I'll make my way along the south wall directly towards where they are standing. Paul, you go through the center aisle, and Jennifer, you go along the northern wall. There's enough large machinery in there so that we should have no problem staying hidden. You'll be tempted to peek above the machines to see where you are exactly, but don't do it. The worst thing that could happen is if they see or hear us before we want them to."

He removed his hands from our shoulders and became more animated. I couldn't help but notice the thick, bulging biceps, about the size of my calf muscles, as he moved his hands and arms. He spoke just above a whisper, but his tone impressed upon us the importance of what he said. "Have your guns out, but if we do this right, no shots will need to be fired. When I think the time is right and I'm at that last grinding machine, about twenty feet from them, I'm going to jump up with my gun drawn and yell at them loudly. As soon as you hear me, and not before, pop up with your guns pointed right at them. Stay where you are so you can use the machines for cover in case they decide to start firing, but I'm hoping they'll be caught off guard and give up quickly."

Jake had assumed control, and that was a good thing. Whatever experience he had with this type of thing was certainly more than I had. With nothing further said, we returned down the hallway to the door leading to the plant. Jake went first, slowly opening the door, getting on his hands and knees to stay below the height level of the machinery, and crawling to the right towards the southern wall. I went next, copying Jake, but going straight ahead down a path between two rows of large metal grinding machines. Jennifer followed me and headed left to the far wall, leaving the office door open rather than risk any additional movement which might be detected.

I crawled methodically, hearing the seemingly casual conversation between the Russians. The next movement of my bare knee on the concrete floor landed in what felt like a bed of sharp pointy needles. I stifled an "ouch" and looked down to see that I had found a bunch of metal shavings, remnants from the machine shop. I lifted my knee and brushed them off. Going back to all fours, I was about to continue forward when the silence stopped me. The conversation had ended. *I hear footsteps!*

They're moving! My heart leapt into my throat. I went to one knee and pointed my pistol down the aisle, holding the small gun with both hands to keep it steady. Frozen in place, my heart pounded so loudly I was afraid they could hear it. The Russians passed my field of vision, crossing from right to left, their faces directed straight ahead, not noticing me. They moved towards Jack, close to the northern wall. No longer hearing the footsteps, unsure where they had stopped, I agonized over how their change of location would affect our plan.

A couple more minutes and I had crawled to where the last metal cutting machine stood. Any further and I would be exposed. The Russians were once again talking, but I couldn't tell where they were. I remembered Jake's advice to avoid the temptation to poke my head above the machinery. There was nothing more I could do now but wait. Wait for Jake.

But the Russians were too far away from Jake. I knew it would be risky for him to attempt to subdue them from that distance. I perspired freely, in spite of the coolness of the bare cement floor.

Suddenly, Jennifer screamed, *"Freeze!* Put your hands straight up in the air!"

Next I heard Jake. "C'mon! *Now!* You heard her!" The pounding of his footsteps raced from right to left.

Recovering from the shock of Jennifer initiating everything, I jumped up from behind the machinery and pointed my weapon at them, slowly stepping towards them. The two Russians stood with their hands in the air as Jake disarmed them, stunned expressions on their faces. With no further words spoken, I commenced to do what I did best. I picked up the same duct tape roll that had been used on me and walked towards our two prisoners. Jennifer kept her gun aimed at one of them as Jake held down the guy I was taping. When both were firmly secured, I went to Jack and began to undo the tape that had held him motionless and speechless for over two weeks.

He raised his battered face, looked at me with exhausted but happy eyes, and said, "A man could get old waiting for you to save him."

I wrapped my arms around Jack and gave him a firm embrace, burying my head on his shoulder. Tears crawled down my cheeks. "You alright?" I asked.

"Couldn't be better. Seeing those two guys on the floor over there ... yep, couldn't be better. By the way, where's my other two buds?"

"They'll be here in a minute, wearing the same attire as those boys."

Seeing my tears, Jennifer approached me from behind and patted me on the back, consoling me. I stepped away from Jack, giving his shoulder a final squeeze. "Jack, meet Jennifer Ryan."

Bewildered would probably be the right word to describe Jack's face when I introduced him. His mouth was half open as he looked at me for an explanation.

"Well, you see, Pops, it all started with this paparazzo who came down to Sorrento one day." I paused and glanced at Jennifer. "You know what? It's a long story."

Jennifer grinned broadly. "A really long story."

Jack leaned up against one of the grinding machines, happy but exhausted. "And how about this guy?" He pointed at Jake, who was checking my tape job on the two prisoners.

Jake walked over and smiled at Jack. "Hi, I'm Jake Morris, the hired help."

I briefly explained to Jack how I had taken Sokolov and Viktor to Jennifer's house, leading them to believe it was Moberg's house. I told him how Jennifer had pulled out the gun and disarmed them. Then I explained that Jake worked as Jennifer's bodyguard, and that she had called him to come help us.

Jack gave me another quick embrace. "There might be hope for you yet, boy." As he spoke, he winked at Jennifer.

I JOGGED BACK to the rental car by myself to move it to the parking lot behind the warehouse. Just like I'd done earlier, I scoured the street, searching for witnesses. The road was empty. Good thing nobody was open on Saturday. I hopped in and drove to the rear of the building, parking in the same spot the car had been when I arrived last night.

I opened the trunk and Jake came out to help me remove the Russians. They didn't squirm, probably exhausted, but their eyes were alive and angry. An unexplained pang of sympathy entered my mind as I looked down at them, claustrophobically bound in the trunk. But the feeling left me quickly, recalling the kicks to the head and the cigarette burn. We hoisted them from the car and into the building, laying them next to their partners.

Jack took a few steps over to where the bodies lay and stared down at Sokolov. He scowled at the incapacitated Russian. "Fuck you," he said. "Fuck *you.*" He gathered what little strength he had and kicked him in the ribs with his bare foot. Then he planted his right foot squarely in the middle of Sokolov's face and stood on him like his head was a stepstool.

I grabbed him by the arm and pulled him away, afraid of what he might do next. His wrath relented and he regained his composure. Looking at Jennifer, he said, "I apologize for the language."

My hands were on my hips as I looked in turn at Jack, Jennifer, and Jake. I clapped my hands together once, and said, "Whadda ya say we get the hell outta here."

Jake nodded in agreement, stepped over to me and asked for the keys to the Cutlass. He went out to the car and began wiping down the steering wheel, door handles, and anything else which might have our fingerprints.

"What are we gonna do with these guys?" I directed the question at Jake as he walked back in from the parking lot.

"Leave 'em here for now. Let's give it some thought and deal with it later." He finished wiping the keys with the Windex and held them in a paper towel as he stuffed them into Sokolov's front pocket.

"Maybe we call the cops anonymously. They just committed felony kidnapping, so I don't think we have to worry about these guys talking," I said.

Jake looked at me blankly for a few seconds, apparently stopped in his tracks by my suggestion. "Maybe. C'mon, let's go," he finally said.

Jack listened to our exchange dispassionately, and didn't render an opinion.

THE FOUR OF US headed out the rear man-door of the warehouse, turned the corner, and made our way towards the street. The early afternoon sun beat down on the side of the metal building, creating a pocket of hot air where we walked. I beamed inside, the realization of my accomplishment sinking in. I edged closer to Jack and put my arm around his shoulder.

"Welcome back, Pops."

His face was a mess, he had lost a lot of weight, and he walked slowly with great effort, his leg muscles atrophied from the inactivity. But the life was back in his eyes. He stopped, turned to face me, and we embraced. Heretofore, there had been no crying from Jack, but his emotions seemed to reach a breaking point and tears welled up, finally escaping down the side of his face.

"I'm not sure what to say. I ... I ... can't thank you enough ... all of you. You saved my life. I'm sure of that."

Jack hugged Jennifer and Jake. I think everyone shed a tear. I didn't think I had any left.

"So how long did those bastards have you tied up like that?" Jake asked.

"I couldn't tell you if it was four days or four weeks. It's like I lost track of time completely."

I interrupted and told Jake it was about two weeks.

Jack continued in a hoarse, raspy voice. "First they took me to a hotel room for a few days, then here. It wasn't till we got here that they started to get nasty. I'm afraid they got a little impatient with me." He paused and gave me a wink. "They gave me just enough water and a few bites of whatever they were eating to keep me going. Once a day they untied me to let me go to the john. I needed to lose a little weight, but next time I think I'll go to a different fat farm."

Everybody laughed as we reached the street and began moving south along the sidewalk towards my car. Abruptly I stopped in my tracks. "Man, I almost forgot. I've still got these guns. I've gotta go back and leave them in the warehouse with our friends."

Jack grabbed my right elbow and said, "Paul, I'll do that. You go ahead and open up your car for everybody. I'll be right back."

"You sure? I hate to make you walk all that way."

"No, I'm fine. It feels good to move around. Plus, I need to say my good-byes," Jack said, a thin smile crossing his lips.

"Alright, here you go. Oh, let me engage the safety on this one." I flipped the safety latch and handed him the two pistols.

"And here, you better take this," Jake added, handing Jack the bottle of Windex and a paper towel.

WE WERE WAITING in my car when we heard the gunshot. The three of us gasped simultaneously and looked around, unsure of what exactly it was and where it had originated.

"What the hell?" Jake said from the backseat.

Then we heard a second shot. I looked at Jennifer and mouthed the words without saying them, "Oh, shit."

When the third shot rang out a few seconds later, we all flinched, as if we had collectively received an electric shock. We knew what was happening.

I put my head in my hands, closed my eyes, and said softly, "Oh, my God."

The fourth shot came as expected, another punch in the gut. Nobody said a word. We sat in silence, waiting for Jack to return.

40

Santa Monica, California
Wednesday afternoon
August 24, 1977

It was as close to a perfect day as you're going to find at Sorrento Beach. Bright white ribbons of clouds streaked the deep blue sky and a slight breeze rustled the seventy degree air. I had just arrived with Tommy and Lori. It had been four weeks since the attack and he was recovering well, although not yet one hundred percent. Lori was still staying at our apartment, nursing Tom back to health, and he loved every minute of it. Sometimes I think he acted a little more helpless than he actually was. Lori felt guilty and responsible for the attacks. We tried to ease her mind, but she felt if she hadn't come to California, then Max wouldn't have followed and the attacks would never have occurred. She was right of course, but to take the blame for the actions of a psychopath was silly.

She and Tommy were really hitting it off, and in spite of his injured state, I had never seen him happier. Lori enjoyed taking care of him, whether it be out of guilt or true love, only time would tell, but for now, I felt a little like the odd man out at the apartment, they were so enamored with each other.

Today was the first trip to Sorrento for Tom since the attack and the first time for Lori to ever come. She wore a skimpy red bikini top and a pair of blue denim shorts over the swimsuit bottom. Walking with her from the parking lot I could feel the gaze of every guy on the beach upon us ... upon her, I should say.

We set our stuff down next to Jack, who had already played a game and was three bites into his tuna sandwich. Engrossed in his lunch, he didn't notice us until we were upon him. Finally he looked up, raising his eyebrows in surprise. "Well, they'll allow just about anybody at this beach. How are you, Tom? Good to see you. And who is this beautiful young lady?"

"Jack, meet Lori. Lori is a friend of Paul's from Kansas, out here for a while," Tom replied.

I leaned down and pretended to whisper to Jack, but spoke loud enough for all to hear. "You know, Pops, these women follow me everywhere. This one all the way from Kansas."

Jack chuckled. "In your dreams, boy, in your dreams."

IT HAD TAKEN two weeks for the Russian bodies to be discovered. The Santa Monica Outlook and the Los Angeles Times both featured the story on the front page with a large headline. The articles said that a machining company had occupied the building, but had abandoned it after a Chapter Seven bankruptcy. A guy from Kennedy-Wilson, an equipment liquidator, had discovered the dead men when he entered the building to evaluate and inventory the equipment to be auctioned. The apparent execution-style murders were the talk of the town. The articles said that the bodies had yet to be identified and that there were no suspects at this point in time.

Later in the afternoon of the very same day of the shootings, I had met with Buck and told him the whole story of what happened. Aside from the four of us at the scene, and Tommy and Lori, who I had to tell, he was the only one to know the truth. It didn't take long for the FBI to come see Buck. After the bodies were found, they contacted the property owner, who told them Buck had arranged for the Russians to lease the building for a movie shoot. They interrogated him for over two hours, but he just kept telling them that all he did was find the building and hook Sokolov up with the owner. He said he was a little surprised by getting paid in one hundred dollar bills, but had no idea if they were doing anything other than shooting a movie. Buck gave them the name of his director friend who originally referred Sokolov to him, but never mentioned my name or Jack's.

It came out in the papers that Sokolov really did work in the film industry, but not as a producer like he told Buck. In addition to his affiliation with the KGB, Sokolov made regular trips to Southern California to learn about the art of filmmaking. As a representative of the Soviet government, he legitimately tried to learn as much as he could, and then passed along the information to industry leaders in Russia. Jack told me that, in addition to his deliveries in Germany, he had specific instructions on how and when to deliver Moberg's rolls of film to the Ocean Plaza Hotel.

I remained anxious about my role somehow being discovered. I replayed the events of that Saturday over in my mind, trying to think of any evidence we may have left at the scene. Footprints, yes ... fingerprints, probably somewhere. I wasn't even sure if Jennifer, Jake, and myself had done anything wrong. After all, we were rescuing Jack from men who had kidnapped, beaten, and tortured him. We had no intention of harming the men, only subduing them.

But if any of us were discovered, we would have to tell what happened and incriminate Jack. And if he were identified, he would no doubt be convicted. In spite of being the original victim, there was no excusing the killing of his captors after they had already been rendered helpless.

None of this worried Jack. Since the day we freed him, he had been in a great mood. For obvious reasons, he had not told anyone the true explanation for his two week disappearance. His story was that the guy in the suit at the beach was his German contact for buying cars. The German was upset over a car that he said Jack had committed to buy, and had reneged on. Jack said he had forced him to fly to Germany with him to meet the seller of the cars and make it right. It was a little far-fetched, I thought, but from what I could tell, everybody at Sorrento seemed to buy the concocted tale.

I FINISHED securing the umbrella in the sand, leaned back in my beach chair, took a deep breath, and the tension in my neck and shoulders began to melt away. My head still lay on the canvas backrest as I turned towards Jack. He took a long swig of his Olde English 800. "Hey Pops, something I've been meaning to ask you. How did you decide to name yourself Jack when you came to America?"

He chuckled and got a faraway look in his eye, remembering another time and place. "Pretty simple story really. I knew I wanted to change my name. Isaiah Rosenberg was a little bulky. Plus, I wanted a fresh start—you know the whole story. I was trying to forget the past and move forward. The boat trip over was a long one, and we did a lot of drinking, mostly out of boredom. One night I was drinking with this guy I met, and we started dreaming up possible names for me." He shifted in his beach chair and turned to face me. His smile widened as he spoke. "Seems like the more we drank, the more we fell in love with that whiskey bottle. And the name on the whiskey bottle was Jack Daniels. Well, my friend thought I should take that name just the way it was on the bottle. So I almost became Jack Daniels, but the next day after sobering up, I decided I wanted to keep part of my surname. I was trying to decide between Rosen and Berg, and finally decided on Jack Rosen. So there you have it ... named in a drunken stupor from the label of a whiskey bottle."

I put my interlocked fingers behind my head. "Huh. Well, that worked out pretty well. I hate to think what my name would be if I did that. Probably be Jose Townsend." We both laughed at that.

I NOTICED Doug Williams sitting about ten yards to my right with a woman and young boy. Wondering if it could be possible, I strolled over and said, "Could this possibly be Mrs. LJ?"

LJ laughed and nodded his head. "Paul, I'd like you to meet my wife, Marissa."

"The pleasure is mine," I said, and spontaneously leaned down to give her a kiss on the cheek. I felt like I knew her even though we'd never met. "You know, Marissa, all of us here thought Doug was making up the fact that he had a beautiful wife and a son. We just figured he was a lonely old man trying to convince us he was normal."

"You are right on one count, he's pretty old. But he's definitely not lonely and just as definitely, not normal," Marissa said, laughing.

I sat cross legged in the sand, facing the two of them in their beach chairs. "What enticed you to come to lovely Sorrento Beach after all these years?"

Stray wisps of her silky long, black hair fell into her face—she wiped them back carelessly. Her loose fitting, sheer white cotton top covered a one piece, dark colored bathing suit.

"You know, Paul, Douglas and I have been married eight years now. Throughout those years I always felt like he was trying to get away from us when he came here. I kind of knew not to ask to come. It broke my heart, but I tolerated it because it seemed so important to Douglas. Yesterday, he asked me if I wanted to come to the beach with him. I just about fell out of my chair! First time he has ever asked. It was like he wanted us again ... wanted *me* again." Marissa stopped abruptly and had an embarrassed look on her face. "Oh, my gosh, why am I boring you with all this? Here I just met you and I'm rambling on and on."

"Hey, I'm the one who asked," I said.

LJ chimed in, "Paul, it's like this—you guys are all like family to me, you really are. I finally decided I wanted my real family to meet my beach family. Looks like we might be doing this more often."

LJ's son, who had just turned four years old, interrupted his castle building and said, "Daddy, can you bring me here every day?"

"Not every day buddy, but we'll definitely come again, okay?" LJ replied.

"And can I say hello to the beach, like the man did?"

We all chuckled. "Yes, you can yell out 'hellooo beach!' just like Scott does."

I got up and extended my hand to Marissa. "Welcome to our beach. Any wife of LJ's is a friend of mine."

I TOOK OFF my t-shirt, settled in the beach chair, and started to apply sunscreen to my face. Jack looked in my direction, but his eyes were focused beyond me. He said, "Check it out, Paul. Look who's emerging."

I turned my head toward the wall in time to see Jennifer close the gate which leads from her backyard. She began striding in our general direction and I waved at her, but she seemed to already know where we were sitting. The entire beach stopped what they were doing to watch her make her way over.

I stood up and gave her a hug. "Whadda ya know. If it isn't the famous movie actress, come to hang out with the low-lifes." Jennifer noticeably blushed. I had continued to see Jennifer often since our rescue of Jack, but this was the first time she had ventured onto the beach.

"Shut up, Paul. You know I'm self-conscious enough as it is," Jennifer said, as she sat down next to Jack. "You go on your way. I'm just going to sit here with Jack. He's nice to me."

Jack's mouth stretched in a large, toothy grin as Jennifer moved closer and put her hand on his forearm. I introduced Tom and Lori, then offered Jennifer my beach chair, which she accepted. Before sitting, she removed her tank top and sarong to reveal a tiny, pink, flowered bikini.

"Before you get too comfortable there, what do you think about trying your hand at some volleyball?" I asked.

"Yes, yes. I want to learn. Will you teach me?" I reached down to pull her up from the chair and we walked the short distance to Court Four. For the next few minutes we hit the ball back and forth and I gave her some basic instruction. Her athleticism surprised me. She picked it up quickly.

Diving after a ball that was just out of reach, she remained in place, sprawled in the sand. She took a deep breath, exhaled, and looked up at me with a big smile. "This is so great."

"What? What's great?"

"Just being out here. Thanks for encouraging me to come out ... out of my house and onto the beach with you guys." She propped herself up on her elbows and leaned her head back, gently shaking it to remove the hair from her eyes. "Sometimes I feel like a captive in there. I can't tell you how great it is—no photographers and without a bunch of people gawking at me."

I stood over her, my shadow covering her face. "Oh, they're gawking alright. But not because you're Jennifer Ryan, just because of that bikini."

She laughed. "When they stop looking, that's the time to worry."

I settled in next to her, gently brushed sand off her stomach, then leaned down and gave her a quick kiss. "Whadda ya think? You ready for a game?" I reached across her to grab the volleyball.

She rose up and brushed more sand off. "Sure, why not?"

I jogged back over to where we were camped, asked Jack if he wanted to play, and then yelled over to LJ. They both agreed and began to make their way over to Court Four. I tossed the ball to Jack as he approached.

He stopped a few feet away, staring at Jennifer on the sand, holding the ball against his hip with one hand and a lit cigar in the other. "I want to let you know before we start playing that I think you have an unfair advantage, and I'm not happy about it."

Jennifer looked puzzled. Jack seemed so serious. "What advantage?"

"I'm gonna be so busy lookin' at you in that bikini that I'll never be able to hit the volleyball," he said, then put the cigar back in his mouth.

She stood up and strutted seductively toward Jack. "Then that's a good thing. I need all the help I can get."

Jack turned his back and stepped to the other side of the court, shaking his head. "No fair."

We warmed up for a few more minutes and then started the game, with LJ being the first one to serve. Showing no mercy, he served the very first ball to Jennifer. She passed the ball nicely toward the net. I gave her a good, low set about five feet off the net. She reached high and took a mighty swing. But she did not connect solidly and the ball went off the side of her hand, hitting the top of the net and trickling over, a few feet in front of where Jack stood.

"*Move!* You fat old Jew. *Move* for the ball!" Jack yelled at himself. We all fell to the sand in laughter.

EPILOGUE

Jack Rosen: Three years after he had murdered the four Russians, Jack remained a free man. The Santa Monica Police Department had turned the case over to the FBI because of the victims' nationality. From the information we read in the papers, it appeared that the case would remain unsolved. Neither Jack nor any of us had ever been questioned.

Jack showed no remorse for his actions. Quite the opposite. He seemed to have a new energy about him, an increased zest for life. I had had several long talks with him about the whole incident. He talked to me about the wife and son he had lost, about the murder by the Russian soldiers of his mother, father, aunt, and uncle. He commended me for my detective work in finding Jerry Moberg, and gave me more insight as to how their partnership worked. He bragged that he had been feeding false data to the Russians for nearly two years before they discovered his deception.

I admired the fact that Jack had refused to reveal Jerry Moberg's name to his captors even though they had tortured him for two weeks. Although I didn't agree with it, I came to understand why Jack had returned to the warehouse and killed the Russians. He told me he thought that killing them was the only way to guarantee that all of us who had helped rescue him would not be in danger of retaliation. And maybe he was right. But beyond that logical reason, he had an emotional need to exact revenge. The killing of his tormentors seemed to appease his anger and he was at peace with himself thereafter.

He took no more trips to Germany and he was no longer in the car business. Most of his days were spent as they had been for several years, on the sands of Sorrento Beach. His new friendship with Jennifer Ryan had done wonders for his acting career. In addition to the occasional commercial, Jennifer had gotten him parts in four of her movies in the past three years.

Doug Williams (Little Joe "LJ"): LJ continued to be a Sorrento regular between jobs. He had always been a happy guy at the beach, but I got the sense now that he was happier with the rest of his life. There was no more talk of divorce. You know the saying, "Happy wife, happy life." Well, Marissa Williams was now a much happier wife. She didn't come with LJ to the beach very often but that was by her choice. She knew she was welcome to come, and that was all that mattered.

More often than his wife, LJ would bring Travis, and occasionally even bring his baby daughter Kelsey, now two years old. Travis was seven years old and starting to bump the volleyball around a little bit. Doug played less volleyball when the kids were with him but he didn't mind the sacrifice. When I first met LJ, he was reluctant to give up the freedom that he had when he was single. Not that he was unfaithful. He wasn't until that night after Tampico Tilly's with Michelle Santos. But he thought he could be married, have children, and still have the independence to do what he wanted, when he wanted. And as any of you who have been in a relationship know, that is not how it works. But now he had matured into a proud father and a much better husband and was finally at peace with himself in this role, this new phase of his life.

Buck Braddock: If Jack Rosen was my substitute father, then Buck Braddock was my grandfather. I am forever grateful to him for not revealing my name to the FBI. He saved me from possible prison time and from having a felony conviction on my record. It goes without saying that he saved Jack, and probably Jerry Moberg, from a lifetime in prison.

In July of 1979, Buck sold the 9th and Wilshire property to a Japanese group who planned to build a high rise, office/retail complex on the site. He struck a favorable deal with the buyer to lease the ground floor retail space to Buck's Sporting Goods. Now, one year after the sale, the developer had received final approval from Santa Monica's City Council to proceed with the project. Demolition is scheduled for next week. Buck's Sporting Goods will be disappearing for about fifteen months.

Tommy Ruderman: After graduating from UCLA in Spring of 1978 with a degree in Psychology, Tom began playing beach volleyball in earnest and last summer he was the seventh leading money winner on the tour. He even played a couple of tournaments with Jim Marlowe, since Andrew Lee had taken some time off to try to get back in the NBA. There wasn't much money in beach volleyball but Tom had done well enough to get by without a full time job. To supplement the volleyball earnings, he worked several nights a week as a waiter at Moonshadows, a nice steakhouse right on the beach in Malibu.

Tom's father had made great strides. He began attending all of Tommy's volleyball tournaments. He stopped criticizing everything he did. I could see the change in Tommy. He felt like his father finally appreciated him for who he was. I think that it may have been the attack on Tommy that was the turning point for his father. After almost losing him, I guess he decided he should start treating him a little better. So maybe that was one good thing that came of the whole business with Mad Max.

Tom and I continued to live in the same apartment on Kelton Avenue. And believe it or not, Lori Lewis still lived there too. But I'll save the really big news for my update on Lori.

Lori Lewis: Maybe you already guessed it. Tom and Lori got engaged. It just happened two weeks ago. Now, of all the people I know that would get hitched at the ripe old age of twenty-five, Tom Ruderman would be about my last guess. Mr. "I've Never Been Able to Keep a Girlfriend Longer than Three Months" is getting married. Wow! I have no doubt that they will live happily ever after. They are perfect for each other. And I should know. One is my best friend and the other is an ex-girlfriend who I've lived with for the past three years.

Lori, who received her RN at Mount Saint Mary's Nursing School about six months ago, is now working at St. John's Medical Center in Santa Monica as a nurse in Labor and Delivery. We made a makeshift bedroom for her in the corner of our already tiny living room. We picked up a couple of those moveable office partitions at a used office furniture store to use as walls. She is a tremendous roommate, cheerfully cleaning up after us, cooking for us from time to time, and pretty easy on the eyes.

There is no wedding date set but they are aiming for next spring. I guess the writing is on the wall for finally getting out of our apartment.

Jennifer Ryan: The last two movies she has starred in have been blockbusters at the box office. She is one of the most sought after, and highly paid, actresses in Hollywood. But the thing she loves doing more than anything is spending time at Sorrento Beach. In the beginning, she would crack open the door leading from her backyard to the beach, peek out and see if I was there. If I was, she would come out, sit with me, and I would play a game or two with her. She loved volleyball and was rapidly improving. After meeting most of the regulars, she eventually felt comfortable coming out even if I wasn't there. She loved that she was just a regular person at Sorrento, just one of the gang. She didn't have to worry about paparazzi and she wasn't stared at or hounded for autographs like everywhere else she went.

My overnight visits with her continued for several months, but ended when she found a more serious suitor, a forty-two year old screenwriter named David Sulpor. They have been a couple for over two years now and Jennifer, now thirty-five, is anticipating they will soon marry and start a family.

Originally I was very jealous of Mr. Sulpor, but eventually my brain prevailed over my heart and I understood what I knew from the very beginning, that we were at very different stages of our lives. Plus, I had always been careful not to be seen in public with her. I hated the idea of my picture being splashed all over the tabloids and gossip magazines. Jennifer convinced me that being famous was the last thing I wanted to be.

I remain good friends with Jennifer, see her often at Sorrento, and will never forget the intimate moments I was fortunate enough to spend with her. I will always hold a special place in my heart for Jennifer Ryan.

Paul Townsend: As for me, I have delayed growing up about as long as possible. After graduating with my B.A. in Economics, I took a year off from school, continued working at Buck's and played a lot of volleyball. I began playing competitively in the tournaments, had good success in the lower level tournaments, winning one, but realized that doing well enough to make any money was probably not going to happen. So after the year away, I returned to UCLA to go to business school, and two months ago graduated with an MBA. Now I'm done with school and Buck's is being torn down. Ready or not, I'm being thrust into the real world. Next month I'm starting my first full time job, as a financial analyst at TRW. Yes, you heard that right … TRW. Me and Jerry Moberg. Don't expect I'll be selling any secrets to the Russians, however.

Six months ago I called Renee Ayers and, attempting to be funny, asked her if she was old enough to go on a date. After she hung up on me, I called her back and begged. She agreed. Renee had stopped working at Buck's when she graduated from high school, a semester early as she had planned. She is living in La Jolla attending University of California at San Diego and I have been making frequent trips south to see her. I'll confess that I am hopelessly in love with her and I believe she feels the same way about me. I have no doubt in my mind that we will be together the rest of our lives. I just have to convince her. Like when Dustin Hoffman tells his parents in *The Graduate* that he is going to marry Elaine Robinson, but "she doesn't know it yet".

Renee Ayers: We learn by example from our parents. Many of our parents' traits we decide to emulate and other behaviors we tell ourselves we will do the opposite when we are parents. For Renee, at least for the time being, she was following in her father's footsteps, a pre-med major. But my guess is that, when she becomes a doctor, she'll choose a specialty that allows her to work more normal hours. She's often told me that she doesn't want to be gone all the time like her father.

She turned twenty a couple weeks ago and just finished her junior year. Why someone like her puts up with the likes of me is a mystery. Maybe she's not as smart as I always thought she was. Maybe when she gets older she'll wise up. Or maybe love really is blind. I'm banking on the last one.

AUTHOR'S NOTES

Although *Sorrento Beach* is purely fiction, the geography I wrote about is real. Apartment 239 of the book is the same one I lived in for four years. I played volleyball at Sorrento Beach several days a week throughout the late seventies. And lastly, I worked as a racket stringer, not at the fictional Buck's Sporting Goods, but at Tex's Sporting Goods, at 9th and Wilshire in a dilapidated, old, L-shaped building.

The story's characters are modeled after a mixture of real and fictional people. Even the names, in some cases, are formed from multiple real people. For example, at Apartment 239, I had several roommates over the years, normally three or four at a time crammed into the tiny place (to save on rent). The name of Tom Ruderman was put together by taking the first name of Tom Jasek, one of my long-time friends and roommates. The "Rud" came from George Rudnicki, a fellow volleyball player and roommate who lived at 239 with me for the entire four years. Bob Weaver contributed the "er", a small piece, I know, but all he deserves (just kidding Beav). The "man" is from Scott Wells, my roommate in the dorms, and then in 239 afterwards. Everybody calls him Wellsman, hence the "man".

At the beach, Jim Marlowe was a combination of Jim Menges and Chris Marlowe, Sorrento regulars and two of the all-time greats of beach volleyball. Andrew Lee combined Andrew Smith and Greg Lee, two more great players. And so forth.

The first name of my true love in the story, Renee Ayers, is the middle name of my true love in real life (and my wife), Sherie Renee Grote.

The story didn't start out to be such an obsession with girls, but the more I put myself into the mind of a twenty-one year old male, the more "hanky panky" (as Lori Lewis would say it) made it into the story.

The inspiration for this book was more from my days at Sorrento Beach than anything else. When I moved to Southern California from Fresno (not Winfield, Kansas, but maybe just as dramatically different), I was introduced to beach volleyball and soon was hooked. I spent hours and hours honing my volleyball skills and enjoying the camaraderie of the large community of regular attendees. Just for the heck of it, I decided to put together a list of all the Sorrento regulars I could remember. And with the help of Steve Baer, a long time regular, I think I did pretty well. And I guess this is an acknowledgement of sorts, since without them, I wouldn't have been so inspired.

Here you go: Andrew Smith, Andrew Doubroff, Annie O'Rourke (Annie Fannie), Annie Park, Alan, Bill Fiers, Bill Sharman, Billy Berger, Camillo Passarelli (Blackie), Bob Eickes, Bob Feinberg, Bob Parucha, Bob Vogelsang (Vogie), Bobby Jones (BJ), Bobby Ramos (Boots), Bobby Ramos Jr. (Little Boots, LB), Brian Rofer, Brodie Greer (Bambi, Bear), Bruce Sellery, Chris Marlowe (Cy), Courtney Grossman, Craig Rodgers, Dale Eickes (Goose), Dan Doubroff, Dave Puretz (JD), Dave Beck (Herman, Ben), Dave Doubroff, Dave Heiser (Heiz), Dave Mochalski (Big Mo), Dave Grote (Groteman, Spock), Dave Siebel, Davy Hilton, Debbie Dick, Debbie Feinberg, Doug Anderson (Dougger), Doug Rabe, Ed Kerns, Gayle Fiers, Gene Pfleuger (Pfleugie), George Rudnicki, Georgie Smith (Peaches), Greg Lee, Guy Roach, Hank (Hammerin' Hank), Heidi Feinberg, Howard Feinberg (Howie),

Jack Kerns (Pops, Father, JK, The Penguin), Jack Lipps, Jay Hanseth, Jay Moore, Jean Brunicardi, Jim Hoback, Jim Menges (Cookie), Jim Smith (Beaver), John Harkrider, Kathy Gregory, Ken Stovitz, Kirk Rodgers (Muscles), Lan Kerns, Lisa Lee, Liz Masakayan, Lynn Shackleford (Shack), Marco Ortega, Mark Eller (L-Dog), Mike Deroache (Leo), Mike Kramer (Spoon), Michi, Mike Normand, Mike Stanton (Teacher Mike, TM), Mike Wilson (Willie), Mike, Mokie, Nancy Passarelli, Nina Grouwinkle, Pat Powers (PP), Paul Smith (Pablo), Peter Horton, Peter Bigler, Peter Eaton, Phil Bersinger, Phil Mitchell (Tarzan, Mitch), Randy Niles (Whale), Randy Sievers, Rich Feinberg, Rich Van Horzen (Horse), Robert Chehoski, Ron Von Hagen (Von Yogurt), Roz, Sally Bartell, Scott Tibbetts (Curly), Sharon Feinberg, Singin Smith, Steve Baer (Bum), Steve Marks, Steve Olen, Steve Salmons (Sambo), Steve Stovitz, Suzanne Feinberg, Teddy Grossman, Teddy Morse (The Commander), Tom Chamales (TC), Wally Busby (The Mayor), Yoshi Busby, and Zenon Brodzki (Z).